PRAISE FOR KARISS LYNCH

"A scarred hero and heroine, both seeking to overcome their past. Family ties and loyal friendships. I was drawn in by both the characters' struggles and Kariss's authentic and modern storytelling voice. An author to watch!"

— BECKY WADE, AUTHOR OF FALLING FOR YOU

"The heart is easily deceived when truth fails to rise to the surface. *Heart's Cry* shows one man's journey to rediscover the man who once held courage and faith in his hands. Kariss Lynch is a masterful writer who practices the art of creating emotional intrigue that weaves love, danger, and faith."

— DIANN MILLS, CHRISTY AWARD WINNER

"Assertive dialogue, strong leads, and power punches of peril continue to be the foundation of Lynch's storytelling. She's an author not to be missed!"

— NICOLE DEESE, AWARD-WINNING AUTHOR

"Kariss Lynch's writing, rich in detail, and strong characterization captivated me from the opening paragraph. The spiritual truth she weaves throughout the story to combat her characters' lies stirred my spirit, causing me to continue thinking about the story long after finishing the last page. The depth of emotion she layers into her story created multi-dimensional characters who felt more like real-life friends. I was sad to say goodbye. Lynch's books have a permanent place on my keeper shelf."

— *LISA JORDAN, AWARD-WINNING AUTHOR FOR LOVE INSPIRED*

"Brave but broken heroes, savvy but sweet heroines and compelling dramas that touch the heart—Kariss Lynch knows how to create a story that will stay with you long after you close the book. I'm making space for this new writer on my bookshelf!"

— *SUSAN MAY WARREN, USA TODAY BEST-SELLING, RITA AWARD-WINNING NOVELIST*

"Intriguing, relevant, and most of all, heart-tugging—Kariss Lynch consistently wows me with her storytelling. I love how she pairs romance and slices of suspense while weaving in military life and shaping characters who feel real. She writes with an authenticity that never fails to pull me in. I can't recommend her books enough!"

— *MELISSA TAGG, CHRISTY AWARD-WINNING AUTHOR OF NOW AND THEN AND ALWAYS*

HEART'S CRY

KARISS LYNCH

LIONHEART PRESS

Copyright © 2020 by Kariss Lynch

Cover Design Copyright © Chasya Kiewit

Author Photo by Andrea Bradshaw Photography

All rights reserved.

No part of this book may be reproduced in any form or by any electronic or mechanical means, including information storage and retrieval systems, without written permission from the author, except for the use of brief quotations in a book review.

Most locations are fictional and created for the purposes of the story world only.

To Grandad, Aunt Carrie, Uncle Fred, and Uncle Tommy
You didn't live to see this book published,
but you cheered me on during its making.
We miss you.

"To love at all is to be vulnerable. Love anything and your heart will be wrung and possibly broken. If you want to make sure of keeping it intact you must give it to no one, not even an animal. Wrap it carefully round with hobbies and little luxuries; avoid all entanglements. Lock it up safe in the casket or coffin of your selfishness. But in that casket, safe, dark, motionless, airless, it will change. It will not be broken; it will become unbreakable, impenetrable, irredeemable. To love is to be vulnerable."

— C.S. LEWIS

CHAPTER 1

The only easy day was yesterday, according to the United States Navy SEALs, but Micah Richards felt that was the understatement of the century. Every day felt equal parts hard with a teaspoon of borderline crazy brought on by nightmares. Nothing was easy. Not even yesterday.

He wasn't a SEAL anymore. And this journey was part of his penance.

Mountains towered around Micah as his beat-up black mustang winged its way into snowy Colorado. The black sky crowded around him, the Milky Way smearing the sky with the lack of city lights. Mountains slashed through the twilight on either side of the twisting road, standing as silent sentries observing Micah's solo journey. He didn't like being solo. Micah took a deep breath of crisp, cool air. His breath puffed in the car, illuminated by the lights on his dashboard.

Granger Smith's "Backroad Song" lyrics blared through the car, prompting Micah to check his phone screen. Hawk. His hand tightened on the wheel in the narrow mountain passes.

He pressed the green button, ending weeks of silence with

his best friend and brother-in-law. "I know you are not calling me at eight p.m. beach time on a Monday when you have a wife who is an early riser and is probably already getting ready for bed."

"You know your sister well." Nick Carmichael's familiar voice drifted over the phone, and for a second, Micah felt his old normal return—the normal that had existed when he was a United States Navy SEAL, part of a team, a brotherhood, and his life had been in California. Up until a month ago when he could no longer live with the guilt.

"Bulldog?"

"Yeah?"

"I asked how you were, but I guess the silence answered that question."

Micah sighed. His concentration was an issue on phone calls lately. "I'm fine, Hawk." His brother-in-law had the best eyes on their team and was a trained sniper, earning him the nickname "Hawk" among their peers.

"Uh huh. Giving up your life and packing everything into that run-down Mustang to drive off to no destination in particular sounds like the Micah I know, minus the quitting part."

"Watch it, Hawk. I'm not a quitter," he bit out, his teeth grinding so hard his jaw ached.

"I didn't say you were. I just said you quit."

"Did you call for a reason, dear brother-in-law of mine?" Micah couldn't contain his sarcasm. His knuckles glowed white on the steering wheel.

"Just checking on you. How was your adventure with Ben Strider?"

The ghost of a smile tugged at Micah's lips. "Ben is a chip off the old block. It's a pity Harrison wasn't here to fulfill his promise and take his baby brother bungee jumping for the first time."

Silence on the line. Micah hated the silence.

"We all miss Harrison, Bulldog."

Bulldog. A nickname he'd earned for his terrible morning mood but also his dogged loyalty and defense of those he loved. He would do anything for his people.

But Harrison was another painful reminder of Micah's failure.

"Bulldog, did I lose you? You're not alone in this."

His chest squeezed tight. Micah forced a breath and took a turn slowly, snow pelting his window shield.

"This was my fault. Now, it's my responsibility."

"Micah, it wasn't your fault." Hawk's voice rose in time with the snowy attack on the glass. Micah slowed another five miles per hour.

"I'm not going to argue with you, Hawk."

"Then don't. Come back to California. We'll work through this together. Kaylan misses you. Our whole team misses you. Logan and Kim's kids keep asking for their 'cool Uncle Micah,' though why they think you are cooler than me, I haven't determined."

Micah snickered. "Please. I out-cool you every day of the year."

"I think just by using that phrase you lose."

And he had lost. His home. His life. His very identity. Without a team, who was Micah "Bulldog" Richards? Nobody. His path was no more clear and purpose no more defined than the winding mountain trails he traced now. He slowed even more as snow nearly obstructed his view.

"I need to get off the phone, Hawk. Go be with your wife. And if she calls me mad at you, I'm coming back to kick your butt into next year."

"Bulldog, is that all it will take to get you back here? I make her mad on a daily basis. Start driving."

Micah laughed. "Just take care of her."

"You know I will. She misses you, though."

"She doesn't need me anymore. She has you."

Micah had lived in the same town as his sister and brother-in-law for two years of their marriage and almost a year of them dating beforehand. They had been a normal part of his week, and withdrawals from their company hit hard, especially in the quiet. But it was time for Micah to move on. To what and where, he didn't know. He had one more stop to make on this journey. Just one. And then he would decide. But the last stop would be the hardest of all.

Nick's answering laugh sounded more like a bark. "Don't kid yourself. She will always need you and Dave and Seth. Y'all are her world, the men she looks up to next to yours truly. And your dad. And Pap." Micah smiled at the mention their dad, a doctor in Alabama, and their grandfather, a retired state judge and the patriarch of the family. The man oozed wisdom and never worried about stepping into the lives of his grandchildren to set them back on the straight and narrow.

"That is quite a lot for you to live up to. How in the world did you make the cut?" Another turn in the road sent his lights cascading over another rocky sentry. He turned the heater up a notch, the flurries so large he could see their sharp patterns. Just looking at the icy white sent a shiver crawling up his spine. He missed the sun, sand, and ocean. He missed surfing with Colt, a SEAL on his Support Activity team, hitting the waves right as the sun peaked over the horizon. Surfing with his friends had been one of the few things that dragged him from bed before sunrise—that and the job. The job he had loved.

"I had a glowing recommendation from my best friend."

"Yeah, remind me why I did that again?" Micah laughed. The car shuddered and he let up on the gas. A quick check of the gages revealed smooth sailing. Now would not be the time for his old car to act up.

"It was my charming personality and roguish good looks."

"No, that's me," Micah retorted. "I asked why I recommended you."

Micah heard a scuffle on the other end of the phone and then a groggy voice that still made every brotherly bone in his body melt. "Micah? Come home." Kaylan. His sister. His responsibility. Well, not only his anymore. He didn't mind sharing the responsibility with Nick. As much as he teased, no one would love his sister more.

"Did you just steal the phone from your husband?" He could just imagine his auburn-haired, green-eyed beauty of a sister sneaking up on her six-foot-four, Navy SEAL husband, flashing her sweet smile, and taking the phone right out of his hand.

"He was sweet enough to hand it over."

"Whipped," he coughed into the phone. But truth be told, his baby sister had Micah wrapped around her finger, too.

"Seriously, we need to find you a girl." Her old mantra made him smile. Micah had dated but never really been serious about anyone. Truthfully, he hadn't found a girl that could handle his life, who stood as a warrior in her own right. Micah had always been a hopeless romantic, but that didn't mean he would settle.

"That's what you keep telling me." He'd always wanted a girl he could protect and love, someone he could have fun with, build a life with. A best friend. A teammate. His sister had set the bar high.

The car shuddered again, and Micah could swear steam drifted from the hood, but it was difficult to tell in the increasing snowfall. *Please, Lord, no,* Micah silently prayed as he urged the car along. He didn't know when he would hit the next town, but he needed to get there quickly.

"Micah Matthew Richards, did you hear me?" Just like their mom pulling that middle name business. Kaylan's Alabama southern drawl lengthened in her drowsy state. He heard Nick chuckle on the other end of the line.

"I heard you, and you need a new line."

"I do not. I'll retire that one when you actually find a girl to settle down with."

He chuckled, the sound foreign to his ears. "Night, Sis," he murmured softly.

A heavy pause hung between them, and he wished he was in California to make her laugh and get a hug. Something about his baby sister brought out every protective instinct in him and healed the broken parts just a little. She made him feel a little more like the hero he'd once been. But he was far from a hero now.

"Micah, are you really okay?"

The car stuttered again, and the grinding of metal broke the stillness. "Kayles, I really do need to go. Love you."

"Micah, I . . . we . . . stay . . ." He glanced at the screen. No service. Great. He hung up and tossed the phone in the passenger seat as he rounded a corner and fought to maintain control of the car.

With a pop and rattle, the car died, and he coasted to a stop on the side of the mountain road, snow immediately taking advantage of his disabled windshield wipers.

"Great." Micah sank back into his leather seat, a shudder rocking through him as the chill immediately permeated the car. Snowflakes barraged the windowpane, each crystalline flake caking and stacking against the glass. He leaned forward to watch their twirling pattern. He knew just enough about cars to know his was about to be toast, and this one was worth more selling to the junkyard.

"Well Iron Man, did we just take our last journey together? Fifteen years of cross-country trips and too much time at the beach and you've finally had enough."

He rubbed his hands together and eyed the piling snow. He silently cursed his hoodie, jeans, and cowboy boots as he crawled from the car. "Good grief. Forget fire—my hell would be ridiculous cold," he muttered.

The hood of his Mustang groaned as he dislodged the accumulating snow and propped it open. "I knew I should have listened to all Jay's talk about engines," he grumbled, thinking about his hot-headed fellow SEAL. The brains of his car looked like metal boxes and organs pieced together with a bunch of pipes and chords. "This is a mess."

He slammed the hood and traipsed to his trunk for his flashlight, warmer clothes, and emergency supplies. The SEALs had at least drilled that into him—be prepared.

One second he was moving toward his trunk, and the next he landed hard on an icy slab of road. He sucked in a harsh breath, the mountain air thinner than his familiar ocean home. He lay flat on his back staring up at the swirling white snowflakes trying to kill him with their icy beauty. Boots and ice didn't mix. Ice and Micah didn't mix. He needed to get out of the cold fast. His back stung with the instant chill seeping through his hoodie.

The purr of an engine and slice of headlights careened around the curve, and Micah scrambled to get out of the way. He fought to get on his feet, but his boots refused to find any traction on the stretching patch of black ice. *Move, Micah.* But nothing worked. The car sped closer. He gave up and did the only thing he could to move. He rolled closer to his Mustang and prayed.

The headlights came straight for him. There was nothing he could do but wait.

CHAPTER 2

The beat-up wood floor pulsed with the movement of dozens of couples two-stepping their way to Blake Shelton. Casey Stewart stood in the corner, sipping ice water from a glass and watching the action move around her. Her friends, Teagan and Shawn, cut up and laughed in the middle of the dance floor, weaving between couples like pro, Texas two-steppers. Not even in Colorado for a few hours and already they had found the most Texan thing to do on their annual vacation.

Teagan's red-orange hair whipped around them as Shawn twirled and dipped her with a familiarity that spoke of years of friendship. Heads turned toward her friends, studying their footwork, spins, and dips. Casey smiled. The two of them could really dance. It had never really been her thing, despite Shawn's best attempts.

Well-worn, round, wooden tables circled the dance space with chairs haphazardly scattered, abandoned. Water pitchers and half-empty glasses littered tables, their owners demonstrating varying levels of intoxication on the dance floor.

A small bar sat off in the corner, manned by a cute blonde

flipping through her phone and eyeing a redheaded guy goofing off a few tables over. Casey could tell by their green and gray Colorado State jackets that they were athletes of some sort. Judging by the build of the redhead and a few of his buddies, she guessed football. Too bad they couldn't help her with the new sports league she was trying to start or find her the coach she needed to hire before the holidays. She had roughly seven weeks before Christmas. Seven weeks to hire someone and get them settled before sports leagues kicked off in January. She shoved the thought aside quickly. *Vacation mode, Casey. Vacation.*

One ogling gaze turned in her direction had Casey slipping further into the shadows. She shook her head. No way. Her party days were long over and her taste for cocky athletes had died a quick death in high school. She ran fingers through her shoulder length, layered, brown hair, pulling it over her shoulder.

"Case, it's your turn to dance with Shawn." Teagan Ray skipped up to Casey in all her bohemian glory that only she could pull off in a Colorado winter. Her ivory sweater belled at the sleeves. Her jeans tucked into red-brown, ankle, moccasin boots, and jewelry dripped from her wrist and ears. Her long, curly hair hung loose and wild, like Teagan—bright and free. Shawn closed in on the two of them, his plaid shirt hugging his broad shoulders and his jeans hiding his cowboy boots. His naturally olive skin, dark hair, and dark eyes kept female eyes glued to him wherever they went, but he'd never paid much attention, something that endeared him to Casey and Teagan even more.

"I'm having too much fun watching the two of you."

Shawn's crooked smirk cast Casey's way made a girl nearby look twice. Casey could practically see her drooling.

"Seriously, Shawn, can you try to tone the cuteness factor down just a tad?"

Shawn drew himself up tall. "Casey Stewart. I am a man."

Teagan nearly spewed the sip she'd just taken.

Casey attempted to match his pose, her five-foot-two frame dwarfed by his size. "And?" Her own smirk danced on the corners of her mouth, but she sucked it back.

"And that means I am not cute. Hot, handsome, gorgeous, or even good-lookin' I will take. But not cute." He crossed his arms over his chest, his shirt stretching tighter. He must have been hitting the weight room with the football team he coached.

Teagan patted Shawn on the back. "Casey was being sarcastic, Shawn." She shook her head with a dramatic sigh. "I'm afraid you are just average."

He turned the full weight of his charm on Teagan. "Oh yeah?"

Teagan shot Casey a look, but Casey only shrugged. She'd been the middleman between the two of them since childhood. The three of them had been best friends for years, united by dysfunctional home lives and the desire for something different. Teagan and Shawn had both been foster kids, eventually adopted by the families on Casey's street. Casey almost wished she'd grown up in a foster home, but she didn't wish for Teagan and Shawn's experiences. They all bore scars from childhood. Casey's mother had definitely left her fair share. Speaking of . . . her phone lit up with another text from her mom and another rant about how Casey was a terrible daughter. She'd been on a roll since Casey, Teagan, and Shawn had landed.

Teagan grabbed her arm and tugged, sloshing the water from Casey's glass and splashing a few drops on Casey's cherry red sweater. "Time to get you on the dance floor. No sulking, no thinking, nothing but fun. Those pretty brown eyes of yours are far too shadowed right now. Time to lighten up."

Casey laughed at her friend's dramatics. She squeezed Teagan's hand. "I'm finishing my water, Teag. Go have fun. I'm good."

Teagan did a double take over her shoulder, and a sly grin

stole over her face. "Well looks like you don't have an option. Dust off those boots because here comes a guy who could rival Matthew McConauhottie himself."

Casey snapped her head in the direction of Teagan's gaze and fought back a groan. Sure enough, the jock had decided to dethrone himself and head her way, another buddy strutting across the room at his side.

"First of all, I'm not wearing boots. Second, you need to come up with a new, good-looking actor besides Matthew McConaughey. And third, I am not dancing with either of those guys and you know why. Besides, I can't move my feet to the rhythm, and I don't want them dropping me on the fl . . ."

"Hey, gorgeous, I saw you eying me over there. Care to dance?"

The guy, who looked a little more like Zac Efron than McConaughey, towered over her. Dressed in a white, long-sleeve shirt that hugged his athletic frame, he crossed his arms, making his muscles bulge even more. His eyes drifted down the length of her body. Her back ached and her muscles tensed, ready to respond. She hated his roving eyes. Time to revert to "distract the step-dad" mode. Fortunately, it worked to keep other guys at bay, too.

She took a step toward him and gave him a once-over, smirking. "I think you're mistaken. I was just talking to my friend here. I'm set." She raised her now almost empty glass in a toast and spun on her heels, reaching for Teagan. She took a quick inventory of the room, Shawn now over at the bar ordering a soda and the door on the other side of the dance floor. She angled her body that way.

A hand grabbed her forearm in an iron grip, and she found her body spinning before she slammed into a rock-hard chest. Apparently, he had more coordination in his current state than she gave him credit for.

"I love a girl who plays hard to get," Mr. Asking-for-it slid his hand down toward her waist. Blood filled her cheeks as he played with her belt loop and began to move his hand lower down her backside. With a quick jerk, she threw her knee up and between his legs.

His hands flew off as he doubled-over in front of her. She fought the urge to push him the rest of the way to the floor. Any modicum of kindness leached from her as her defenses locked in place.

"Your mother must not have taught you manners. When a girl turns away from you, she isn't begging you to chase her. Now be a good boy and run back to your friends." Asking-for-it's buddy choked on a laugh and grabbed his friend's arm. Shawn had appeared quietly in the struggle, but he'd known Casey long enough that he provided his presence and let her fight her own battles. Just like she'd been fighting them alone since the age of fifteen. Maybe even before that.

With a groan and grimace, Asking-for-it unfolded himself to his full height. Casey could see the effect of the alcohol in his system. Great, an angry drunk. Why had she ticked off an angry drunk? Too many nights in her mom's bar in Austin, Texas, slammed into her, knocking her back a step. Too many nights of deadbeat men and stepdads hollering through the house after a night of binge drinking and watching a game on television.

She threw up her walls and prepared to fight, her fingers balling into fists at her side, ignoring the fact that this guy could knock her down without trying. Her phone buzzed in her pocket. Probably yet another text from the woman who had aided her distrust of most guys in the first place. Casey could only fight one battle at a time.

The guy took a step forward, his jaw locked and eyes brimming with anger at being humiliated in the growing crowd. Casey felt Shawn tense next to her. She reached for a rickety wooden chair, ready to swing it if necessary. Shawn took another step closer. This guy had about five seconds before the situation would leave Casey's hands and Shawn would cease to stand in the background.

"Whoa, whoa, whoa. Calm down there, Sanders." The ginger decked out in his football jacket arrived on the scene. His swagger spoke of confidence bordering on arrogance, but no alcohol inhibition. His grin could have melted the heart of any ice queen, but Casey had learned not to fall for a charming smile long ago. Ginger grabbed Asking-for-it's arm and nodded at his friend to do the same. "My apologies for my friend here. I think it's time we call it a night. He's normally a charming southern gentleman." Ginger grinned at Casey while tugging at his friend.

Casey nodded her thanks. "You'll have to forgive me if I don't take your word for it."

He nodded. "Fair enough. Can I make it up to you?" The hint of hope lingering in Ginger's gaze made her cringe, but at least he was more of a gentleman. No more boys tonight.

"Only by taking care of your friend here. Thanks." Bending, she retrieved her glass from the floor, dismissing him with a final glance, and turned to Teagan and Shawn.

"You don't always have to be sassy to the guys, you know. Some of us do have good intentions." Shawn threw his arm around her shoulders, his plaid shirt pulling tight against his chest and his buttons gaping to reveal his t-shirt and the emblem of a mustang, the mascot of the school he coached for. She grabbed his wrist, her fingers closing around the tattoo peeking from below his sleeve on his olive-toned skin.

"You are the exception to the rule." She shifted her feet on the scuffed oak floor. "He was asking for it."

Teagan hugged her waist on the other side. The only people who could get away with hugging her this much were these two. And her little sister. But that's it. She really needed to text Emery tonight. If things were heating up with their mom, Casey might need to step in.

"One day, some guy is going to knock through that sarcastic, homely thing you got going on," Teagan tugged at a strand of Casey's dark hair, "and he's going to haul you over his shoulder and ride off into the sunset while blaring that pop rock junk you like so much."

Casey chuckled and tugged away from her friends, reaching for her black down jacket hanging on the back of a chair. "There will be no sweeping off the feet, no hauling, and no charming. I swore off men in high school. You know that."

Shawn grinned and dropped a quick kiss on her head. "Thou doth protest too much."

"That doth soundeth lameth coming from thou, Coach."

Shawn grinned, his white teeth gleaming red in the dingy light of a neon sign mounted on the wall. "That sounded worse. How are the kids you work with ever going to learn to speak proper English with you talking like that?"

Casey sighed and slipped on her coat. "I don't think that is their biggest concern right now." Casey and Teagan both worked at Ellie's Place in South Dallas, Texas, a nonprofit organization intent on restoring hope to a community caught in bad patterns of poverty, socioeconomic issues, crime, and hopelessness.

They started with the kids, providing mentors, after-school programming, tutoring, and a safe place to come and stay out of trouble. They hoped by caring for the kids and partnering with them in their daily life that the community would learn they could reach for more. Slowly but surely, they would change. That's why Shawn toughed it out at the local high school, Teagan led the mentor program, and Casey handled the leadership program and some counseling and worked with Teagan on the fundraising events. Al, the founder of the center named after his late wife, counted on them to keep things running smoothly. Being away for even a few days when they planned to launch the sports leagues so soon made Casey feel like she was letting someone down. What if one of her kids needed her? What if parents or guardians had trouble with the registration? What if she didn't find someone in time for the new year? Ellie's Place was not for the faint of heart. You had to feel called to work with kids who needed a little more TLC.

Teagan turned a playful smile to her friend and bumped her hip. "Let it go, Case. You're on vacation. You can mother all your little chickens and host all the interviews you want for the new position when we get back to Dallas. But for now"—she shoved her friends closer together—"dance with Shawn."

Casey held up both hands. "I'm outta here. I'm going to call for an Uber."

"Take the rental. Teag and I can call for a car later." Shawn tossed her the keys.

She snapped the ring out of the air and released a quiet breath. The benefit to having two friends who had known her since the age of seven meant they knew when to let her go. Her demons knocked, and she wanted to get away from the conduit for the memories. She cast one last look over at Ginger's group. The guys seemed to still be talking Asking-for-it down from his heated seat. Someone had been dumb enough to put another beer in his hand. She sighed and wound her way to the front door.

Silence descended as the heavy wooden door closed behind her. Casey leaned into the stillness and took a deep breath of cold mountain air. She loved living in Texas, but there was something strong and calming about the mountains that loomed like dark shadows behind the buildings across the street. White flakes fell from the sky, twirling in the orange glow of the street lamps.

Casey ground her snow boot into the ground, tracing a pattern in the fresh powder. She could relax, she could let go for a few days. And then she would go home and jump back into her life and back into the fight. She glanced at the quiet street, shops now closed, buildings quaint and attractive for tourists in the small ski town of Deacon, Colorado. Maybe the break would be good. Maybe the mountain air and hitting the slopes with her oldest friends would give her a bit of the peace she craved. And maybe a good night's sleep would erase the memories of another handsome jock who had ripped out her heart so long ago. Her phone buzzed again. Casey took a deep breath of the cold mountain air and finally checked the messages. Mom. Mom. The last text made her heart plummet. Emery.

Please get me away from Mom. I can't do this anymore.

So much for a break. No matter how far she went, she couldn't get away from the wreckage her mother left in her wake. Casey had been collateral damage, she'd picked up the pieces, and now she was worried about her fourteen-year-old half-sister. She couldn't—wouldn't—allow her sister to grow up like she had. Emery had Casey, and Casey couldn't let her down. With her back to the bar, she headed toward the car, snowflakes thickening above her in the black sky. Time to call her mother.

CHAPTER 3

Casey definitely hailed from Texas. The snow was beautiful, but her bones ached with the deep cold. She tugged her coat closer.

"Heat. I need heat. Lots and lots of heat." She fumbled with the buttons in the rental car, punching them more forcefully than necessary. The short phone call with her mom still rang in her head. Mother dearest had only wanted to tell Casey how rebellious her sister had become—that she was acting out, just like Casey. Oh, and that her latest stepdad and Emery's father had moved out. On to the next guy. Casey had lost count of the men who had cycled through her doors as a kid. Emery's father had been on and off with Mona Rodriguez since Emery's birth. Casey really wanted to get Emery out of that home.

Music blared through the car as she tapped the wrong button and flinched. "Stupid, fancy, rental car," she huffed, missing her own Toyota back home. All her stations programed, all her dials familiar and easy.

Her mother confused her to no end. When Casey made a bad grade or had a minor problem at school, her mother disciplined Casey for being rebellious. When she had her first drink and spent the night throwing up her guts, her mother had mocked Casey's inability to hold her liquor. Nothing made sense. Nothing except Mona had been a terrible role model and a terrible mother. Casey had practically raised herself. Maybe she could raise Emery now.

"Continue straight for five miles," Siri blared over the enhanced speakers, cutting through Casey's reverie.

"Thanks, Siri, I can see that on the display," she talked back. She shouldn't be so morose. Not on vacation. While verbally and emotionally unhealthy, Casey's mom had never physically hurt either of her girls. But Casey still wanted better for her little sister. She knew the most painful scars weren't physical marks. That's why she fought so hard for the kids at Ellie's Place. She was to them what she had longed for growing up: someone to love her and fight on her behalf. She shook her head, dispelling the gloom. She couldn't change the world or her little community all at once.

"How do you turn up the heat on this thing?" She took a quick look at the road and then turned her gaze to the dashboard, softly illuminating the interior.

Casey glanced back up at the road and jerked the wheel, a curve sneaking up on her. The wheel tugged slightly as her tires fought for traction on the gathering snow. She tapped the brakes, gaining a bit of control. "Whoa, that was close," she exhaled. "Wait is that . . ." She slammed on her breaks, the gears grinding and squealing. "Stop, stop, stop!" She tugged on the wheel, sliding to a parallel stop next to a black Mustang that sat fuming and blocking part of her lane.

Casey couldn't move. Her breath filled the air in heavy puffs. She jerked around to make sure another car wasn't going to come out of nowhere and hit both of them.

"What the . . ."

A body flew up from the ground, stumbling and arms flailing. She shrieked and immediately clamped her hands over her mouth. The figure straightened and turned to face her, squinting in the glare of her headlights.

Not an it. A him. A very handsome him. And she despised herself for noticing.

She shoved her door open and whirled on the guy. "Are you crazy? I could have hit you! What in the world were you doing on the ground?" She stalked around the front of the car, the headlights casting her shadow on the road. Casey took a quick assessment for injuries but saw none. Only dark hair, day old scruff framing a handsome face towering nearly a foot above her five-foot-two frame. "Can you speak or did you have a heart attack?"

A slow grin spread across his face. Good grief. His hot points just sky-rocketed and so did her hesitance. A sliver of rational fear penetrated her bravado. She was alone on a mountain road with a strange man. Had he been laying on the road on purpose? She backed up a step, preparing to run if necessary.

"Easy there, short stuff. You almost hit me." His smile and stance hid the slight bite she heard coating his words.

Was he seriously trying to flirt right now?

"Let's start over." He rested a hand on his chest, like she was five and needed him to speak slowly and point. "I'm Micah."

She crossed her arms.

"You," he pointed at Casey, a grin emerging amidst the dark stubble dusting his cheeks and chin, "almost hit me with your car. My noble steed," he turned to point to the smoking car behind him, "decided to die a very untimely death, and then the ice tried to kill me, too. So this might be one time when I need the damsel's help to rescue the stranded knight."

Casey smirked. She was pretty sure this guy was just stuck, not a creeper, but he was definitely a charmer, which meant even worse than a creeper in her world. "You know, it's a real shame I didn't hit you."

"Then you would have missed out on my friendly personality." She caught a wink in the lighting from her headlights.

She snorted and shook off his charm. "Well it seems like you do need my help. Where are you headed?"

He straightened and rubbed his hands together, breathing into them. "Well that's the thing. This was a bit of an unexpected stop. So at this point, I'm interested in any place that has a bed and a heater." Sincerity rang through his tone, all sense of joking abandoned. How long had he been out here?

"Oh okay." She thought fast. "Tell you what. My friends and I are staying at Mountain Home Ski Resort a little ways up the road. You can come with me and either sit in the lobby while you figure out your next step or see if they have any rooms available."

"I'll take it."

She put her hands on her hips, taking a step toward him in the dim light. Snow now coated the hair extending from her beanie, and the chill seeped through her down jacket and layers of sweaters. Her own Texas blood was ready to abandon the cold. "Why were you lying on the ground? Any chance you are a stalker or psycho-killer?"

He winced at her words, and Casey wondered which part hit a chord. The more she studied him, the more she felt like he was safe. She had to be a pretty good judge of character in her line of work. Working with teenagers and their families in a rough neighborhood cured lingering naiveté. And apparently any sense of self-preservation.

He leveled her with a stare and cocked his brow, his chiseled jaw popping with some emotion she couldn't quite read. She silently groaned. He truly was handsome. Even in the dim lighting. While not blind, she hadn't noticed a guy like this in years.

She didn't like it.

"The black ice tried to kill me. And unfortunately, cowboy boots are not made for snow." She glanced down at his feet.

Southern maybe? She didn't hear much of an accent in his tone. Maybe she'd met another wannabe cowboy. Without answering her first question, he walked to his trunk, carefully navigating the icy patch she now saw in the light of the headlights. No wonder he hadn't been able to stand quickly. He opened the creaky lid and tugged out a huge duffel, clearly military, and slammed the lid. So probably not stalker, possibly still killer?

She nodded slowly. "I'm actually headed to the resort now." She walked to the driver seat of her rental car and searched for the button to pop the trunk. "Got anything else you need to get out of the car?"

He turned slightly, his profile illuminated, and his shoulders deflated for a second. Gorgeous, snarky, and sad? With a pop, the trunk sprang open. She met him at the back of the car.

"I travel light." He pointed to her feet. "Watch the road. There are patches of black ice everywhere." She immediately froze and glanced at her feet. Sure enough, another patch lay inches from her boot. Add chivalrous to his list of qualities. With precise steps, she stepped closer to the car.

"Micah. Got a last name to go with that?"

"Richards. May I?" He pointed to the bags already in the trunk and she nodded. He began shuffling to make room for his bag, shifting Teagan's heavy bag with little effort.

Casey pulled out her phone, the screen's glow casting an eerie light on the falling flakes now caking Micah's dark hair.

"You won't find me on Google or Facebook or any of those apps."

She glanced up into hooded, dark eyes, shielded by the shadow of the trunk. "Well I guess that would mean you aren't a known stalker or escaped convict. Glad we ruled those out. But who escapes Google now days?" She offered him a small smile, which he returned. She sent a quick text to Teagan and Shawn to let them know where she was and what had happened while

Micah finished shifting the bags and retrieved his from the snowy ground.

"Navy SEAL. Was," he amended with another wince. "Was a Navy SEAL. I stayed off all those social media sites to help with privacy and security. You know you never told me your name. What if you're a stalker or an escaped convict? I might get into a car with a crazy person."

Casey barked a quick laugh. "Touché. Casey. Casey Stewart."

"Nice to meet you, Casey Stewart." He extended his hand, which she reciprocated. His grin glowed red in the shine of the taillights. Even hidden slightly by shadows, her stomach did a small flip. Probably just a result of the dark and potential of cars rounding the curve and hitting them. Definitely that. She scanned the road. No lights.

She pointed to the embroidery as he slipped his bag around the suitcases already occupying the trunk. "Bulldog, huh?"

He nodded. "That's what they call me." He tested the trunk lid. "How many clothes did you bring?"

Nosy. A bad quality to add to the list. Unfortunately, not bad enough to negate the handsome and chivalrous positive qualities. But charming tipped the list heavily to the negative side. It didn't matter anyway. She would drop him off and never see him again. Casey didn't date.

She fought for a measure of control. Five minutes with Micah Richards and he had managed to mess with her head. "Clearly Bulldog stands for jerk. What knight school did you graduate from?" she shot at him, only drawing a smirk. Awesome. He liked girls with a little fire. She toned it back a bit. "I have two friends back in town. We haven't checked in yet, hence the trunk full of luggage."

She slammed the trunk and made her way to the driver's seat. Something intrigued her about Micah. She didn't like it. Tall, dark, and handsome guys were a dime a dozen. But Micah seemed to have something . . . more. She opened her door, the scent of pine wafting to her from the passenger's seat now hosting the man in her thoughts. She shuddered and dialed up the heater.

The sooner she waved goodbye to the handsome stranger, the better. Single was better. Single was safer. Single was all she'd known since her teens. No reason to change that now. No reason to allow any margin to turn out like her mom, to choose the wrong guy . . . again. She started the car and navigated around Micah's Mustang as he placed a call to a tow truck company to let them know the location of the car using his phone's GPS. With one more call to 911 to let them know about the road hazard, they were on their way.

Micah blew heat into his frozen fists, once again cursing his insufficient clothing.

"Mind if we turn up the heat?" The slight chatter of his teeth chipped at the shreds of his pride. Could he be any more embarrassed? So much for the always prepared SEAL. Just one more indication of his failed status. He was just no longer that guy. But oh how he missed that guy—a team behind him, a calling before him, and a purpose to live for every day. Now he was team-less, calling-less, purposeless, and now carless. He sank back into the seat. He needed a job, a hobby, a destination. Something to plan on, to find purpose in after his last visit with Whitney and her little girl. If only Juan . . . He shoved the thoughts aside.

"Of course." Casey fumbled with the dials until the rock music dimmed to a dull bass and the heater poured feeling into Micah's frozen limbs.

He peered through the windshield at the rapidly falling snow. He would think it was beautiful if not for his nearly blue extremities.

He shivered and held his hands close to the vent. Heat pricked digits that no longer wanted to respond, leaving a stinging sensation in their wake. Why, oh why, hadn't he packed warmer clothes?

"Guessing you don't like the cold?"

He smirked and glanced at her, taking the opportunity to study her profile as she focused on the winding road. Dark brown hair peaked from beneath her gray beanie. Choppy layers and the mid-length short style made him wonder if she was a low-maintenance, sassy kind of woman. If their conversation back at his car was any indication, he was willing to bet sassy didn't even cover it. Her skin glowed a beautiful tan tone, washed out in the dash lights. Eyes hidden in shadows flashed his way. Her brows quirked in amusement.

Right. He needed to get better with his response time tonight. "Let's just say I was made for precipitation of the melted variety." He nodded to the flurries beating a frenzied path to the road. "This stuff is a little too cold for me."

"Me too. Texas is home, and we don't get too much snow. Mostly ice where I live. If anything." She relaxed back in her seat, but her hands clutched the wheel in a death hold. His presence, or something else, made her uncomfortable.

Micah had the sudden urge to reach over and soothe her grip. He ground his teeth and shifted so he could look at her, his fingers now bending without the frozen ache. "I grew up in the South. Alabama. We have fairly mild winters, but every once in a while, we get true winter weather. I've been in California since I graduated high school and left home. No winter there."

"In Dallas, people freak out when it snows." She smiled, and he liked the way her nose wrinkled just a bit. "Roads close, schools shut down, cars are stranded. A few years ago, we had a storm come through that iced people in for days. People called it 'Icepocalypse.'" She chuckled. "My friend and I were snowed in for two days. We drank hot chocolate and watched movies and put a puzzle together that we actually had framed and put on my wall." She stopped and glanced at him. "Sorry. Probably too much info."

Micah shook his head. "I know. I was sitting over here thinking you talk *way* too much."

Her eyes cut in his direction, a smirk tilting her lips. "Well at least I wasn't lying on my back in the middle of the road at night."

He chuckled. "That black ice had it out for me."

Her fingers tapped on the steering wheel as the car rounded another mountain curve. "I hate to break it to you, buddy, but the ice won."

"Ha ha. You almost performed the victory lap."

Her laughter floated softly. "True. So what brings you out here? Skiing?"

He sank further into the seat back, the seat warmers soothing the chill he couldn't escape. "Actually, just passing through on my way to Fort Worth."

Casey cast him a quick look. "Oh? I didn't think this was the most direct route from California."

"You're right. It's not. When I left California, I hit Idaho, then Arizona, then a spot just north of here. Next stop on the road trip is Fort Worth."

"Is this trip business or pleasure?"

"Neither. My mom would call it a pilgrimage." He cleared his throat. Her quiet questions felt probing despite their innocent nature. He hated the reason for his trip. His position on SEAL Team 2 based in Coronado, California, had been a badge of honor, his life. He'd lived with his buddies, been minutes away from his best friend, Nick, and Nick's bride and Micah's sister, Kaylan. He was a frogman, a teams man, an operator.

Had been.

Since then, he'd chased adrenaline highs across the country, while visiting the homes of team members, saying goodbye. The last one would be the hardest. Then harder still . . . figuring out a new purpose when his calling was no longer an option. He felt like a hazard to the people around him.

Casey pulled the car into a lot and eased into a parking space in front of the massive wooden building that stretched in an arc in a snowy glen. "I'm guessing your noble steed breaking was not part of this pilgrimage?"

Micah laughed and unbuckled his seat belt. "That it was not, but I may take a few days to enjoy this beautiful castle we just pulled into. Wow. *This* is a resort."

She laughed. "It's our one splurge a year. But it's not peak ski season yet, so I bet they still have rooms if you plan to stick around."

In the glow of the parking lot lights, he could finally see her eyes, the color of chocolate with tawny flakes that reminded him of caramel. She wasn't a bubbly girl. She seemed strong, quiet, guarded. But kind. Not many girls were sassy, kind, and intentionally didn't pursue him. He was intrigued. He felt like there was more to Casey Stewart, and with that, he considered staying for a few days. Maybe.

They stepped out of the car, the dry cold immediately attacking his bones. He shivered. "Thanks again for not running me over."

"I mean, it's not every day I get to rescue a knight. Now I have a good story to tell. Does this qualify me for honorary SEAL status?"

Micah swallowed back the ache and summoned his bravado. Tapping his chin, he regarded her. Short, beautiful in a natural way, and the way her body stayed angled away from him . . . definitely guarded, yet helpful. "I bet you could give some of those guys a run for their money. But . . ." He shrugged. "You might just be too short. I'm not sure they allow pint size SEALs."

A dangerous grin lit her features right before she bent and popped up with a snowball flying his direction.

"You did not just throw snow at me."

"You did not just call me pint size." Another snowball flew his direction over the car.

He ducked, laughing. "I give. I give. I'll do anything to get inside those doors." He looked longingly at the heavy wooden doors and the glow of warm light filtering through the large windows on the bottom floor.

Casey's soft chuckle floated from the back of the car where she'd popped the trunk and lugged out one of the roller bags. "Coming, Soldier?"

The sudden use of the nickname made him grit his teeth.

"After you, Doll Face." He winked and fought a laugh as she threw her hands on her hips. He could almost see steam float off her in the frigid air.

"You need to work on your nicknames."

"Right after you work on your driving technique."

He lifted his duffle from the car and swung it over his shoulder. "You want help with these other two bags?"

"What a gentleman."

He swept into a deep bow, then began pulling the other two bags from the trunk, one huge and one more like an overnight suitcase. "I wouldn't want you thinking us southern boys don't know how to treat a lady." He let the full impact of his southern drawl slip through his normal control. Like his sister, his accent bled stronger in exhaustion and when at home.

He straightened and caught her smother a smile. "There's that accent. I was wondering if you had lost it completely out in Cali."

He fell into step next to her pulling the suitcases with his duffle stacked on top of the largest bag, their boots crunching through the thin layer of snow blanketing the cement. The resort loomed before them with a black backdrop and the faintest trace of a mountain peak in the distance behind it. He imagined the view would take his breath away in the light of day. Lights glowed from large windows spaced every few feet on all three floors. Wood paneling coated the outside giving it the appearance of a cabin on steroids. Balconies jutted out from multiple rooms, a few glowing with what looked like private fire pits centered in the middle of outdoor lounge chairs. Cozy, warm, inviting. For the second time in an hour, Micah took a breath, thankful for his Colorado detour.

Micah tugged the wooden handle of the giant barn doors and motioned for Casey to slip through with her suitcase into a lobby designed right out of a catalog. A fire roared in the back of the room, surrounded by distressed, brown leather couches. Young adults joked around a bar off in the corner and played games at several of the tables off to the side of the room. Several chandeliers made from antlers and a mix of crystals and twinkling lights hung from the ceiling. Rugs draped painted concrete floors, and guests lounged around the room, talking and carrying mugs clearly from the drink station in the corner. Resort staff dressed in hunter green wool jackets checked in a couple and their two kids, too sleepy to stand up straight as they leaned against their parents.

"This might be the nicest place I've seen since I left California."

"Been staying in run down motels on this pilgrimage of yours?"

"Pretty much. But I think I could treat myself for the next few days." And maybe just get to know this small, confident woman who was kind enough, and maybe just crazy enough, to care for a stranger.

"Reservation, ma'am?"

She blinked and handed her printed reservation to the

smiling desk clerk cloistered behind the stained wooden counter. "It's under Casey Stewart."

She had picked up a stranger and then actually kind of flirted with him . . . without knowing anything about him. What had she been thinking? *Dumb, Casey. Really dumb.* This was totally out of character for her. Her focus shifted to Micah now talking with the tow truck company on his cell. Micah Richards. A SEAL with something missing. That much was clear.

Micah Richards. A man who intrigued her. Amused her. Despite his charm, she suspected he wouldn't push her.

Micah Richards. An enigma. Different.

"Your room keys, miss."

"Thank you." Casey accepted the two keys to their rooms upstairs then turned back to the large room. The fire crackling off to the side called her name. But she really should get upstairs. Jump in the shower and clean up from her day of traveling and wash off the lingering memories of the bar.

And yet . . .

She turned one more time to find Micah pacing near one of the couches. Something made her not want to turn in for the night, not say goodbye.

Interesting.

She'd wanted nothing more than to leave the guys at the bar.

Even now, she could see a similar rowdy group in the corner. She looked closer. Great. The same guys. How had they beat her back to the resort? Siri must have taken her the wrong way. And then Micah. And now they were here and he was here, and she oddly didn't know what to do. She gripped the gold metal bar of the luggage cart laden with all their luggage, intent on heading to her room. It had been interesting, nice even, to feel a spark for a guy. But that was it. Just nice. No reason to stay.

Except.

The fire called to her. The drink bar in the corner begged

her to grab a mug of hot chocolate, the kind with the little marshmallows on top. The kind that made her remember campfire nights with Teagan and Shawn as kids. It had been their way to end a bad day on a good note. Something about a fire, a night sky, laughter, and a cozy drink that chased the shadows and chill away.

And now she was craving chocolate. There was only one solution.

She angled the cart toward the drink bar to the side, which stood right next to the bar where the football players were laughing and chugging glass mugs full of amber liquid.

In the middle stood the redheaded guy from the bar, the guy who had interceded. The guy who now listed slightly to the side, his stance less confident than before, slightly . . . tipsy. And she'd wanted to give him the benefit of the doubt. Spoke too soon.

But that chocolate . . . maybe she could just slip over there unseen, grab a cup, and escape to her room.

"Ma'am, do you need help with your bags?"

A bellhop dressed in the forest green uniform offered her a smile, probably a local working to put himself through college. His boyish face had begun the transition to manhood, his blond facial hair still patchy in some places. Maybe a late bloomer.

She smiled, relieved not to lug the cart everywhere in the lobby. "Could you take these to Room 304, please?" She would have Shawn pick his up from her and Teagan's room later. She pulled a few dollar bills from her pocket and stuffed them in his white gloved hand.

"It would be my pleasure, Miss."

Her phone rang as the bellhop moved toward the elevator.

"Hey, Teag."

"Hey, we're on our way to the resort. And you won't believe this. There was this car in the road and a tow truck and a state trooper blocking a lane and we almost hit them and then went off the cliff."

"What?"

"Teagan." Casey heard Shawn's exasperation bleed through the phone.

"Okay, okay." Teagan sighed. "We didn't almost go off the cliff. But we did almost hit the tow truck. That was a terrible place to break down."

Casey cast another glance toward the fire and the drink bar. Her heart felt set on what she couldn't bring herself to do—walk past the jocks to fulfill her longing for chocolate. "I know. I almost hit the driver. I brought him back to the hotel."

"You what?" Teagan started talking ninety miles a minute, Shawn telling her to chill out on the other end of the line.

"How could you pick up a stranger? In the middle of the night? In a foreign country?"

Casey rolled her eyes, shifting slightly closer to the chocolate. None of the guys had noticed her yet. The subject of her conversation remained locked in his own just couches away. She wondered what had triggered his journey. She shook her head. She didn't need to know. She wouldn't see Micah again.

"It's not a foreign country, Teag. It's Colorado. We come here every year. And trust me a bit. He's all right."

"Anything that isn't Texas is a foreign country, Casey." Teagan sighed in exasperation. "And where is he now?"

Casey looked at Micah finishing up his phone call. She was curious if he would stay.

"He's here, Teag."

She shifted closer to the chocolate. Most of the guys had their backs turned. Now was her moment.

"Teagan, there is chocolate and baby marshmallows calling my name. I gotta go. I'll see ya when you get here." She hung up and took her last step forward, surveying all of the yummy toppings. Was she in the mood for marshmallows, whip cream, and chocolate shavings on top? Or did she want to go the cinnamon-y red hot direction? Or . . .

An arm landed on either side of her against the buffet cabinet. "Well, hey there, beautiful." The "l" slurred from his lips. Casey flinched and slowly pivoted finding herself boxed in and all too close to the blonde from the bar.

"Do you have any rooms available?" Micah leaned over the wooden counter in the grand lobby, now finished with the tow truck company.

"Let me check." the girl behind the counter asked without looking up from her screen. "Only a suite. It will be eight hundred dollars for the night. Would you like me to book it?"

She kept typing, giving him info about the suite, but Micah was focused on Casey as she approached a beverage buffet. Something in him felt . . . disappointed. More than anything, he wished he were the guy from a year ago who had it all together, could step in and charm her, bust through the walls he sensed were stacked sky high, and sweep her off her feet. But he had nothing to give her. Nothing. And the last year had taught him his friends and family were better off with him far away. Then he couldn't hurt them. Destroy their lives. Even by accident.

"Sir?"

"Uh, no that's okay." He chuckled. That was a little out of his price range during unemployment. Or even with employment. He really needed to figure out the job situation soon. Guess that eliminated staying for a day or two.

"I'll figure it out. Thank you." He stepped away, fiddling with his phone, wondering who to call or what to do next. Maybe another hotel nearby? He could call for an Uber. Raucous laughter sounded from the small corner bar and the chant of "chug, chug, chug," filled the lobby as other guests chimed in.

Micah watched a blonde guy in a football jacket slam a glass down on the counter. The guy tossed his hands in the air and turned to face his admirers as they cheered. Then the guy spotted Casey.

Micah hefted his bag over his shoulder, watching. Waiting. The guy pushed past his friends, his eyes fixed on Micah's beautiful savior. Judging by the guy's swagger, it wasn't his first drink. Micah had seen too much alcohol abuse with his buddies. Drinking he could handle. Drunk was another story. Drunk and fixated on a girl rarely ended well. Micah slowly moved toward Casey, preparing to help if necessary.

Before he had taken two steps, the guy pounced, his arms bracketing either side of Casey's small frame. Micah quickened his pace, the look in Casey's eyes as she turned around—fear and anger—urging him forward.

"You need to back off. Now." He heard her say as he reached her side. His bag slipped from his shoulder, leaving his hands and arms free.

"Hey, man. Do what she says." His tone stayed calm but firm.

The guy turned his head to face Micah, his eyes unfocused. "Back off. I saw her first."

He was like an animal marking his territory, or a toddler defending his toy. Micah almost laughed.

"She's with me, man. And she doesn't want to be pinned like that." He placed his hand on the guys shoulder and tugged. "Just back up."

The guy fell backwards, his arm swinging towards Micah. "Man, I saw her first. I swear. You can ask anybody." He righted himself and waved his arms towards his friends.

"Like he said, you need to back off," Casey chimed in, standing as tall as her short frame would allow. Micah saw fire in her eyes, hiding the hint of fear. He took a step in front of her, blocking her from the guys view.

The guy swung. Micah ducked. With a quick pivot, Micah

had the guy facing away from him, his arms braced behind him. "Just calm down, man. No need for this to get ugly."

"You're taking my woman." He tugged, but Micah held firm.

"Your woman?" Casey emerged from behind Micah.

"Casey . . ." Micah warned, praying she wouldn't complicate this. By now the whole lobby was watching the guy struggle. Micah hollered to some of his less inebriated friends to come take him.

Within minutes, hotel security and a few of the guys from the football team were in deep conversation.

Micah turned to face Casey, arms crossed. "Want to tell me what all that was about?"

She shrugged, turning back to the hot drink station, but not before he saw her hands shaking. "I could have handled it."

"I'm sure you could have."

He grabbed a mug next to her and began to fill it with hot cider. He added a cinnamon stick and stirred.

Her hands still shook as she grabbed the whip cream can and tried to press the top down.

"Let me."

"I've got it." Casey jerked at his brief touch. He reached for the other can and sprayed a quick swirl in her drink then raised his hands and backed off. Her glare only made him smile.

"You didn't run over me on the road or let me die from frostbite. I rescued you from a drunk jock and covering yourself with whip cream. Let's just call it even."

A small smile graced her lips. "Fine. We'll call it even . . . for now."

His grin deepened at the possibility of later. But he let it go, picking up his mug and taking a sip. Not as good as his Gran's, but it was in the running.

"Soooo . . ." He followed her to a couch and sat down on the opposite end, his bag between them on the floor.

"Sooooo . . ."

"How do you know him?"

"He was at the country bar tonight. Just got a little too . . . flirty. But I took care of it."

"Uh huh. That's it?"

"You're so nosy."

"You are a terrible storyteller."

"Sometimes there isn't much to the story."

He was quiet for a moment. "There's always more to the story."

She swallowed hard, the crackling fire replacing their conversation.

"So did you get a room, or are you moving on?"

"Well it seems like they are full except a suite I can't afford. I'm not sure what I'm going to do for the night. But I'll figure something out." He always did.

She set her mug down and stood, and Micah followed suit. "I think I might have a solution to your room problem as long as you're willing to bunk with my friend, Shawn. And if you stick around, you are welcome to join us on the slopes tomorrow."

He reached down and swept his bag off the floor and onto his shoulder. He was weary to his bones. The memories weighed heavy, the emotional drain of the day tugging on him. But hitting the slopes. Not going it alone for a couple days. It sounded like heaven.

"Lead the way. I'll let you be the knight in the equation this last time. As long as I don't have to sleep in the car, I think I can handle your friends. Quick question." He flashed her a tired smile. "Are they as crazy as you?"

She threw an elbow into his side.

"Oof." He rubbed his ribs. "I'm just saying. You pick up strangers in the mountains and face down drunk dudes at bars. That's quite a record for one night, Champ."

"Running you over with the car is still an option." She glanced up at him, a smirk lighting her face.

"Then you'd miss out on the epic nickname I come up with. I'm not quite sure 'Champ' fits completely."

Her lips turned down at the corner as she hit the button to call the elevator. "I'm holding my breath in anticipation. But we don't have long before we bid a fond farewell, so you better make it quick. We're only here until Friday."

Micah chuckled and leaned against the wall, letting it hold him for just a moment as he studied her. He was weary to his very soul, but something about Casey roused a semblance of anticipation. Kind. Strong. Selfless. Those traits made him want to stick around. Maybe just for a day. Or two. Or maybe he would just stay until Friday. A few days of fresh powder and a pretty girl couldn't hurt. Especially while he figured out the car situation.

"Casey Stewart, I think it will be worth the wait," he said as the elevator doors swung open. Micah stepped in after Casey, and she immediately held it open.

"Teagan, Shawn, hurry!" A redhead and tall dark headed guy jogged the last few feet to the elevator.

"Thanks for holding, Case," the guy who must be Shawn said. He turned to Micah, his hand out. "You must be my roommate. Casey texted me."

Micah took his outstretched hand as the doors closed. "Looks like it. That okay for the night?"

"Casey is a fairly good judge of character. If she thinks you're alright, then it's fine by me."

Micah nodded. "Well anything that will make you feel more comfortable, feel free to ask. I really appreciate it."

"And I'm Teagan." The redhead shoved her hand out for Micah to shake as the elevator doors swung open on the third floor. "How in the world did your car break down on the side of the mountain? How long are you staying? And where are you headed?"

Casey jumped in to answer some of the questions as they

navigated the carpeted halls to their rooms. Micah grinned at the friends' exchange. It made him miss his buddies back in California. Another wave of exhaustion hit Micah as they arrived at their rooms and Casey distributed the keys. Micah was ready for sleep and wondered what the next day might hold with the firecracker who'd rescued him. He had a feeling he was in for an adventure.

CHAPTER 4

The mountain bustled with skiers carving new tracks to the valley below. Ski lifts cranked overhead depositing skiers and skis in a tangle of limbs and bodies. Casey could spot the inexperienced from the experienced based on their landing. Ever since her college graduation six years before, Casey, Teagan, and Shawn had booked flights to Colorado for fresh powder and the cool mountain air. They had been determined to learn how to ski. It was their "family time" full of laughter and adventure and rest. And in that time, Casey had gotten pretty darn good. But after two days of skiing with Micah Richards, she knew she'd met her match in a ski partner. Micah thrived on danger.

He'd rented gear and skis and hit the slopes, starting somewhat easy but quickly dusting the rust from his muscles and hitting the big leagues. And Casey had been crazy enough to go with him. Something about that stupid, charming smile, the permanent five o'clock shadow, and his constant teasing made her stomach weakly flop. No guy had managed to pique her interest since high school, and Micah barely made the cut. Not even mentionable.

But that smile.

It annoyed her.

She could still hear Teagan whispering in her ear when Micah had invited her to ski: "Girl, if you don't spend the day with McGorgeous, I will." A sick feeling curled in Casey's stomach, a feeling she didn't particularly like. And just like that, she'd accepted Micah's challenge. Based on his annoyingly cute grin, he'd known she wouldn't turn him down. Either that, or he'd heard Teagan. She really, really hoped that wasn't the case.

"You ready for this, Ace?" Next to her, Micah adjusted his multicolor goggles and tugged his floppy red beanie firmly over his ears.

"Keep trying with the nickname, Hotshot."

"Hotshot, huh?" His warm chuckle melted the chill around her. "I like that one."

"Well then I guess I'll have to keep trying." She bent to check her skis, her heart racing at the sheer drop of the double diamond she'd agreed to.

She straightened. Took a deep breath. She blamed that annoying grin for this suicidal mission. Next to her, Micah whistled. His goggled gaze turned her way reflecting the pinch of her lips and tick in her jaw.

"Hotshot might be a good one for *you*."

Casey groaned, his smooth voice doing things to her nerves that she wanted to boycott. "Come up with something original there, Soldier."

Micah stiffened like a switch had flipped. His grip tightened and vibrated on the poles in his hands. His chest rose and fell in quick heaves. And his focus lasered in on the course before them. Trees dotted the path all the way down the mountain, obscuring the trail from view at certain points. The powder glistened in loose mounds nearby.

Dumb. This was a really bad idea.

"You sure you want to do this, Micah?"

His fingers flexed on the poles, then tightened again.

A sharp nod.

"I don't quit."

Sweat trailed down his cheek, despite the chill. "Micah, are you sure . . ."

"I'm good," he snapped. "I'll see you at the bottom." He shoved off, careening out of view.

Something felt . . . off in his response. Nerves were normal. She was shaking in her boots. But Casey had watched Micah face down every challenging course in the last couple days with a wild laugh and "What's next?" Something had changed today, and she wasn't at all sure what had triggered the shift.

Casey didn't know what to think of Micah Richards—handsome, adrenaline junkie, mysterious, confident, kind, protective. And wounded. He felt broken somehow behind the smile and charm. She'd seen it when she picked him up. She'd noticed when some of her comments felt a little digging, something Teagan and Shawn rebuked her for constantly. She'd seen it in the way he spaced out at breakfast over coffee for just a moment, the distance in his gaze when Teagan or Shawn asked him a question about the last few months. Something had hurt her tough warrior.

She shook her head, bringing that rabbit trail to a screeching halt. He wasn't hers. Definitely not hers. Too much time with this guy the past couple days had developed an attachment she would sever as soon as she jumped her plane back to Dallas tomorrow. But another part of her—the part that jumped in to help her hurting kids—that part wanted to help. Just as much as she wanted to run. Experience, wisdom told her to run.

She rolled her shoulders, shaking her muscles out as she peered down the mountain trail before her. A patch of evergreens sat farther down the course to the right. Ski marks dented the snow in front of her. Her skis hung over the edge, ready for the plunge. She rotated her neck, her side braid tickling her exposed skin. She shifted her toboggan. "Alright. If Hotshot can do this, so can I. You can do this, Casey. Just don't," she placed her skis in place and took a deep breath, "overthink it."

With that, she pushed off. Powder kicked up on either side of her as she wound down the mountain at what felt like a near drop. Brisk air whistled past her, ringing in her ears. The sound of vacation. The sound of a challenge. "Whooo!" she shouted to the mountain, loving the freedom that zipped through her as she controlled every motion. Micah swerved into view below her, his leg swinging out wildly. "Reign it in, Soldier," she muttered. She sped past a tree, looking for obstacles and a red ski cap.

A yell. Then a thud.

She rounded a sharp twist in the trail and skidded to a stop. Micah lay crumbled and curled up near a tree. Skid marks tracked in the normal pattern until the snow split and gaped where he had landed, flipped, and rolled.

"Micah? Micah!" She pushed out of her skis and shoved them into the snow. Powder flew around her as she stumbled to Micah. She dropped at his side.

"I'm all right, Slugger," he groaned, shifting to lean on a tree. "Just an old muscle injury that flared up in my leg." Acid laced his voice. "I'm usually a much better skier."

"I bet you are." She did a quick scan. No blood. No protruding bones. His pride appeared more bruised than anything she could physically see. There was that haunted look again but only a flash before it disappeared. It was a mystery that tugged at her.

Don't go there, Case. She resumed her physical assessment, steering clear of any hidden scars.

Micah grabbed her searching hands. "Casey."

He waited until she stilled.

"I'm fine."

She pulled her hands into her lap. "Does this injury tend to have bad timing?"

"Story of my life. At least since high school. For some reason it has acted up ever since my . . . accident almost a year ago now." He tripped over the words, averting his eyes.

Another secret. Casey bit her lip. She was used to asking the tough questions. Her kids back home needed her to ask, even when they didn't want her to. But Micah? She had a feeling he was the kind of guy who, once he opened up, would demand that vulnerability in return. And she wasn't willing to share that. Casey's past, her secrets, were in a lock box marked "do not disturb" and buried deep underground. Never to be touched. Ever. Period. No, Micah's secrets were better left alone. They would go their separate ways soon.

Casey shook her head and pushed to her feet. "Let's get you up."

Micah waved her off as he leveraged the tree at his back. "I don't think you can carry me, Rocky."

"Yo, Adrian." She popped both hands on her hips. "I may be tiny but I am fierce."

"I have no doubt about that." His molten chocolate eyes could melt snow. "And when did I become Adrian in this equation?"

"The second you called me Rocky. Don't be a macho male." She put her arm around his back and tugged. "Let me help you."

"Casey, don't." His weight tipped. She fought for traction but met only air. Casey landed in the snow, Micah sprawled sideways across her stomach. That scruff. Now it was close enough. He was close enough. He smelled like mint and forest and cold. Her wall fissured. Just the tiniest bit.

She felt every sweep of those eyes over her face. Deep with flecks of the lightest brown, now focused on her lips. Her breath caught. She wondered if he would make a move. Wondered if he would take advantage of the moment and be just like every other guy who had forced an opportunity. But he held still. Just watching her, the weight of his body felt unnaturally safe. No pushing. No demanding more.

"You okay?" Breath puffed against her cheek in the frigid air, but all she felt was warmth.

Too warm.

No, no, no. She wasn't going to be fooled again. She couldn't be.

But something about Micah made a small part of her want to be . . . desired. Protected. Cared for. That was her role, though. Her lot to be the protector. Never the recipient.

She didn't mind the sacrifice. Not really. It kept her safe.

She shoved a layer of steel against the wall and pushed against Micah's chest, rolling him into the snow. Cold air rushed over her again. For the first time, she felt the chill seep through her ski pants, numbing her back and legs.

"Would you like to go to dinner with me?

Casey sat up so fast, her braid slapped her on the cheek, strands sticking to the chapstick coating her lips. She swiped at the strands. "Now?"

Micah chuckled and tossed an arm over his eyes where he reclined in the snow. "Sure, now's good, Ace. Anything out here look particularly appealing? Maybe we could find a rabbit. Apparently, they are good eats."

She shoved to her feet. "Did you want me to say yes? Because you are . . ."

"Casey." She stopped talking and stared down into those eyes again. "I would like for you to come to dinner with me. Please say yes?"

"I . . .I don't date." The dull roar of a motor edged into the silence before a snow patrol pulled into view.

"You two okay here?" A man in a red jacket unloaded and shoved his goggles onto his head.

"Yeah, man." Micah hobbled to his feet, his foot extended in front of him. "Banged up a weak muscle a bit. It should be fine with a little ice and elevation, but I don't think I'll make it down the rest of the trail. Could you give us a lift down?"

The man wrapped Micah's arm around his shoulder, his jacket swishing in the quiet. Casey watched, still trying to wrap her mind around Micah's questions. He'd passed up on kissing her but asked her out?

He probably didn't mean anything by it. Just a hang out.

He didn't want to eat alone.

Yeah, that was it. That had to be it.

"Casey, did you hear what Greg said?"

She shook her head, clearing the argument. "No, I must have missed it."

"He can only give one of us a lift down the mountain. Are you good to finish the course?"

She walked to her skis and started punching her feet in place. "Absolutely. I'll see you at the bottom."

"Hey, Ace, about dinner."

She checked her gloves and waved in his direction as he straddled the snowmobile. "Dinner. Great. No problem. We both have to eat. And Teagen and Shawn want to go dancing again, so it all works out." She adjusted her goggles as the engine roared to life again and drowned out his next words. In seconds, they were gone and Casey was left alone.

Wind whistled through the tall pines. A few needles drifted down around her skis. The air smelled crisp, cold, with the hint of cedar.

She'd said yes to an almost date. With a guy she barely knew. What was she thinking? The cold mountain air must be getting to her. She just needed to get back to Texas. Back to normalcy.

She pushed off the snowy mound, navigating the steep angles with care as she raced to the bottom, the adrenaline a welcome rush from the anxiety. She only had one more night before heading home. Only a little longer until retreat. It had never sounded so good. And so wrong all at the same time.

Dinner had been the smoothest non-date she'd ever been on. Heck, it'd really been the only non-date she'd ever been on as an adult, barring that catastrophe she'd agreed to to make Shawn happy. After her date knocked her dinner into her lap and then tried to take her home afterward, she'd never let Shawn recommend another guy. But with Micah, she'd laughed until she almost cried. She didn't remember the last time that had happened. Time with him felt easy for the most part. Easier still, because away from the responsibility of her kids and launching this sports league, in this place full of good memories, she felt a little freer.

Hot chocolate warmed her hands and marshmallows danced on top. Micah grinned next to her on the couch telling another story of his Navy SEAL team in his glory days. "Then Jay lost control for half a second, and Colt tossed him under the waves and kept pushing him under until he came up swearing he would never substitute shaving cream for whipped cream on Colt's coffee again." His laughter bounced off the beams in the corner of the sitting area of the hotel lobby. A few people shooting pool turned and grinned in his direction. Casey smiled into her mug and took another sip.

"Are they all back in California?"

Micah nodded, a heaviness shuttering the joy that had sparked in his eyes only moments before. "They're still there. Training. Working." He smirked. "Antsy to surf, I'm sure."

She poked at a marshmallow and studied him over her mug, trying to pinpoint the darkness he kept hidden just below the surface. Maybe it was only a figment of her imagination. "Do you miss it?"

"Miss what?"

"Your team? The ocean?"

He took a big gulp from his mug, avoiding the chip on the rim. "I miss the ocean." Longing coated his face, a longing she envied. "I miss the sound of the waves. The way they rush in and then foam and smooth out on the shore. I miss the way the water cools my skin on a hot day. I miss days in the sun surfing with the guys. I miss the way I can feel the power in each wave, the way it washes through you. And I like that you never know if the wave will win or if you will, but you try to beat it anyway."

"Sounds like you had a great life there. Why leave?"

He cleared his throat. "I . . ." the phone vibrated on the wooden center table. She'd never seen a man lunge for a phone like that.

"Hey, Hawk."

The baritone sounds of a man's voice leaked from the speaker, but Casey couldn't discern the words. She snuggled into the leather and studied the fire.

"Nick, I'm kinda stranded in Colorado right now." He paused. "The car broke down and the guy just called. It's going to be more to fix it than it's worth. So the car is officially dead. I've got to get to Fort Worth somehow, but I'll figure it out." Another beat. His hand balled into a fist before he rubbed his forehead. "Come see me, huh? Not sure when I'll be there, and I don't think you should come with me."

More murmuring.

"I'm not going to argue, Hawk. I'll see you the next time we are all home." His hand fell limp in his lap. "Tell Kayles I said hi and that I love her. And I guess . . ." This time the pause hung heavy. "I guess I'll see you when I see you."

He ended the call and tossed the phone between them on the couch.

She waited, but Micah only stared into the fire. The joy of the night evaporated. "So no car, huh?"

He shrugged. "There are worse places to be grounded. I'll figure it out."

"And Fort Worth?"

This time, he was slow to speak. "My buddy's family lives out that way. Nick, my brother-in-law, wants to meet me for a visit, but I need to go see them on my own." He waved her off. "But let's not ruin our last night."

And just like that, the charm was back in place, his grin captivating. She sank further into the couch, reminding herself to breathe, have fun, and get ready to run tomorrow.

"So tell me more about these kids you teach at Ellie's Place."

Teach was such a loose term. She was protector, coach, counselor, friend, mentor, teacher, a lifeline. Mostly their lifeline. "They are pretty great, although they require a pretty firm hand. Some of the guys love basketball, so we raised enough money to fix the court on the property. Right now, we are about to launch our last fundraiser to pay for a few more things before we start our own sports leagues in the community for kids of all ages. We are planning to start with baseball and basketball since the older guys have football over at the high school with Shawn. He's been filling in when he can, but coaching is a heavy load, and we need someone totally dedicated to this.

"We also help with their homework until their parents get home. And I run an after school leadership program for some of the kids. This guy, Al Jackson, had the idea for a safe haven for teenagers. He and his late wife couldn't have kids of their own, but they had a lot of money. He lives in this really ritzy part of Dallas. Story goes that they loved kids but wanted to go where there was a need. Enter in South Dallas. They tend to be forgotten sometimes. But they are incredible people, a lot of whom are caught in a tough cycle.

"This one kid, TJ . . . We aren't supposed to have favorites, but he's one of mine. His dad left when he was young. Oldest brother was killed, and his mom . . . Well, she has taken to some unhealthy occupations to put food on the table. He's trying to help, but he's only fifteen with a bright future ahead. I'm really worried that he's going to resort to something terrible just to help make ends meet. Selling drugs or something. He's the only freshman in my leadership program, and I'm hoping for big things for him and his family. He has two younger brothers. If they watch him succeed, I hope they will want to fight hard for that, too.

"Then there's Bianca. She's so talented. She's in my leadership classes and just blossoming as she leads her cheer team at the high school. I think she could get a scholarship, go to college, and really do well. She loves helping the younger kids with their homework, too. But she's dating this guy who is not the nicest kid I've ever met, and I'm concerned he's mixed up in some bad stuff."

She grimaced, aching at some of the things her kids had seen, some that she had seen as a kid. She wanted to protect them. "When Al's wife passed away, he sold his big house, moved to South Dallas, and bought this run-down, small elementary school. He refurbished it and turned it in to Ellie's Place. It truly is a safe haven for them. It's hard, but I wouldn't trade it for the world."

"Safe." That faraway look returned to his eyes, the longing intensified. "Sounds like a great program for the kids."

Her phone beeped and Casey checked the text. "Looks like Teagan just got back and needs my help wrapping up some packing. She and Shawn want to get to the airport early in the morning." She placed her mug on the table and looked at Micah. Time to say goodbye. Yet in that moment, she found she didn't really want to run.

He stood and held out his hand. She ignored it and pushed off the couch. Micah shoved his hands in his pockets. "I guess this is goodbye?"

She nodded, ignoring her racing heart.

"Can I at least have a hug?"

Casey grinned. "Is that all you want?"

He opened his arms wide. "Wouldn't want to scare ya with anything else, Buttercup."

"Buttercup? You call me that and expect me to hug you? You really need some new nicknames there, bud, because . . ."

"Oh just come here." And with that, he hooked an arm around her waist and pulled her tight against his chest. "See? It's not so bad. I've enjoyed the last few days, Casey Stewart. Thanks for not running over me." His words fanned over her cheek.

"It's not too late." Her voice was muffled against his jacket. She quickly pulled away.

Micah chuckled and took a step back, shoving his hands in his pockets. Casey shivered. It had to be the cold. It couldn't be that she missed being in his arms. She'd only known the guy a few days!

"Well, I guess this is it. Take care, Gorgeous."

She couldn't remember the last time someone had called her gorgeous. Maybe never. And somehow, she thought Micah just might mean it. "That one is slightly better. But only slightly. You take care of that leg."

"It just aggravated that old injury. I used an old brace. I'll be good as new in a few days." Even now, he favored his left leg.

"Let me know if you make it out to Fort Worth." She grabbed her jacket from the back of the couch, the chill now seeping into her bones as she took a step away from Micah.

"I'll figure it out. See ya, Ace." Sadness raced over his eyes before it disappeared. With a small smile and a nod, he turned toward the concierge desk.

She took two steps. Her heart hammering, her palms clammy. This didn't have to be goodbye. It needed to be. But . . .

"Come back with me." It was out of her mouth before her brain could stop it. She froze.

No sound.

Casey didn't dare turn around to face him. Bad idea, such a bad idea.

"I'm sorry, what?" She heard the muffled scuff of his boots on the rug and felt those eyes boring into the back of her head.

She squeezed her eyes shut and refused to turn around. She could keep walking. Pretend she hadn't said anything.

Micah's hand on her arm jerked her from her silent debate. "Casey?"

Time to dig out of a hole.

She could help him and still run. That was it. She could do both. That's all it was. She just wanted to help. No way was she interested. She couldn't be. Not to a gorgeous charmer with a southern accent and a protective streak a mile wide. Not to a daredevil who could break her heart. No way. She nearly groaned. Who was she kidding? Fine. She could be appropriately intrigued and not do a thing about it. Just . . . help.

She opened her eyes and squared her shoulders. "Well, it's only logical." *Think, Casey. What are your options?* "You need to get to Fort Worth. You don't have a car. Renting one sounds crazy. Tickets are cheap. I know someone you could stay with in my neighborhood. We've all landed at Mama Rosie's house at one point or another. Yeah, it all makes sense. You might as well fly back with us."

"That sounds like a lot of trouble, Case."

"No trouble, really." *Really, Casey? Lots and lots of trouble if this kind and handsome man is in the same state, let alone the same block. What are you thinking?*

"I guess that would work. If you really don't mind. It might be good to find an odd job or something in the meantime. Just while I figure things out. And a car."

"I'm sure Shawn could help with all that." Shawn. Right. Not her. Because that would be a bad idea. But she could volunteer Shawn. He owed her anyway.

"Okay. Okay, yeah this could work. I guess let me see if there is a spot open on your flight."

Within minutes, Micah Richards was booked on her Southwest flight in the last open seat bound for Dallas. And Casey wondered if she'd just made the second biggest mistake of her life.

One look at Micah's face, and she wanted to step into his arms and run all at the same time. She needed to get home and fast. To normalcy. To responsibility. And to her fortress where she could lock her heart up again and just focus on protecting her kids and her sister.

Emery needed her. Her kids needed her.

And she couldn't need anyone.

CHAPTER 5

The engines roared as the plane zoomed down the runway. Micah's chair rattled. He gripped the armrests, his knuckles whitening around the cheap plastic. Flying didn't bother him but the images did. The sound. The memory of his greatest failure—of helicopter engines hovering over turbulent waves, the blades whirring as he clutched his buddy, Harrison, in his arms, yelling at him to hang on. Harrison's eyes had glazed over before staring up at nothing. Yet above Micah, the sky roared.

"Didn't know you were such a chicken, Soldier Boy," Casey chided from the seat next to him.

Micah clamped down on a retort. He could taste the salt, hear the slap of the water as the waves white-capped under the slice of airborne blades hovering overhead. He could still see faces. Four. Gone. Micah sucked in a deep breath.

"Soldier Boy is technically incorrect," he ground out, his teeth clenched, heart racing.

"Micah, seriously, are you okay?"

"Fine," he managed to whisper before memories choked him again.

And for two hours he squirmed under their relentless tide. If only he'd been faster. If only he hadn't tripped over that boulder when firing over his shoulder. If only.

If onlys couldn't bring back his team. *If onlys* couldn't ease the guilt. Nothing assuaged the pain. The memories hit at the worst times, all reminding him of the man he used to be, the man he no longer was—surrounded by a team, living for something bigger than himself.

Now? Now, he just wanted to make it through a day. Figure out who he was apart from his team. Micah Richards, no longer a SEAL. Micah Richards, uncertain. Lost.

Most of all, he wanted to stop hurting the people around him, which now included Casey. He couldn't—wouldn't—do that to her.

"God, please," he whispered. He longed for the peace he had once known intimately to drown out the memories. He'd once known his place, his people. But lately, it felt like even God was distant. Now he felt utterly alone.

Casey stiffened next to him and shifted away. He glanced over, his mind clearing for the first time in a couple hours as the flight attendant announced their descent into Dallas. "You okay?"

She nodded. "Looks like you finally snapped out of it." Her tone stiff, more distant. Her fingers no longer soothing the back of his hand.

He didn't feel like explaining. He released a breath. "That praying thing helps."

Her lips pursed but she didn't respond. Micah didn't have any energy left to follow through. Battling his demons sapped every bit of stamina.

"What's the plan?" He focused on logistics. Details. It's what he did in war. It seemed appropriate here.

"I called Mama Rosie last night." She fumbled the phone in her lap. Micah reached to still her fingers, but she jerked from his touch. He was too exhausted to figure out what he'd done to offend her.

"She has a room open, as always. Shawn is staying with her right now while he tries to find a place closer to the school, so you'll have a buddy." Micah glanced across the aisle at the guy bobbing with his Beats on. He'd spent a little time with Shawn in Colorado, skiing and rooming with him. They'd shared a couple meals and several conversations about sports. Easy guy to befriend.

"Awesome. Thanks for calling her."

"She also said she might have a lead on a car for you."

"You didn't have to mention that."

"Well, I've never called and mentioned any other guy besides Shawn before, so she demanded details. And you don't tell Mama Rosie *no* if you know what's good for you." She smirked, a bit of playfulness returning to her tone.

The plane smacked the runway, the engine roar grounding him firmly in the present this time. He had nothing left in his mental tank. He went through the motions of deplaning. After catching the shuttle to the long-term parking, they hopped into Casey's Toyota and pulled into Dallas traffic. He sank into his seat in the back as Shawn and Teagan carried on a running dialog.

"Next year, we need to stay a full week," Teagan said.

"You know we go during the week to get cheaper tickets. Plus, I only get one weekend off during football season, Teag, and even that is pushing it. And this year, playoffs, baby! I can't believe they made it. With a little more discipline and training, we might go all the way. This coaching gig is a big responsibility."

Teagan rolled her eyes and tossed her red hair. "Responsibility is so overrated, don't you think, Micah?"

He only grimaced in response. He liked the responsibility that used to be his, the freedom of a nation, of his loved ones, propelling him forward. Now, he was responsible for nothing. And he hated it.

"You should swing by and see the kids practice, Micah. Didn't you say you used to play in high school?" Shawn asked.

Micah nodded. "I was quarterback in high school and was second string for the Trojans in college."

Shawn whistled. "That's big time."

"Not too much." Those memories carried a bad taste, too. "I pulled a tendon in my ankle my senior year of high school after I'd already committed. I did a lot of conditioning and fully recovered but could never quite earn that number one spot." He released a breath, finally feeling his muscles unwind.

"Did you ever want to go pro?" Shawn asked.

The car came to a stop in front of a white brick house; a white picket fenced rimmed the outside with two trees shedding the last of their red and golden leaves in Texas style faux fall.

"That was always my brother's dream. Mine became the SEALs." The old dream weighed heavy.

"Alright boys, you can chat inside. Mama Rosie is waiting. Micah, take care, and good luck with everything."

Micah halted his shuffle and tried to catch Casey's eyes in the rearview mirror. Her gaze stayed fixed on the road, her fingers twisting around the steering wheel. She was saying goodbye. Permanently. Gone was the comradery of the ski slopes and plane.

Weary, he mumbled, "See ya," and scrambled from the car. Shawn tossed him his duffle and led the way to the front door, waving at the girls pulling away.

"Dude, what did you do to Casey?"

"I have no idea. Things were going really well last night. I thought when she invited me back here..."

Shawn stopped him at the door. "First of all, that shocked all of us. Casey isn't exactly friendly toward guys, except me. So you did something right." Shawn narrowed his gaze, his broad shoulders squaring. "But you better figure out what you did wrong. I would hate to get a call and have to ruin our budding friendship and all that."

Micah smirked. Shawn was alright. "Duly noted. I would hate to kill the possibility of a bromance."

Shawn unlocked the door and held the screen open for Micah. "Well, then, after you, handsome. But don't you dare get too cute. I don't do this bromance business."

Micah sighed. "Missing out, man. It's a whole new world."

"There is something wrong with . . ."

"My boy is back. ¡Hola! Welcome home, mi amigo." One of the shortest women Micah had ever seen bustled into the small entryway and yanked Shawn into a hug. Her once-black hair now held streaks of gray, and her brown skin creased with a million wrinkles as her smile and eyes danced.

"You must be my new one." She tugged Micah down into a hug and kissed both cheeks. Shawn grinned over her shoulder as Micah doubled over to return the hug.

"Nice to meet you, Ms. Rosie. Thanks for letting me stay for a bit."

"It's Mama Rosie to you." She wagged a finger in his face. "And you can stay as long as you like. Once you stay at Mama Rosie's, you never get rid of me, huh?" Her grin was contagious, soothing his frazzled nerves.

Shawn wandered down a short hall decked in photos to his room as Mama Rosie walked Micah to the room next door. She waved him in. "Get settled and then I have food ready in the kitchen. You better be hungry." She patted his stomach. "Oh, all muscle, no meat. Mama Rosie will fix that." She bustled off, leaving Micah staring after her.

Shawn appeared and lounged in his doorway. "She really will try to fix that, too. You better take out a gym membership while you are here, or she will have you rolling home in no time. Better yet, you can come work out at the high school gym."

"That sounds like a good plan." He dropped his bag and surveyed the room. A double bed, nightstand, and short dresser were the only furniture. More photos hung from every wall. Simple, but all he needed. It was better than a hotel. Better than his car. And home cooking sounded like a dream come true. He plopped on the bed. "I don't think I've been inside a school gym since college."

Shawn crossed his arms. "Well, this one isn't much to look at. The school is pretty rough and there isn't much funding. The kids are pretty rough around the edges, too."

"I'll take teenagers over terrorists any day of the week."

"You might change your mind," Shawn chuckled. "By the way, got any weight training experience?"

"I've never trained anyone personally, but between high school, college, and the SEALs, I have some experience." Micah sat up and studied Shawn. "Why?"

"The coach who normally does all the training lost his dad and asked for time away the rest of the year to take care of things. Apparently, his dad has a large estate and some business dealings that will just take time. I could use a temp in the gym and on the field if you are interested. As in, I'm kinda desperate, and you kinda owe me for sharing my room in Colorado." He grinned.

Micah hesitated. He didn't want to set down roots. He wanted to pay his respects to his buddy's widow and then leave again. Scratch that. He didn't even want to go pay his respects. This one would be the most difficult. She'd just given birth to their first child a few months earlier. A little girl. Caroline. A name seared in his memory. And after this final visit, he was finished. And his buddies would really, truly feel gone. And then he would need to figure out his next move. A job. A state. His life. It all seemed too much. He'd had his dream. What did he do now?

Shawn offered a hand and pulled Micah to his feet. "Think about it and let me know. The offer stands. The boys could use a little SEAL training, a little discipline. This might be right up your alley. You told me in Colorado that you were trying to figure out what to do next. Maybe this is a good step." He shoved Micah out the door and led him to the kitchen where spicy and sweet scents mingled in the air. "But if we don't get to the kitchen pronto, Mama Rosie will come give us an earful, and trust me," he gave Micah a knowing look, "you don't want that."

"Duly noted."

Micah and Shawn stepped into a kitchen painted in a sunny yellow with rose accents. It was the farthest thing from updated but the closest to home Micah had tasted in months. He didn't know what he was doing in Texas. He'd hopped on a plane to follow a girl who now wanted nothing to do with him to stay with a woman he'd never met and potentially coach and train teenage guys. He was the farthest thing from a role model for these guys. He didn't know what he'd gotten himself into, but maybe this could be a fresh start. At least right now. It would at least keep him busy. The barrage of memories was becoming more than he could handle.

"Girl, you better get it together, or I'm going to get it together for you." Teagan tugged on Casey's braid. Casey didn't need to look at her best friend to know her green eyes fired as much heat as her red hair.

"I have no idea what you're talking about." Casey jerked to a stop as the light shifted to red. She tapped a quick rhythm on the steering wheel, praying for a green.

"Well, then let me spell it out for you, Casey Denae Stewart," Teagan drawled, sass dripping from every syllable. "Hot soldier boy shows up. Gives you attention. He's a total gentleman. And good grief, that grin could stop traffic. By the way, the light is green."

Casey threw her foot on the gas. The car leapt forward. Micah's grin could do more than stop traffic. It had the ability to punch holes in her walls. But she didn't want Teagan to know Micah had that potential.

Teagan whistled. "Girl, you got it bad. At least as much as you are capable of crushing on someone, which isn't much. The worst part is you don't want to admit it. You never would in a million years."

"There's nothing to admit." She pulled to a stop in front of Teagan's apartment building. "Micah will be gone soon. He's just passing through."

"Then why invite him home with you?"

"I suggested he fly on the same plane with us to Dallas, Teag. That's it. Very different from inviting him to come home with us."

Silence greeted her. Casey finally faced her friend to see the very look she'd avoided, the one that said, "I've known you since we were seven. I live behind your walls. Quit lying to me."

"It's more than that and you know it." Teagan grabbed her backpack and motioned for Casey to pop the trunk. "Make nice with that boy, or I will do it for you."

"Don't you dare."

This time Teagan paused. Casey rarely put her foot down with her friends. She would literally do anything for them, including jump in front of a herd of stampeding elephants. Or teenagers. But this she wouldn't let Teagan touch. This was an area she didn't let her two best friends see or examine.

"One good reason, Case." Her voice gentled and she leaned through the open window. "Give me one reason why you can't at least try. He's one of the good ones. And they don't just slip in front of your car in a land far, far away every day of the week."

Casey wilted. "He prayed, Teag."

"What?" Her friend leaned through the window to hear.

This time Casey snapped. "He prayed, Teagan. To God. He trusts the guy."

Teagan pulled back. Her teeth worried her lip, and Casey knew she was chewing on her words before she released them. But this time, only one sentence emerged. "You can't hate God forever, Case."

Without another word, Teagan grabbed her suitcase and turned her back, her red hair stark against her navy sweater. Casey stared after her friend long after she'd lugged her suitcase up the stairs. Asking Casey to trust Micah already bordered on impossible. Asking her to trust God? Wouldn't, couldn't happen. Micah would want her to know his God. And she had. Once upon a time. Before he broke her heart and left her alone, too. She'd built her wall after that. If God wouldn't protect her, she'd have to do it on her own. And she'd looked out for herself ever since.

CHAPTER 6

Saturday morning dawned with Micah in need of figuring out his car situation, a problem which Mama Rosie quickly remedied. "Follow me, mi amigo." Mama Rosie motioned Micah to hurry behind her as she wound through her small house, packed tight with furniture, bric-a-brac, and photos. Photos everywhere. Black and white photos dated back to her childhood. Current photos of families, teenagers, and kids decorated every wall and surface. Micah halted in front of a framed photo on the wall. Casey hung suspended mid-jump, yelling from the sidelines as a group of kids engaged in an intense game of basketball.

"They had a neighborhood tournament last year. It was the first time Casey tested the waters to see how a league might work through Ellie's Place. The kids practiced for months. I was on the sidelines for every game. I am neighborhood mama. They are all my kids." Pride rang loud and clear. "Casey sent me that after the game as a souvenir. That," she pointed at the photo, "was a good day. It changed lives."

"How did it change lives?" Micah studied the small woman next to him. She'd dressed in some sort of pink dress overlaid with an apron today. Her loafers were built for work and comfort.

"These kids, mijo, their parents don't care. That's why Casey provides them with other opportunities. She wants them to know they belong, that they are more than they have heard and seen. That day, some of the kids played as a team for the first time and liked it. Some learned that they were winners. Some learned what it looks like to cheer for the kid from the rival family. The game. It brought the kids together. It changed perceptions, emotions, hearts. So, it changed lives that day." She kissed her fingers and brushed them across the glass. "And that is why it is my favorite."

The way she talked about Ellie's Place, Casey, the community they were trying to build, it was something he longed to be part of again. But he feared he would only mess it up.

She started toward the door at the end of the hall. "Now hurry. We don't have all day."

He shook off his melancholy. A car. That was a problem in his control to solve. One step at a time. Micah followed her into the garage. A tarp covered something in the center of the cracked cement floor. Boxes and a tool bench lined the sides covered in layers of dust. Mama Rosie tossed the tarp into a corner, revealing an old, beat-up, red Chevy truck. "Meet your new ride."

Micah just stared. This piece of junk probably ran worse than the car he'd laid to rest in the mountains of Colorado. "Does it run?"

"I don't know. That's for you to figure out. It belonged to mi amor."

"Is he . . ."

"He went to be with the good Lord ten years ago." She popped her hands on her plump hips and gave him a look that even his mother would have been proud of. "You need a way to get around. This is it. Dallas isn't a small city. We don't just walk or ride our bikes. We're commuters down here, and you need a car, or you'll have to ride the bus."

"Mrs. Rosie . . ."

Her eyes could have shot him dead. Micah shuffled back a step, his hands raised. "Mama Rosie," he corrected, "I'm not planning to stay that long. I'll just hop a ride with Shawn or call Uber."

She marched across the garage and stood toe-to-toe with him, her tiny frame even shorter than Casey's five-foot-two, yet somehow more intimidating. "Then consider fixing this truck as rent."

She pointed to the corner as she stalked out of the garage. "Tools are over there. Skill is in your hands and in that thick head of yours. And any questions . . ." she cast a look over her shoulder. "Young TJ usually stops by around dinner time. I'm sure he can show you a thing or two. That boy is a good mechanic and he's not even sixteen yet. He's gonna go places with his skills. I just know it."

Micah heard her mumbling as she exited the garage. He stood in front of the truck. It was the beat-up, old, red pickup of all his country, non-childhood fantasies. And now he was the proud owner. Renter? He didn't really know. He wished he'd paid attention when his dad and older brother, David, had tried to show him the ropes of fixing up a car. For them, it had been therapeutic. For him, it had been next to torture. He felt around the hood of the car until a latch clicked and he could pop the top. The metal groaned in protest. Micah empathized.

"Well, you big ole rust bucket." He patted the dinged, dusty car door as he circled the hunk of steel. "Looks like it's just you and me. Let's figure out how to bring you back to life." He winced, glancing at the tool box. "And maybe forgive me if I break something before you get better."

He rolled up his sleeves and slipped his watch from his wrist, dropping it into his pocket. He heard the slight scrape as the watch slipped over something. His fingers brushed over plastic. Holding it up to the light, he caught a glimpse of Casey's faint smile, warm brown eyes, and dark hair falling around her shoulders. Her license. She'd asked him to put it in his pocket in the rush of shuffling bags and removing layers when they arrived at the airport in Colorado. Before she'd told him to get lost.

"Well, Casey Stewart. Looks like you aren't quite rid of me yet." Armed with his excuse, Micah abandoned his new wheels and went in search of Mama Rosie for an address and a game plan. Maybe he could convince Casey to talk to him again. Something about her sparked his interest. And that hadn't happened in a long time.

After agreeing to chauffeur Mama Rosie on all her errands, Micah borrowed her car and followed the directions to Ellie's Place later that afternoon. He pulled up to a small building. The center's name identified the building in red letters just over the entrance. Teenagers hung near the doors. Around back, he heard shouting, cheering, the faint scuff of shoes on concrete, and the slap of a rubber ball greeting the ground. He shifted his trajectory, aiming for a chain-link fence peeking around the corner.

One of the most competitive shirts-versus-skins basketball games he'd ever seen raged in the cordoned court. And, with her toes edging onto the court from the sidelines, was Casey, yelling and jumping as she kept pace with the ball. The kids played rough and seemed to range from ninth to twelfth grade. An older man sat in the middle of the bleachers, teens surrounding him on all sides. The hint of a smile was just visible beneath the shadow of his fedora.

Micah paced the fence, looking for a gate. Casey hadn't noticed him yet, her attention firmly fixed on the court. "Pass it TJ. Nice steal, Coleman."

He choked on a laugh. She was coaching both teams. Skins

went in for a basket and the stands erupted. Before Micah could take a step in Casey's direction, a scuffle broke out on the court. The kid, TJ he assumed, swung at Coleman. In one quick move, his neck was trapped in Coleman's much stronger arms, his back bowed and arms flailing.

Micah hopped the fence in one move, his body groaning from his lack of exercise. But years of training put grace and power in his movement. He made it halfway across the pavement but Casey was already there.

In one move, she ripped the boys apart and stood with her arms stretched between them. "That's enough, you two." If Micah wasn't so worried one of them would punch her he might have laughed—a tiny mouse caught between two angry jungle cats. Micah stalked closer, Casey still oblivious to his presence. TJ swerved trying to punch Coleman, but Casey was in his face. "Cool it, bud. You know that's not how we do things here."

"Nah, bro. Not at all. You gonna let this tiny woman fight your battles for you?" Coleman egged him on.

"Coleman, that's enough," Casey spat without ever turning to look at him.

His slow grin made Micah's skin crawl. He was about ready to throw a punch. Micah took another step, but the older man in the stands caught Micah's eye and gave one subtle shake of his head. Micah clenched his fist and stood his ground, watching the stare down.

"C'mon, TJ. You always going to let Casey fight your battles for you? I thought you were a man now. The only man left in your house because your brother went and got himself . . ."

With an angry cry, TJ launched himself past Casey and into Coleman, knocking Casey backwards onto the asphalt. He heard a crack as her head connected with the concrete. Micah's temper slipped. With a yank he pulled Coleman from TJ. The older man appeared, grabbing the other wiry teen around the waist and holding him fast.

"C'mon, Al. Let me go!" Anger radiated from TJ but Al held fast.

A dark chuckle tore through the kid knotted in Micah's arms. The sound grated. With a firm squeeze from Micah, Coleman stopped chuckling and wheezed for air. Micah released him and patted him on the back. His voice slipped to a deadly calm as he whispered in the teen's ear, "Disrespect Casey or any guys on this court again, and you'll have me to deal with."

"What are you going to do about it, old man? I ain't scared of you." Coleman's smirk lit a fire in Micah.

With a quick snap, Micah had Coleman's wrist twisted and his arm folded awkwardly behind his back. "Where I come from, a man treats others with respect," he whispered. The court was deathly quiet. "A man knows how to fight for others instead of picking a fight." He tugged harder and the boy winced. Kids around him shifted, but he could tell they were listening. He raised his voice so they could hear. "You want street cred, you'll be fighting your whole life to earn respect. You want warrior cred?" He shoved Coleman away. "Learn how to earn respect that lasts."

Coleman backed away from him and spat, his eyes reminding Micah of a jungle cat. Crisis averted. For now. The crowd slowly disbanded, and the thunk of the ball slapping the court signified a truce. No one would be fighting again today. The adrenaline rushed out of Micah, leaving behind the echo of the man he'd once been.

The label of a warrior—honor, courage, respect. He no longer felt he measured up. His life felt like a lie. He turned slowly and came toe-to-toe with Casey.

"What do you think you're doing, Hotshot?"

"Whoa." Micah held up his hands and took a step back. "Now you're mad?"

She grabbed his shirt and yanked him after her, beating a quick line to the building. Micah choked back a chuckle. "If you wanted me to go with you, all you had to do was ask."

"It's more satisfying for me to drag you around." She shoved his chest as soon as they walked inside. She had some muscle. And more than a little fight.

"You undermined me."

"Excuse me?"

She stood on tiptoe to get close to his face, her finger poking his chest. "You heard me."

He stood his ground. "You were flat on your back with some angry, strong teenagers going at it right next to you." He crossed his arms, forcing her back a step. She needed some serious awareness training. Maybe a dose of reality while she was at it. "Where I come from, you stand up for those you care about, and you don't let a man mistreat a woman."

"I am not a damsel in distress. I can take care of myself. And you barely know me. Don't pretend you care."

Something in him snapped. He took slow steps toward her, forcing her to back against the wall. He stopped when they were toe-to-toe. Her only option was to stare at his chest or meet his eyes. And Micah knew she wasn't a coward. His voice lowered to a whisper. "Who hurt you so bad that even the prospect of someone defending you forces you behind your walls?"

Her brown eyes practically glowed. She tried to shove his chest, but he anchored his arms on the wall, closing her in. "I will not ask your permission to protect you or anyone else if the situation calls for it, nor will I smother you if I see you have it handled. But you need a serious reality check if you think you can handle things on your own all the time." He took one step closer, a breath from touching her. "As for the caring part, I spent several days with you and your friends. How much time do you need to spend with someone before you know you enjoy their company? Who dictates that standard?" He leaned down and whispered in her ear. "But if you're too scared, I understand." He took a step back, watching her exhale. Her wary eyes fixed on him.

"I'm not scared. Nor am I stupid."

Adrenaline pumped through him. Something about her beauty, her strength, the care she radiated to those kids as he watched her coach from the sideline—it had every protective bone in his body wanting to stand between her and the world. That small taste of his old self—the protector no matter the personal cost—it unnerved him. The last time he had been the protector, he'd gotten his friends killed.

He took a deep breath and backed up a few paces, finding the opposite wall and allowing it to bear his weight. She held his gaze. Slowly, he watched her body unwind, her knuckles return to their tan color, her breathing even. "We'll agree to disagree on one of those statements."

This time, she advanced but stopped in the middle of the hall. A door slammed nearby, but her eyes didn't leave his.

"You're leaving, Micah. I don't know when, but you're drifting through. You've made that clear. And I know you're tough. I know you can handle those kids. But they don't need someone who can handle them. They need someone who will care about them, someone who will stay." Her voice lowered, a challenge leaking through her words. "Let's not pretend I'm the only one who's scared. I may hide behind a wall, as you put it, but you hide behind your charm and calm and this journey you are on."

His jaw popped as he ground his teeth.

"You say you care? Maybe." She cast him one last glance, but this time he saw an echo of his own brokenness in her eyes. "But those are just words. If it's true, you'll have to prove it." With a quick pivot, she was gone. Back to the kids she loved and the job she hid behind. Back to the remnants of tension she shouldn't referee alone. Back to a local battlefield. The kind of field he never wanted to enter again.

The kind of minefield she had just called him to tread if he wanted to prove his feelings. His feelings. He had them, and he didn't know what to do with them. Micah slapped the wall, his palm tingling against the cinder blocks. Casey was cute and sassy and fun and a fighter—everything he was attracted to. Everything he secretly always wanted. But he was a mess. He had nothing to give her

He touched his forehead to the porous cement blocks, their cool texture absorbing his anger, his confusion. He cared. But . . .

People around him wound up hurt or dead. And he couldn't let Casey be a casualty.

"Lord, you've been quiet lately, but a little help here would be great," he whispered, feeling a wave of calm ease his racing thoughts. Though the Lord seemed silent, Micah constantly felt his presence. A little direction now would be nice.

A door slammed, jarring him from his thoughts. A heated basketball game brewed on the court just outside the window. Casey cheered right in the middle of her kids again, so small in the midst of so much attitude. These kids were angry. And she was fighting for them. She needed a champion, too. Someone to step in when her back was on the ground.

But was Micah the guy for the job?

"You must be Micah." The soft sound of loafers paused behind him, and he turned, stepping away from the wall.

"And you must be Al." He extended his hand. "It's a pleasure to meet you, sir. Shawn, Teagan, and Casey have spoken highly of you."

He chuckled. "Well, I can't say the same for Casey, but the other two mentioned you this morning when I saw them. You're from California?"

"Alabama, originally."

"Ah, just passing through?"

"Probably." Micah ran a hand through his dark hair. "Not really sure what I'm doing right now to be honest with you."

His eyes twinkled, reminding Micah of his Pap back home. "You don't exactly strike me as a man without a plan."

Micah chuckled. "Well that used to be true."

Al tipped the rim of his fedora up, his cool blue eyes piercing. "And why not anymore?"

Micah shuffled. "Let's just say my original plan came to an unexpected end, and now I need a new plan."

"Or someone to plan for." A smile hovered on his face.

Micah grimaced. "I'm not too sure Casey wants me to plan on her. Or even plan on staying for that matter."

"Mmmhmm. Well, I've known Casey for a few years now, and I can tell you that Ellie's Place is all about second chances. And future chances and dreams. Maybe you being here isn't a coincidence."

Micah stared at the man. Was it even possible to replace what he had lost? To start over? Find a new dream? Another team? A purpose? He wasn't sure. But the thought tugged at him.

He shoved his hand in his pocket, producing Casey's license. "Would you give this to her for me? She was a little too riled up."

Al took the license from his outstretched hand. "Casey is riled because you fought hard enough to get into her space. And that scares her. Few of us have survived the climb behind her walls." He rested a hand on Micah's shoulder. "But something about you says you may have what it takes. We could use a guy like you around here. Think about it." He squeezed and exited through the glass door to the court.

～

The Tried and True Trio had a strong Sunday brunch game. Over the past few years, it had become the thing to do on a Dallas morning, and the lines stretched for hours. But Casey had a strategy. While Shawn drove from church and Teagan came from wherever she'd been, Casey drove down to the Bishop Arts district, parked her Toyota on a neighborhood street, and walked a couple blocks to Oddfellows, one of their favorite brunch places in the city.

The people watching only enhanced the experience. An old, seventies-style van sat in front of Oddfellows, boasting outdated and gently used clothes. A thin sheet in the very back allowed people to browse the tight space with a couple of clothing racks and then try on their finds. The space was too claustrophobic and heated for Casey's taste, but some days she would order a coffee, sit on a stool at the outdoor bar counter, and watch people stumble from the tie-dye, painted van with new treasures from decades past.

A woman wearing a fedora and a blue, crushed velvet vest strolled past Casey walking her cat on a leash. A guy with tight jeans and gigantic ear gauges swerved down the street on a longboard, dodging cars and morning brunchers.

Casey asked for a to-go mug at the coffee bar, double-checked her phone number on the list, then wandered down the block, popping in shops selling trendy t-shirts, knick-knacks for homes, and an assortment of jewelry and art. Sundays were sacred—her mornings to breathe, think, and enjoy.

But this morning, she had only one thing on her mind: Micah Richards. The handsome guy whom she had literally almost run over with her car. They'd only spent a few short days skiing and enjoying the small Colorado town with her friends, and then he'd panicked and mentioned God on a flight to Dallas. It made her curious. And wary. Now, she couldn't seem to get rid of him. In fact, he had even tried to protect her this week. What was he thinking?

Her phone buzzed with an incoming text: *Your table is ready.*

Casey hurried back to the white restaurant front, the picnic tables gracing the sidewalk now packed with people waiting their turn to move inside. Casey greeted Shawn and Teagan at the front door with a hug.

"Y'all ready for another tasty and successful Sunday brunch experience?" Teagan rubbed her hands together as she scooted into a booth.

"I'm always ready for brunch with you ladies." Shawn picked up his menu and quickly rattled off their coffee and drink orders to the waitress.

Teagan perused the menu, even though she knew it by heart. "How goes the coach hunt, Casey?"

Casey steepled her fingers over her menu and leaned forward. "Well, I had two phone interviews on Friday afternoon when we got back from Colorado. One with a guy named Marco in Memphis, Tennessee. He's coached baseball there at a middle school and is looking for a change, but it's a big move. I put the ball in his court to let me know if he is still interested. He was going to talk with his wife and get back to me.

"The other candidate is this local guy named Brad. He graduated from SMU about a year ago, great athlete. Played on their basketball team. But he's really young, and I'm not sure how he will handle our kids. He's coming for an in-person interview on Tuesday, and then I may see if he can help with the upcoming fundraiser. Test him out with the kids a bit."

"Sounds like some promising leads," Shawn said.

"I'm content for now. But we can talk work later. Teag, you ready to order yet?"

"I think I'm feeling pancakes. No, an omelette. No, the special. Shoot, I can't decide."

Shawn and Casey grinned at Teagan. The hippy redhead could eat an entire pig and not gain weight. Casey despised her friend's metabolism.

"Come on, Teag. Just order all of it. We know you won't gain an ounce."

Teagan let her menu fall and pointed a finger at her friends across from her. "Hey, I work out."

"It's okay, Teagan. We all know you hate to sweat."

"Well, true. But I do work out."

"Since when?" Casey took a sip of her coffee, smirking at Teagan.

"Since I found this new boxing gym."

Casey could have sworn Shawn's eyebrows had just permanently buried themselves in his hairline.

"You? Miss Flower Child? Boxing?"

"Listen here, Muscle Man." Teagan leaned across the table.

"Oh no," Casey muttered.

"One, I resent that name. Just because I like nature-y things does not mean I'm a flower child. And two, I can box. And I'm actually pretty good at it."

Casey had been wrong. His eyebrows could go higher.

"I somehow can't picture that."

"Well why don't I show you?" Teagan stood, a challenge in her eyes and a wicked grin gracing her pixy features. "Outside, now."

A waitress with a full tray skirted around Teagan as Shawn grabbed her wrist and tugged her back into the booth. "How about you show me later, killer. And since you are actually working out and I've been trying to get you to do that for forever, I salute you."

"Thank you." Satisfied, Teagan returned to her menu.

"Speaking of new things. What's with this Micah guy sticking around even longer? I heard maybe Christmas?" Casey complained.

This time Shawn's raised eyebrows turned her way. She would have to help him rearrange his face later if he kept doing that.

"Don't call him 'that Micah guy.' We all know y'all have some ridiculously crazy chemistry going on," Shawn said.

Casey had to pick her jaw off the floor. "I'm sorry, what?"

Teagan closed her menu. "Pancakes, I've decided. And maybe a side of bacon. And eggs. And seriously, Case, don't pretend like you don't feel the chemistry. Everyone sees it. I heard he totally defended your honor yesterday."

"Whoa." Casey held up her hands in the all stop sign. "I think y'all have confused chemistry with supreme aggravation and annoyance."

Both of her friends sank back into their chairs, arms crossed, smirks firmly intact.

Wrong move.

"Uh uh. No way. There is not chemistry." Her voice raised an octave. The guy sitting a few feet from her turned and winked. Weird. A bar hung through his nose. Nope. Definitely not interested.

She turned back to her friends. No way did she and Micah have chemistry. Except . . . that one time. And maybe. No. No way.

Teagan reached for her hand over the plastic, sticky menus. "Hon, it's okay if you do have chemistry. It's okay if you like him." The tease lighting her eyes quickly turned to understanding. "And frankly if you do, it's about time."

"Messed up, running from something he won't talk about, occasionally freaks out for no reason. Yep, he's a keeper. He won't hurt me at all." Sarcasm dripped.

"Hold that thought." Shawn held up a hand as the waitress returned. Teagan complimented the bright blue highlights in her chestnut hair before rattling off all their orders. Casey sat there, quiet. It wasn't okay to like Micah. She didn't even know what to do if she did like him. The last guy who had liked her had taken everything from her and then painted her in a bad light. So had every guy who had paraded through her home as a kid. She'd never dreamed about the white picket fence, two point five kids, and a golden retriever. That was a fairy tale. Prince Charming didn't exist. Animals didn't talk. And romantic love only brought pain.

But dreams . . . those she believed in. Dreams bred hope for something better. For her. For her sister. For Shawn and Teagan. Maybe even Micah. Maybe that's really why she'd invited him back. Dallas had been the place she'd rediscovered hope. Maybe he would, too.

She chewed on her lip. If she were truly honest, her deepest, most secret hope was that a guy, any guy besides Shawn, would prove her wrong someday. But as she approached thirty, those embers had begun to burn out.

"Okay," Shawn shifted in his seat and threw an arm over the back of her chair. "Let's look at Micah in a different light, shall we?"

Casey didn't respond, wasn't sure she could.

"He's the guy who has stepped in to protect you not once, but twice in the last few weeks. He liked you enough to come to Dallas, even if he had a broken-down car and other reasons, as well. Mama Rosie likes him, which should say everything right there. He has treated you with consideration. He served our country as a SEAL. Those guys aren't playing around. I don't know many guys who serve in the capacity he did and don't come back battling personal demons. Does he have things to work through?" He narrowed his eyes on her. "Don't we all? But I don't think he is quite the mess you are painting, and I don't think you truly believe that either."

"More coffee?" Blue streaks was back. Perfect timing.

"Yes, please." Casey practically threw her white ceramic mug at the waitress. Shawn just grinned.

"I think our girl has a crush."

Teagan smiled a dopey grin. "Yeah. We'll get her to admit it one of these days."

"Not likely," Casey protested. But she hated that her friends could climb right over her walls. Heck, she'd made a door for them and given them both keys long ago. She wouldn't trade that for the world, but sometimes . . . sometimes the view they had scared her. They mined the truth she couldn't hide. But this, this felt too deep.

Despite all the Micah talk, brunch was as delicious as ever. Casey felt herself unwind from her coach hunt, plans for the center, and her now churning emotions over Micah Richards.

And then. The peace was shattered with a three-letter word on her phone screen.

Mom.

They exited Oddfellows right as the ringing began. Casey answered as Shawn steered them past waiting brunchers to their cars.

"Casey Stewart, you need to come get your sister or, so help me God, I'm going to kill her."

Casey jerked the phone from her ear at her mother's shouting and slurring. It was noon but it sounded like her mom had already consumed a few Bloody Mary's.

"Mom, slow down. What's wrong with Emery?"

"I'm tired of teenage girls who don't know how to handle their liquor or their men. And I don't have time to deal with the cops bringing her home for underage drinking!" Casey stopped in the middle of the parking lot. Her heart pounding and memories racing.

Her bedroom.

A guy laughing.

And her mom telling her to suck it up while mocking Casey's tears.

Teagan and Shawn stood on either side of her. Casey put the phone on speaker. Just like every other moment of her life, she needed her friends to help her handle her mom.

"Mom, slow down. Where's Emery?"

"I mean," Mona slurred, "you'd think both of you would have inherited a little something from me, learn to handle your alcohol. Or at least not get caught. But, oh no."

"Mom, where's my sister?" Panic tore through Casey. She wanted to wrap her fourteen-year-old sister in bubble wrap. No one should experience what she had.

Please God, no.

The knee-jerk, silent prayer shocked Casey. She hadn't prayed in . . . she didn't even remember how long.

"Your brat sister is crying in her room. The day after the police brought her home, I caught her kissing some high school guy on the couch. Both of them were as drunk as a skunk and on their way to second base. I don't have time for police, but I really don't have time for a fourteen-year-old pregnant girl living in my house."

Casey's heart sank. She knew her mother was exaggerating . . . a little. She also knew Emery was on a path headed to nowhere good. Teagan squeezed her free hand, both she and Shawn feeling the relief with Casey. They'd both been next to Casey in her darkest season—had experienced pretty rough seasons themselves. None of them wanted that for sweet Emery.

"It's time for you to take her. You fix teenagers for a living. Time for you to take a crack at this. And if she gets arrested or pregnant on your watch, maybe you'll get a taste of how hard it was to raise you and have some sympathy for your mother instead of blaming me for everything. I'll be in Waco with her at eleven tomorrow morning. Be there," Mona droned, her sentences slurring more with every moment. "Enroll her in school. Send her to church camp. Just deal with it before she comes back home."

Casey froze. Shawn tightened his fists, his jaw twitching, signaling his silent rage. Color fled from Teagan's already pale cheeks, but her pinched lips told Casey she was about to explode.

"I've had it, Casey. Lord knows I don't need two slutty daughters who require so much attention."

That word. It boomed through the speaker. Two guys walking to their car stopped and looked at their small circle. Casey hunched her shoulders, ignoring their stares. That word wasn't true. It never should have hurt that much. But it did. In her fairy tale, she would have had a dad to protect her. A mother to love her. A sister who knew she was worth more than a drunk one-night stand at the age of fourteen. Instead, they had a drunk mother. Revolving stepdads. And terrible self-worth, reinforced by their mom.

A stinging sensation on her palms let her know her fingernails had dug too deep in her palms. She fought for control, for calm. "I'll be there to get my sister in the morning, Mom. I'll keep her as long she wants to stay." She ended the call before her mother could respond. She needed to figure out what was going on with Emery. Maybe convince her mom to let Emery live with her until graduation. But she needed to do something fast.

Tremors tore through her. Tears burned. She blinked them back. Not here. Not now. Nearby people laughed. Someone road a bike down the street. A horn honked. The scent of coffee clung to the air, along with syrup and the faintest, mouth-watering hint of bacon. Casey felt and saw all of it and none of it. Because the only thing that resounded in her head was the word that had once bled red on her high school locker, painted by the guy who'd promised her the world. The word that had been echoed in every conversation with the school staff and even her mother since that event: slut.

Her sister was better than this. Worth more. Casey. Casey had been worth more. And Casey wouldn't let her sister experience what she had. She'd take her, raise her, teach her, and make her strong so no guy would ever treat her like less than the girl she was and the woman she would be. No more.

Never again.

CHAPTER 7

The clatter of a wrench striking concrete disrupted the silent prelude of the past thirty minutes.

"You trying to give me a heart attack?" TJ muttered, rubbing his chest. "Geez. You mess up everything, man."

Micah mined the wrench from the garage floor and tossed it into TJ's waiting hands. "Mama Rosie didn't tell me you were such a drama queen."

The kid actually rolled his eyes. Micah bit back a smirk. "Mama Rosie's the drama queen." His dark eyes darted to the door. "But don't tell her I said so, or she'll take a paddle to my rear end."

"And mature. She forgot to mention how mature you are." Micah folded his arms over his chest and studied the fifteen-year-old currently leaning over the engine of the car Micah had never asked for in the city he'd wanted to avoid. At least a silver lining existed in the form of a fiery brunette who had him intrigued.

TJ muttered a few choice words under the hood.

"I'm sorry, I didn't catch that." Micah took a quick swig of water and eyed the teen. Lanky yet muscled, TJ hadn't quite come into his height yet stood right at about Micah's shoulder. His dark skin dripped with sweat in the stuffy garage, and his flat-billed cap sat cocked on his head. Micah was surprised it hadn't tumbled onto the engine yet. His fingers made quick work of the car parts. He handled each piece with care as he cleaned, maneuvered, tightened, and fixed.

"Man, what're you staring at?"

Micah settled the water bottle on the hood of the truck and grabbed the dirty rag to clean more black gunk from between his fingers. "I'm wondering why a skilled kid like you is starting fights on the court with a kid twice your size."

TJ's mouth pinched at the corners. Back to silence again. This time Micah refused to let it dominate. Dusk cast its mask despite the open garage door, casting shadows over their rusty project. A car sped down the overgrown alleyway as the stare off continued. Finally . . .

"What do you care? Just because you're Casey's friend doesn't mean I have to like you. How'd an ugly fool like you meet her anyhow?"

"We'll come back to that." Micah lounged against his inherited hunk of steel. "Let's start back at the 'why I care' part. I don't, or I could if you would let me. In my experience, you don't start a fight without a reason." He lowered his voice thinking of the fist fight he'd had with Nick right after deployment.

TJ grabbed the rag and started scrubbing his hands, his knuckles clenched in the fabric. "And you're an expert on fights?"

Micah offered the glimmer of a smile. "I've been in my share of battles."

"No offense, but you don't look like a guy who has seen many street fights."

"My street fighting is relegated to the streets of Baghdad and a few other places I can't name."

TJ slowed his frenzied cleaning, his eyes brightening in the dusty light. "Army?"

"Please."

TJ smirked. "Marines?"

"Do I look like a jarhead to you?"

"Navy?"

"Right branch. Wrong title."

TJ cocked his head, his gaze raking Micah. Micah could practically see the wheels turning. Then came the click. A slow grin spread across TJ's face. "No way. You were a Navy SEAL? Get out of here. I've heard it's crazy hard to pass all those tests." He tossed the rag on top of the engine. "You might be okay, man. You still in, or did you quit?"

The question rolled from an innocent kid but felt anything but. Micah clenched the fist buried in the crook of his arm and shifted his position on the car. "I'm out right now. And I'm here. And I'm hanging with you."

The kid shoved his hands in faded jeans. "Why?"

"Why what?"

"Why be here? Why come to the court? Why break up my one chance to plant my fist in that idiot's face? Why ask me to fix this junk?" He kicked the car, his voice rising in the descending shadows. "Why?"

Micah stood and faced TJ. "Why'd you want to fight that Coleman kid?"

"Because he insulted my brother," TJ spat.

"That's no reason to fight," Micah said, keeping his voice level, even as he shoved down his own guilt. There was a time when he would have done the same.

"It's always a reason to fight. Family is always a reason to fight."

That Micah understood. He would go to hell and back for his two brothers and baby sister. And he wouldn't think twice about it. But he'd learned there were other ways to protect than using his fist or a gun. He took a step closer. "Family is always a reason to fight, to defend." He swallowed back regret, remembering the brothers he'd abandoned, the team he no longer could call family. He shoved it all aside. "Don't waste breath on guys who don't know what they are talking about and are trying to get you in trouble. Don't play that game. That's not honorable."

"And you own the monopoly on what honor looks like?"

Micah stepped back as if he'd been punched. The guilt he'd just shoved away pounded through his gut. TJ was right. He'd messed up. His brothers had been killed on his watch. And then he'd left. What did he know of honor?

This time TJ took a step forward, invading Micah's space. "Around here, we fight for our own. That's honor. My brother..." TJ swallowed back emotion. "My brother didn't deserve what he got. The people around here . . . they don't deserve what they get. But Coleman, Coleman deserves what he gets. My brother isn't here because of him and his crew."

Hurting kid. TJ wasn't just an angry kid trying to prove himself, needing the admonishment of impending manhood. No, he was a hurting kid. A kid who needed to know he belonged, that someone would fight for him, that someone would be there.

"TJ."

But TJ was already backing out into the alley. He swiped his nose and nodded at the truck. "Give her a turn. Should work for you. If it don't, tell Mama Rosie to call me. I'll come back and fix it again." He turned and ran.

Micah let him go. Inside, he ached. Losing a brother to a war he didn't know how to fight? He knew the pain. Not knowing where to funnel that pain? He knew that, too. But in his case, unfortunately, Micah knew exactly who to blame.

He watched TJ's retreating back, wondering if he should leave well enough alone. Why try to help? Why did he keep getting involved?

"What am I doing here?" He kicked out at the bumper, instantly regretting the pain shooting through his toe.

"Well what did that piece of junk do to you?"

Micah chuckled and turned to find Shawn lounging in the door. "Well for starters, it dropped in my lap with a bunch of parts and pieces I can't name and can't fix. So I had to call a fifteen-year-old. Shoulda paid more attention to my dad and brother when I was in high school." Micah slammed the hood and followed Shawn out of the garage, pushing the button to close the door to the neighborhood in his wake.

The scent of cookies lured him into the warm kitchen. "Mama Rosie strikes again." A plate of warm chocolate chip cookies, perfectly shaped and perfectly stacked, sat in the perfect center of the table shoved in the breakfast nook.

Shawn popped a cookie in his mouth and groaned. "That woman is going to make me fat. These are still warm. Try one." He nodded at the platter as he marched to the refrigerator and poured two glasses of milk.

"You don't have to tell me twice." Micah sank into a chair and bit into his cookie. "Good grief, what does that woman put in these? They're incredible."

Shawn handed him a glass filled with milk. "She won't tell me. Says it's some secret ingredient that she will only divulge in her will."

"Well maybe I can talk her into adding me to that will, too."

"Stick around. She probably has everyone in the neighborhood listed in there."

Stick around. The words rolled around in Micah's head. He felt stuck. Stuck in his head. Stuck in the past. Stuck avoiding the last house call he needed to make. Stuck in guilt and shame and a relentless string of goodbyes. Stuck. Did he want to be stuck here, too?

"I told you before, but I'm going to mention it again. I could really use your help finishing out this football season. Practice this week will be brutal since we are one coach short. You would be helping the guys stay conditioned, stay hungry for these last few games."

Micah stopped chewing and stared at Shawn. His University of Texas Longhorns cap sat backwards on his head. A long-sleeve t-shirt and gym shorts told him Shawn had probably just come from a game of pick-up basketball, something Micah learned Shawn loved in his off time.

"I don't know, man. I'm trying to figure out a lot right now. I'm not sure what to do."

Shawn swiped another cookie from the plate. His athletic frame a contrast to the yellow and pink frilly table cloth between them. "Well, you are chasing Casey. Getting to know the kids around here. Fixing a car. And you haven't booked a ticket out of town or made plans to take care of that mysterious business that you came here for. It looks to me like you aren't quite ready to leave. And I could really use your help."

Casey had challenged him. TJ had implied Micah couldn't ever care. Shawn was pushing him. And Micah felt a stirring of something he hadn't felt in a while, the steadying sensation of purpose—a reason to get up in the morning.

He needed something, and a job was on his list. Maybe a temporary one would give him more time to figure out his next move ... and delay this last goodbye to a baby who would never meet her dad and a wife who was now a single mom. Maybe ...

His phone buzzed in his pocket.

I miss you. When are you coming home?

Kaylan.

He missed his baby sister. But California wasn't home. Not

anymore. He didn't know if it ever would be again. He didn't have a home. No roots. Only a right-now.

One more bite of cookie. One more yes to something stable . . . at least for right now. "I'm in. When do I start?"

Shawn grinned and slapped him on the back. "Tomorrow. Get ready for a rough initiation."

Micah grinned back. "Please. How hard could it be?"

A gentle tap on her office door had Casey abandoning her emails to hug Al, the owner of Ellie's Place, and a big reason she'd become an adult who fought for others.

"Morning, Sunshine. You're not usually here so early on a Monday." He sank into the couch near her desk and hung one leg over the other, completely at ease.

Casey plopped in the chair across from him and took his offered cup of coffee. She'd left her house without brain fuel. Bad call. But thoughts of Emery, the need to write a few recommendation letters for scholarships, and two disappointing resumes on her desk had her out of bed and rushing to Ellie's earlier than normal. The sun sat low in the morning sky behind the basketball hoop just outside her window. She hated early mornings, but once she got moving, nothing could stop her. "I have to pick up Emery today."

Al responded with a slow nod, his typical fedora shifted slightly on his bald head, shadowing his eyes. "I see. When did your mom call?"

Casey released a breath. No need to explain her complicated history with Mona Rodriguez to Al. He and Ellie had been her scholarship donors in college. Because of their generosity and a few grants, most of her schooling at Southern Methodist University had been covered. But they'd given her more than money. They'd given her hope. They'd instilled in her the ability to dream despite her past.

"She's been texting. But yesterday she called. It sounds like Emery made some bad decisions at a party and then with an older guy from school."

"I see." Al nodded again and took a sip of his own coffee.

Casey knew he understood. Watching him ponder, she envied his steadiness. Nothing ever rattled him. No matter his endeavor, he radiated peace and positivity. Even when Ellie passed away from her battle with cancer, Al hadn't lost his smile. It just dimmed for a while. He was one of the few Christians who knew her past and hadn't looked at her differently because of it.

"And what did your mom ask you to do?"

Casey took a sip of her coffee, craving the shot of warmth in the crisp November morning. "She wants me to pick her up. She wants Emery to stay with me."

He cocked his head, and the hat Casey had come to identify with her adopted grandfather slid a bit, revealing bright, thoughtful eyes. "And what do you want, Casey girl?"

Casey wrapped both hands around her coffee, her eyes fixed on the glowing sun. "Right now?"

He shrugged. "That's a good place to start."

"I want this sports league to launch. I want to hire a full-time coach and coordinator for these teams."

"And after that? What about for you?"

Casey bit her lip, mulling over what she wanted. "I want my sister to live with me permanently." She tasted the responsibility as she said the words. "I want her to know this." She gestured around Ellie's Place. "I want her to know something different than what I experienced."

"That's no easy task."

Casey shook her head. "But if I don't do it, who will? Who will love my sister more than me? I won't let her ruin her life."

Al only nodded again before leaning forward and resting his elbows on his knees. "Remember the first night you came over for dinner?"

Casey did. It had been a Thursday in her first month of freshman year. She didn't have a major or a life goal. And she didn't know how to behave with rich people who lived in the wealthiest neighborhood in Dallas and could afford to pay a large chunk of her tuition. A black woman had answered the door, dressed in a simple but sweet flower-print dress. Gray streaked her hair and her eyes sparkled as she introduced herself as Ellie Jackson. And the man her physical opposite in every way— white, tall, bald—approached behind her and introduced himself as her husband, Al. Dressed in jeans, a nice button down, and his fedora, Casey immediately felt more relaxed.

"You were so nervous. So guarded. Still are a bit." He gave her a knowing look but didn't push, never pushed. "But I saw a light ignite in your eyes that night."

She'd barely talked through dinner as Ellie and Al shared about his booming business, their desire to help kids from rough home situations, their dreams for a teen center, their struggles to have children of their own, and their hope for her. They saw her spirit in her essays and applications for scholarships and for the school. They were ready to coax it to life.

Ellie and Al wanted dinner. Every other Thursday. If she got an award, they wanted to be there. If she made the Dean's List, they wanted to be notified. When she picked her major, they wanted to be part of it. They didn't care about their financial investment. They cared about her. Casey had never experienced that kind of unconditional love and support from adults before. And she hadn't known what to do with it at first. But Ellie and Al were persistent.

"We wanted the moon and stars for you. But we couldn't push you. You had to find your dreams on your own. You had to fight for it. We just wanted to be in your corner." He chuckled and shook his head. "You were a stubborn one. Still are. And still struggling to choose your own dreams, Casey girl. You dream so well for everyone else. You fight so hard to prove something. But what do you want? I think you still haven't quite figured it out."

Casey snorted and shook her head.

He smirked. "Or maybe you have and you just aren't willing to admit it to yourself yet."

She rolled her eyes.

"No use arguing with me. Even in that lovely head of yours. I can practically hear it."

"I wouldn't argue with you, Al." His brows raised beneath his hat and a small smile plumped his cheeks. "Okay, okay. I don't argue with you much."

Al chuckled again and took another swig of coffee.

"The point is, Casey girl, that sister of yours may be in the same place. She's walking out of a rough situation with your mom with a bunch of baggage and a lot of bad examples to point to. Just like you were. She's going to move in, and it's going to be hard. You'll fight with her, have to discipline and set boundaries, but ultimately you will have to teach her how to dream a bit."

"Just like you and Ellie did for me." Casey smiled at the man who had become her surrogate grandfather.

"You bet. And it wasn't easy. She will have to get there on her own, Casey. You won't be able to make her. Can you live with that?"

"I can try."

Al sank back into the couch again and regarded her. "She's going to have a great example to follow. And you will have Teagan, Shawn, Mama Rosie, and all of Ellie's Place at your back. And maybe this Micah fellow I've heard a bit about?"

Casey fought a blush. "He's just passing through, Al."

"If you say so." But Casey didn't like the spark that lit his eyes. "Do you think he could solve our coach dilemma?"

He chuckled at her glare. "Okay, maybe not the time to talk about that right now."

Al set his cup on the table between them and leaned forward again, faded blue eyes fixed on her. Under his stare, Casey fought against the urge to build her walls higher. Ellie and Al had made it farther than anyone besides Teagan and Shawn, but still trusting others didn't come easy, especially with her pain.

"Are you really willing to do anything, Casey?"

Casey swallowed the lump in her throat and nodded.

"Then I think it may be time to consider trusting God again." His voice barely carried in the silent building, but it magnified in Casey's head. First Micah and now Al, a man who had never pushed her in the faith department, even though Casey knew it was an active part of his life.

"Al," she groaned.

But this time he refused to back down, using the firm tone he normally used on the teenagers. "Casey, do you trust me?"

She bit into her cheek, tasting blood, and nodded once.

"All I'm asking is consider it. You will not be able to care for and love your sister without leaning into the Lord's strength. Lord knows Ellie and I needed it with you." The gentle smile was back in place. "You white knuckle everything, Casey girl. You have so much passion and grit and determination, but your independence, it isolates you. The toll it takes to fight in your own strength, it's weighty. And Jesus says His burdens are light, and His ways are peace."

Peace. Peace from the constant drive she felt to do more, do better, do it alone, even when she knew people loved her. She nodded once again. Where would she even begin trusting God again after she felt his abandonment years earlier? But then again, Al had never steered her wrong.

"I'll think about it."

"That's all I ask." He stood, stretching his thin, long legs. "I have a lawyer friend who could help you with any questions you may have about next steps, if that's something you are interested in. It may be good to seek legal custody if your mom is really serious about letting Emery live with you."

"Yes, please." She cast a quick glance at her watch and popped off the couch. "I'm going to be late if I don't leave now."

Al pulled her in for a hug and walked with her to the door, arm around her shoulder. "Remember what I said, Casey girl. The best way to love Emery, and even forgive your mom, is to receive the Lord's love for you in return and operate in his strength. Otherwise, this is doomed to fail."

Casey nodded as he placed a quick peck on her forehead. His words chased her to the car and haunted her all the way to Waco.

They'd sat in silence for thirteen minutes. Nothing. Not even a peep from Emery. Their mother had said little. Not a hello or a hug or "I'll see you in a few weeks." Just a "fix her" before speeding out of the Waco McDonalds' parking lot. Emery crawled into the front seat, slumped against the window, and hadn't murmured a word.

Casey checked the clock again and then chanced another glance at her fourteen-year-old sister sitting in the passenger seat. Her dark, almost-black hair hung straight as a board around her head, offset only by a single braid dyed hot pink and twisting from the left side of her head. Her dark eyes popped under smoky makeup and what Casey suspected had been a lot of crying and yelling on the way up from Austin.

A black, grungy One Direction t-shirt hung off one shoulder, the sleeve bearing scars of jagged scissor strokes. Bracelets climbed each wrist and too much skin peeked through ripped jeans. She was gorgeous, fiery, and a hot mess. Just like Casey had been a lifetime ago.

"You can stop staring at me now."

Casey hid a small smile and shifted her eyes back to the road. "You want to talk about why your mascara is all over your face?"

Emery's fingers swiped furiously at imaginary black tracts before Casey grabbed her hands and stilled them in her lap. "I'm kidding, Em."

Casey ignored the answering glare. She dealt with teenage attitude all day. This was a picnic to what she normally experienced.

"Seriously, Em. Want to talk about it?"

"Nope," she said, popping her *p* with extra sass.

"Alrighty then." Casey kept her gaze on the road when she felt her sister's dark eyes level on her.

"Seriously? Just that easy?"

"Oh, I didn't say we wouldn't talk about it later. We just don't have to right now."

Emery slumped down further in her seat as Casey wound her way through slower traffic on the two-lane highway. Browning grass and bare trees lined parts of the highway, a testament to encroaching winter, however mild it might be in Texas.

The silence stretched again, until Casey had enough. She punched the button for the radio, filling the car with the sounds of guitar strings, southern comfort, and the feeling of wide-open spaces and simplicity. Country music did that for Casey, made her think of roots and stability and even the possibility of love. She liked when they sang about it, even if she would never experience it for herself.

"Thanks, by the way," Emery mumbled almost too low for Casey to hear.

She turned down the music. "For what, Em?"

"For letting me come stay with you."

She tightened her grip on the wheel. "Can I ask you a question?" Casey only caught a nod from the corner of her eye. "How bad is it at home?"

Her sister, her baby sister, rotated to lean against the door; this time, black streaks marked her sweet face. Casey felt her knuckles crack against the leather as it groaned beneath her grip. "He's mean, Case. And Mom . . . you know how she is. She just makes excuses for him and blames me. One day she's handing me a beer, and the next she's yelling at me for drinking. It's confusing. And frustrating. I just want to live my life. In Dallas . . . with you."

"You aren't going back any time soon. We'll work out the rest later." She reached for her sister's hand, her heart squeezing when Emery gripped hard. Donning her most positive, straightforward, adult-with-teenager voice, she went on, "Here's what we are going to do. The counselor at the middle school near my house is a friend. She transferred all your files this morning so that you can start tomorrow. We'll finish out this semester and then figure out what to do going forward." One battle at a time. One conversation at a time. She planned to keep Emery, but she wanted to see how Emery handled her new set of rules.

"As long as I can get away from Mom, I'm good with whatever," she grumbled. "And as long as I get to keep my phone."

"Deal."

"And try out for cheerleading." She sat up and leaned toward Casey. "If I make the team, can I stay with you next year, too? Please?"

"Cheerleading?" That was all Casey could get out. She'd despised the cheerleaders in high school.

"Not all of us walk around serious and depressed all the time, Casey."

Her mouth actually dropped open. "I am not depressed just because I don't wear a tiny skirt and yell 'go, fight, roar.'"

"Well I don't do those things either."

"Besides, who are you calling depressed, Miss Goth?"

"Stereotyping much? Is that how you counsel all those poor teenagers? Geez, maybe you do need me around to mellow you out."

Casey grinned. "I've missed you, Em." The bantering, the picking, the annoying kid sister. Mostly, watching her grow up. But Casey hadn't been able to handle their mom or the slew of boyfriends and stepdads either. She'd bolted right after high school graduation, and she'd left Emery alone. No more. At least one of those bad relationships had produced something good. Emery.

"I've kinda sorta missed you, too."

"What was that? Couldn't hear you." Casey poked Emery in the rib cage. Giggling filled the car. "No poke backs. Driving here."

"Just wait till you get out of the car, Case."

"Game on, little sis."

For the first time in her life, Casey's mom had given Casey something good: a reason and actual case to fight for Emery. And Casey would fight with everything in her to keep her sister in Dallas—to convince their mom that Emery was better off with Casey. Emery deserved to grow up with someone who loved her. And Casey loved Emery with every fiber of her being. The way no one in her home had ever fully loved her. Emery's life would be different. No more abuse and neglect. Not on Casey's watch.

CHAPTER 8

Sweat crawled down Micah's cheek, despite the sixty-degree weather. Too much pacing back and forth. He shouldn't have worn the long-sleeve shirt. He knew better than that in the south.

He'd been yelling commands for an hour and been met with angry looks, brutal tackles, and one kid cussing him out. Had he had this much attitude as a teenager? He'd had an ego a mile wide, but surely it wasn't this bad.

"Ready to quit yet?" Shawn grinned at Micah from beneath his own hat, this time sporting the school mascot, a mustang. It fit. These kids were wild and untamed. But talented. They just needed to focus their energy and skill on the game.

"TJ, Bates, Lucca run it again," Micah shouted across the field. He'd found TJ's sweet spot after an hour of frustration. The kid could catch and run, an untapped talent since he had been sitting on the bench most of the season. Shawn might have a new varsity wide receiver on his hands. Now if he could just teach the kid a little discipline and affirm him a bit. TJ threw a fit every time he missed the ball, which thankfully rarely happened.

"How long have you coached here?" Micah asked.

"About four years now. I spent two years at a school in the Austin area after college before accepting the head coaching position here. I wondered why they would hire such a young head coach. Turns out filling the position and keeping it filled proved to be a challenge." Shawn chuckled.

"I wonder why." Micah smirked and crossed his arms. "It's alright, TJ. Shake it off and run it again. I want to see you catch it ten times in a row. We aren't moving on until you do."

"Think he can catch it that many times in a row?" Shawn shifted his focus to TJ.

The boys lined up again and within seconds the ball was in play, in the air, and in TJ's hands. Micah whooped before answering Shawn. "He has skill but little confidence. If you can teach him both, you may just have yourself a star."

Shawn's gaze sparked with interest. TJ was on catch three now. His hands scooped the ball out of the air no matter where it went, forcing the quarterback to hone his throws.

"Nice catch, TJ."

Micah whirled at the feminine voice, but Casey had eyes only for Shawn. Micah was starting to wonder if everyone wore baseball caps around here. Casey was just about the cutest thing he'd ever seen in her white t-shirt, thin black sweater with sleeves shoved to her elbows, ball cap, ripped blue jeans, and cherry-red Converse. Her dark hair lay swept over her shoulder, the dimming sun bringing out flecks of auburn. She grinned at Shawn. "When did TJ start playing wide receiver?"

Micah fell for her a little right then. She knew her sports and the positions.

"Micah noticed he was good with his hands. He's been catching passes for the last thirty minutes."

Casey's startled gaze swung to Micah's, noticing him for the first time. "You're working here?"

A slow grin spread across his face as he looked down on her.

"You challenged me to stick around. Practically yelled at me. So I found myself a gig. Temporary gig anyway."

"Don't take it personally." Shawn draped his arm over Casey's shoulder. "She yells at everyone."

"I don't yell." Casey backhanded Shawn in the chest. He had the decency to pretend like it hurt before retaliating. Within seconds, he had her in a headlock, grinning when she squirmed.

"I call her our little firecracker," Shawn joked. This time she elbowed him in the gut. He doubled over chuckling. "And that's about what happens every time," he wheezed

Micah tossed his head back in a laugh. "Firecracker is appropriate. Whoa, hey." She advanced a step on him, her features set in challenge. He threw up his arms and took a step back but couldn't help his laugh. "I'm just calling it like I see it. Nice form, Bates!" He shouted to the field as the kid performed a spectacular tackle.

"Run it again, fellas!" Shawn shouted before addressing Casey. "Did Emery get settled in, Case?" The team lined up again, a little more confident and a little less antagonistic with every play.

"Yep. Administration called me this afternoon to take care of some extra paperwork so just finished wrapping all that up."

"Great. I'll stop by and see her later. Dinner?" Shawn pointed in her direction as he backed away down the field toward the action.

"She'll be thrilled that her secret crush is coming over just to see her."

Shawn's grin flashed in her direction before he turned and jogged a few more feet down the sidelines so he could see all the action on the field.

Micah watched the exchange with growing envy. He missed this. Relationships that ran deep, that shared history and friends and moments.

"Who's this girl that's sweet on Shawn?"

"My little sister." Casey faced Micah with her hands anchored on her hips. "What are you still doing here, Soldier Boy?"

"Well, darlin," he drawled, grinning at her cringe, "like I said, your buddy, Shawn here, offered me a gig. Looks like I'm sticking around until the end of the semester. Cash couldn't hurt." He blew a short blast on his whistle. "Run it again," he shouted to the players on his end of the field. The guys moved into action, a couple shoving one another in the process. No blood, no intervention. That was Micah's new motto. He dropped the whistle and faced Casey.

"I meant why are you staying in Dallas?"

"I thought you were inviting me to stay in your oh-so-inspiring challenge to prove that I care, Ace."

Casey chewed on her nail and faced the field.

Micah leaned down and whispered in her ear, "Challenge accepted. I'm here. What are you going to do about it?"

"What happened to this pilgrimage you need to complete? Why are you really staying?" Her quiet voice drained his teasing. He nudged her with his shoulder, losing the teasing.

"Shawn asked." He ignored the first question. He would figure that out later.

She took a tiny step away, but didn't run. "You could've said no."

He studied her face, her eyes hidden in shadows under her cap.

"Coach!" TJ ran toward the sideline.

"Run it again," he barked, his eyes never leaving her profile. The clash of pads and grunting assured him the boys were back at it.

Casey smirked but kept her eyes glued to the field.

"Casey, I've spent a couple days here now. I do care about these kids experiencing something better. I may not be here long, but I can prove that I care by filling a need for a while."

Her shoulders wilted ever so slightly. "You don't stay in this neighborhood for just a week or just a month." She faced him, turning the full weight of her gaze on him. Passion and conviction and something like experience burned within the earthy brown. "You either stay because you can't get out of it. Or stay because you want to help be part of changing it. But you don't stay just because. There's a war raging on these streets. Poverty, racial division, discouragement, family feuds. And these kids are caught in the middle of a bad cycle. These streets are a war zone. They aren't a retreat." She folded her arms and met his gaze head on. "These kids can't be your reason to hide or another excuse to run from whatever you need to finish. So I'll ask you again. Why are you here? Why are you staying?"

Micah hesitated. Dusty streets, the pop of gunfire, and the screams of women and children running for cover zipped through his mind. He could taste the desperation clinging to ever particle clogging the air, the desire for the war to leave their front doors. War shouldn't happen in front of homes, but in other countries it did.

He shifted, his hands bunched and sweating through their grip on his t-shirt. Apparently, it happened on the home front, too. He'd just never stopped to notice.

He thought of the photos hanging from every free space in Mama Rosie's home, of the kids that trudged through the door after school every day for a hug and a cookie. He thought of TJ and his brother, of Coleman egging him on, of the anger hidden behind each tackle this afternoon, the desperation to be good at something, and the quick defeat in failure. He thought of Casey, small and petite, yet fierce as she cheered for each team on the blacktop. He thought of Shawn staying four years to coach kids who wouldn't listen because no one else would.

He ground his heel into the field, the grass browning and breaking as fall gave way to winter. He watched the kids, running in pads, helmets, and shorts, sweat coating dark and light skin alike. He watched Shawn bend down and whisper in the ear of a kid then slap him on the back and send him back out to the practice field.

Micah's battlefield had looked different. He'd gone to fight in a war so he could come home to peace. But these kids didn't know peace. Dysfunction and conflict were part of their daily lives, and Casey stood smack dab in the middle, fighting against the tide.

He was aware she watched him. Aware she probably saw right through his bravado to the broken pieces he still wrestled with and prayed God would mend. Micah Richards hadn't wanted another war. But this one was worth fighting for, and maybe, just maybe, it was his next assignment. He couldn't be sure. But he also liked a girl who had donned the uniform and stepped into the fray. And Micah "Bulldog" Richards never let someone fight alone, even if he wasn't the man he used to be.

"I want to fill in until Shawn doesn't need it. I can help out with other things if you need it. Maybe help with those sports leagues until you find someone or until Christmas— I'm in. Even if I only help one kid in the process. And, I'd like to get to know you a little more," he murmured.

He thought he saw a glimmer of admiration and a dash of fear flash across her face before she turned to walk away. "We'll see about that last one." She glanced at her phone. "Gotta run. See you around, Micah."

CHAPTER 9

"Teagan, just hold it still."

The redhead wrestled her end of the shelf to make it even with Casey's. "I'm trying, Case. You're the vertically challenged one standing on a desk. I can barely reach this high on the wall."

Sure enough, Teagan was stretched out on her tiptoes, her Toms buckling under her feet. Casey envied her long, pale legs. Teagan was a good six inches taller than Casey's five-foot-two frame, and Casey cursed her friend's height and ability to reach places outside of Casey's reach. And loved her more than she could ever put into words.

"Well I guess height isn't good for everything."

Teagan rocked back on her heel, and Casey caught the full weight of the shelf with an umph. Casey fumbled to keep the shelf straight as Teagan stepped back to observe, a grin on her face. "And that would be why you called Shawn for backup?"

Casey gave up, letting the shelf bump to the floor. She plopped down on the desk, her legs swinging. Anytime she or Teagan needed help, Shawn was their first call. She'd thought about calling Micah, but common sense convinced her otherwise. The guy got under her skin like no one's business. There was that broken thing. That cocky thing. That sarcastic thing. Oh. And that attraction thing. Wouldn't want to forget about that.

Casey couldn't forget about that.

"Hello, earth to Casey. Have you heard from Wonder Boy since you texted him an hour ago? We are no closer to getting these shelves on the wall." Five floating shelves sat in disarray around their feet. Casey loved to decorate—watch a space come alive with personality—and she'd been dying to finish her office at Ellie's Place. Now, she officially hated her decision to use the shelves. But she'd committed, and she didn't back down on a commitment—even if the commitment only extended to sleek, wooden shelves that aggravated her.

She fired off another text to Shawn. "Let's try again, Teag."

Casey stood, trying to balance on the desk. It wobbled beneath her feet. She overcorrected and flailed her arms but no use. She shrieked, tipped backwards. And landed against something much too warm and muscled to be the floor.

"Looks like I arrived just in time."

That smooth, teasing voice. Casey wished she'd just smacked the tile.

She fought to untangle herself from his arms, ignoring how strong they felt, how familiar. How utterly, annoyingly wonderful.

"What are you doing here, Richards?" She snapped.

His brow arched into that rich, dark, annoyingly attractive hair of his. "I believe you rang for a hero? Shawn couldn't make it so he sent the better option."

"You mean his sidekick?"

Point one for Teagan. Casey almost forgave her for being tall and gorgeous. Almost.

"Sidekick? I'll have you know that heroes have other hero friends, which is why Shawn sent me."

Casey rolled her eyes. "Well, Captain America, we need help hanging these shelves. Think you can manage that?"

Teagan snorted. "Correction: Casey needs help hanging these shelves. Her short legs can't keep up."

Micah's mouth tipped at the corner just barely as the full weight of his stare met hers. "I bet she can hack it."

Casey went warm all over. She didn't like it. Most guys who looked at her like that took in every inch of her body, and a hunger grew in their gaze. Micah looked at her and through her, and his gaze felt all too knowing, all too observant. And all too comforting.

Get a grip Casey Denae Stewart. He's not staying. And he's just like every other guy.

But every other guy would have visually undressed her. Under Micah's warm gaze, she just felt beautiful. Strong. Capable.

A throat cleared on the other side of the room. Casey snapped from her thoughts and whirled to confront Teagan. She shot daggers at her best friend, an all too knowing smile gracing her face. These warm, nice, terrible feelings about Micah Richards ended now. The butterflies in her stomach had been replaced by moths long ago. She didn't have room for romance. Didn't have anything to give. It had all been taken.

"Put me to work, Shorty."

A few more comments like that and all the warm feelings would quickly disappear. She just needed to treat him like every other man. Every other red-blooded man who had ever walked through her home as a kid.

One problem. Micah Richards wasn't like every other man. He helped. He teased without expectation. He cared. In another life she could maybe like him but not in this one. Micah waltzed over to the pile of shelves and picked up a smaller one. "Here?" He motioned to the marks on the wall and then began to hammer.

Casey only nodded as she eyed the blank wall flanking her desk, imagining what the space would look like once complete. Rays from the gentle autumn sun filtered through the blinds on the rectangular window set level with Casey's shoulders. It overlooked the basketball courts, her favorite place to watch the kids and do a little mentoring or reading. She shivered a little, the air growing cooler just in time for Thanksgiving week. It was Saturday morning, and they'd cut back on the heater since the kids who visited the center on weekends usually came to play a game outside.

"So what do I get in return for getting me out of bed this morning?" Micah said above his hammer strokes.

"You weren't out of bed yet?" She rubbed her arms, the friction providing temporary heat. She slouched against the wall. "It's ten in the morning. You're wasting good daylight."

Micah winced but hammered another corner of a shelf into the wall. She bent down and handed another shelf to Micah. "Let's just say after years in the military and early morning workouts or assignments on deployment I am experiencing what it feels like to sleep in on the weekends for the first time since high school."

"Ah, back when you were a big star athlete?"

The bang of the hammer smacked the wall harder, louder. Micah's knuckles turned white. Teagan turned around and frowned. "Play nice," she mouthed.

But Casey didn't know how to play nice with Micah. She could handle the sarcasm, the nicknames, the bravado. But this Micah who got up to help, the one who taught the kids, the one who saw more than her body—that Micah was dangerous. Taunting was the only defense she had.

"I don't know about star. What about you, Doc?" He motioned to the graduate diploma on the wall and the leadership and counseling books on her shelf. "Always want to be a shrink?"

Casey held up a nail. A few more strikes and the fourth shelf hung secure. "First of all, not a doctor or a shrink. Just a licensed counselor, which looks a little different in my role here." She studied the staggered pattern of the shelves and nodded in satisfaction. Micah pinned a couple more nails between his lips and held the last shelf in place.

"So why that?"

"I guess you could say high school was a catalyst for me." She tossed a quick glance to Teagan who now studied her carefully. Thankfully, Casey no longer fell apart when mentioning those years. Few knew the full extent of her story. She guarded her past carefully.

One more tack of the hammer, and five floating shelves graced the wall behind her desk in the small office. A decorator she was not, but she knew how to pick out the things others overlooked and polish them until they were something unique, something beautiful. Teagan said it had always been Casey's gift. She'd been alley shopping and dumpster diving more times than she could count, dragging Shawn and Teagan until she found diamonds in the trash.

In fact, her whole office was filled with knickknacks she'd found and refurbished. A bookshelf from an alley in Highland Park. An end table from the dumpster at an apartment complex in Uptown. Lanterns from an alley in the Bishop Arts district. The desk from the front yard of a home in North Dallas. What people threw out, she rescued and made into something beautiful. She studied her office. It almost felt finished.

A chuckle made her spin right into that hard chest again. His arms steadied her before she took a few steps back, her neck tipping to take in his tall frame. Maybe she hated him for being tall, too. "Have you ever heard of personal space?"

His lips spread into a wicked grin. Casey had to force herself not to focus on his mouth. She squirmed. She hadn't wanted a guy to kiss her since high school. And she didn't want Micah to kiss her now. Not even a little.

As if sensing her struggle, he edged closer. "You don't listen well, Doc. I asked what I get for getting up early to come do manual labor?"

Treat him like a friend and kissing feelings would go away. She could do that. Casey patted his shoulder. "Well done, sidekick."

She spun on her heel but was yanked back. That chest and that cocky attitude again.

"Ok, lesson one, Soldier. Put a bubble of space between you and the person you are talking to."

Micah shrugged but dropped her arm. "Space is relative. Besides, it's much more fun to see you squirm." This time, he cast a wink at Teagan.

"Oh, yeah. She's real cute when she squirms." A grinning Teagan stepped up next to Micah, forming a wall of "make Casey uncomfortable." She didn't like this game.

Casey looked back and forth between the two. Now they would make a cute couple. Teagan was tall with ivory skin, bright red hair, and a personality that lit up a room. He was tall, dark, and handsome, with wicked charm and the ability to sweep any girl off her feet. And he smelled good, too—like spice and forest—and she hated him again.

Hated herself for noticing.

And liking it.

"Okay, okay, how about breakfast on me?"

This time, even his grin was dangerous. "Oh, no, princess. You woke me up. I get to pick. Dinner and the drive-in. Tonight. Shawn told me it was a nice way to spend the weekend, and I want to get out of the city."

Casey had to snap her mouth shut. Had he just asked her out on a date? Based on Teagan's glowing smile, she knew her suspicions were accurate.

"Let's just stick to breakfast."

"Don't I get to choose my reward?"

Casey crossed her arms and planted her feet, not caring that he was a Navy SEAL and a good foot taller than her. "No. That wouldn't be fair to Teagan. She helped, too. I can take you both to breakfast as a thank-you."

"Oh, by all means, be unfair to Teagan. This one time it is totally okay." Her best friend grabbed her purse from the chair and practically sprinted from the room with a wave and a quick wink.

Traitor.

"I'll pick you up at six."

"This sounds a little too much like a date instead of a thank-you."

Micah took a step closer, his face now hovering right above her. His voice lowered to a husky monotone. "So what if it is? C'mon, Casey. What have you got to lose? I promise it'll be fun and relaxing. Just what you need right now. Please?"

Again, not like any other man. Despite his closeness, she knew he wouldn't push her, knew he would challenge but back down if necessary, because despite his charm, sarcasm, and annoying ability to set those decrepit moths fluttering, she knew he was a gentleman.

And she wanted to trust him.

What would it hurt to go out and have fun like a normal young adult on a date on the weekend? Just this one time. He was leaving anyway, so it would be an isolated incident.

Casey wrapped her arms around her waist and took a step back. "Fine. I'll be ready at six fifteen."

CHAPTER 10

Micah couldn't remember the last time he'd watched a movie. He really couldn't remember the last time he'd pulled out all the stops for a girl. And he really, really couldn't believe how relaxed he felt, perhaps for the first time in a long time. Micah and Casey had driven over forty miles out to the drive-in, Micah praying the whole way that the truck wouldn't fall apart. But Old Faithful made it intact. They'd brought blankets and pillows to pile in the truck bed and the linked radio station blared through the open windows to where Casey and Micah lounged in the truck bed.

It was a double-hitter 90s night, featuring *The Lion King* and *Forrest Gump*. Forrest was officially up. Casey had relaxed about halfway through *The Lion King*, and with every moment that passed he watched her unwind a bit more.

The Texas fall night cooled Micah's skin, the chill almost too much. Around him cars sat angled up at the screen, enjoying the cooler fall temperatures, sometimes unpredictable this time of year.

Micah tugged the blanket around his legs and burrowed into his coat, getting cozy. He leaned back into the stacked pillows, the familiar movie growing faint as he caught sight of the starry sky. Black and beautiful, pinpricks of light smeared the horizon, uninhibited by city lights this far out of Dallas. Even the stars had brothers. They shined individually, but they did their best work on display together. He remembered nights in the desert with his team, playing cards, laughing, the stars on full display overhead without any light pollution.

A story stirred in Micah's heart of God telling Abraham his descendants would be as numerous as the stars in the sky. He remembered the verse his grandad, Pap, used to tell him about how the Lord numbered the stars and knew them by name. By name. Though part of a beautiful array, each was known by the Creator. Seen. Maybe he was seen, even without his team.

Casey stirred next to him, shifted ever so much closer. Her hand lay limp between them. Sweat dotted his brow. Should he reach out and slip his fingers through hers? Or would she panic? Maybe he could inch just a little closer and see how she did with that first.

Right. He'd try that.

Shifting slightly on the cushions, he moved so his leg brushed hers ever so slightly. He held his breath. Counted to ten.

Nothing.

He exhaled. Now what?

Her hand still lay on the blanket between them, almost as if in open invitation. It wouldn't be hard. Just reach out and slide his palm over hers. Join their lives in the smallest way, the way he'd been wanting to explore all week as he'd seen her on and off at Ellie's place caring for her kids. One move. Just one move. He flexed his fingers and began to slide them across the blanket just as Casey shifted and put her hand in her lap.

Denied.

Micah fought the urge to punch something. *Get it together,*

Richards. You aren't in eighth grade. She's a grown woman. If you want to hold her hand, you go for it and let her turn you down.

Micah wasn't so keen on the "turning down" part. Casey had walls a mile high and twice as thick. And she only opened the door for a few people. Right now, she'd cracked a window for him, let him in just a little by agreeing to tonight. He wasn't sure he wanted it slammed in his face.

His eyes drifted from the screen and slid to study Casey. He caught his breath. The stars had nothing on her. Walls down, joy splashed across her face, totally relaxed—this version of Casey could rival the most beautiful Texas sky. And she would win every time. He wondered what hid behind the walls she'd built. Her loyalty and protection she yielded as sentinels, fighting for her kids and then withdrawing. But this Casey, the Casey few ever saw. Well, she was some kind of beautiful. Micah reached for her hand.

Right as Forrest professed his undying love for Jenny.

Could he have worse timing? Her fingers flexed in his and retreated ever so slightly before relaxing in his grip. She turned, her brown eyes raised in challenge, humor dancing over her features. "How long have you been working up the nerve to reach for my hand?"

Micah rolled his eyes. Trust her to be direct. No gameplaying with Casey Stewart. No subtlety either. He could appreciate that. "Since about halfway through the last movie, woman. Do not make this awkward."

She tried to snatch her hand back, but he gripped tighter. "Really?"

She invaded his space, her lips a breath away. "Call me woman one more time, and you will never be able to bear children, Micah Richards, let alone hold my hand again." She leaned back against the truck and shook their clasped hands. "I could practically hear your heart racing."

"And you didn't help me out?"

The car next to them issued a resounding, "shush," through the open car window. Micah immediately slammed his mouth shut.

Casey's chuckle drifted in the Texas night. "And miss seeing you wrestle? If you couldn't muster the courage to hold my hand, Soldier Boy, there's no way you would have a prayer of sticking around my life."

"Finally! You admit you can't live without me. It's only taken a couple weeks."

The smile slipped from her face, and her hand twitched in his. The movie droned in the background, but Micah no longer cared.

"Case?" Something had just shifted as surely as the faint breeze that now dried his sticky skin.

"I don't remember . . ." she stopped. Her jaw flexed and she swallowed hard. Micah edged closer, rubbing soothing circles on the back of her hand. "I don't remember the last time I let someone in. This . . ." She indicated their joined hands. "I swore this would never happen again." A choke silenced her last words but she shook it off. Her eyes still fixed on their hands resting on her leg.

Micah nudged her chin up, his finger tracing over the pink on her cheek. "Talk to me?"

The last thing he wanted was for Fort Knox to shut again, but he wanted to know— needed to know—how to ease her ache, how to take one step closer. Her eyes met his. He could almost hear the crack of a wall tumble within her. She bit her lip.

"It was my sweet sixteen, and Mom decided to throw a big party. Only, being the kind of mother she is, she confiscated everyone's keys, handed out the booze because she thought she was just that cool, and then ran off somewhere with daddy dearest of the month." Bitterness laced her tone. Micah tugged her closer, ready to defend her against any demons that surfaced. And she'd only begun.

"He was the hottest guy in school, captain of the football team, senior, most popular kid. You get the picture. You know the stereotypical jock in all the teen movies? Unfortunately, he fit the bill and more. And he had eyes only for me." The words flowed, unchecked, like she'd bottled them up her entire life, waiting for the moment when they would finally break free. Her hands shook. Micah laced their fingers tighter, squeezing, willing her to remember he was on her side.

"He kept handing me drinks. All night long. I remember the team egging him on. My friends laughing and telling me I was so lucky to have Tanner Cartwright's attention fully fixed on me."

Micah bit back a roar of fury. The demon had a name and the man, the kid, had hurt this incredible woman before him.

"Before the night ended, we were in my room." She shook her head, her voice raspy. "I sat curled up on my bed for hours afterward. It had been a stupid decision, one I made willingly and then regretted when it was too late. He didn't care that I was upset. He didn't want to hang around. I spent the rest of the night sick from all the alcohol."

Micah fought the anger slicing through him. "Where was your mom?"

Her laugh cut. "She checked in. Laughed. Told me to shake it off and learn to handle my men and my alcohol."

This time Micah didn't trust himself to speak. He eased his arm around her now shaking shoulders. "Casey..."

"There's more."

Micah stilled, bracing for what came next.

"Five weeks later, I was still throwing up. Teagan finally made me go to the doctor. My mom just told me I was weak. And that's when I found out."

Laughter echoed through car doors, but inwardly Micah

burned. He squeezed Casey tighter, willing her to know she wasn't alone.

"I told Tanner. About, you know. He laughed in my face, then called me a slut and told me that's what I get for being just like her."

A drop of something wet bled through Micah's shirt. He wrapped Casey tighter and stroked her hair. Her tears fell silent, but her pain screamed.

"When I told my mom, she called me a tramp. Told me it was my fault and that I would need to figure out how to handle it on my own. Then a rumor started at school. Someone wrote 'slut' on my locker. Guys high-fived Tanner in the hall and asked when I would give them a turn. My friends flocked around Tanner. But not Teagan and Shawn."

Micah recognized the love in her voice for the friends who had stayed. He knew the feeling. He had it in his family, in Nick. He'd had it in the SEALs. That kind of love, that kind of commitment, it didn't happen often. Micah may have distanced himself from all those who once loved him, but he wasn't about to let Casey think her story would push him away. He wanted her to speak of him that way. He wanted to stay.

"I didn't go to school for a week. Between morning sickness and inability to eat because I felt so miserable, I . . ." Silence descended as heavy as the air around them. Micah tucked her head under his chin.

The movie continued, crickets chirped, but Micah could only focus on the sound of her heart breaking. "I lost the baby a couple days afterward. Mom blamed me for that, too. People thought I had an abortion. The looks I got from some." She shuddered. "Well, any remaining friends ran for the hills. After that, I got in with a bad crowd. I did everything to numb the pain, the looks, the names. Everything but let a guy touch me again. You, this . . ." She pulled away but didn't retreat from his arms. "I haven't had someone like me, touch me like this . . . ever. I'm not sure . . ."

He held his breath as the full weight of her gaze rested on him. Raw. Aching. Daring. He wouldn't retreat this time. He tipped her chin up, brushing his thumb over her lips. "You didn't deserve the names, the criticism, the lack of support and care, the blaming. I'm sorry."

Steel hardened her features. "And no kids under my care will ever experience that with me if I can help it. I want them to know support and care and better options than I knew or understood."

Micah smiled. She was a fighter. He cupped her face in his hands, the strength and fragility in equal measure astounding him. "It didn't break you, Casey Stewart. It only made you stronger and more beautiful in the broken places. It fashioned a warrior."

With only a breath between them, he paused. "May I?" he whispered, his focus drifting to her lips. With her hesitant nod, he closed the space, his lips melding with hers under the Texas sky. He kissed her cheek then her lashes, still wet from her tears before finding her lips again. And this time, this time she kissed him back.

He knew he'd met his match. A woman with a warrior's heart, willing to fight for others in a way she'd never been fought for. She was the place he could land after months of running. And maybe, maybe God had allowed him to run so Micah could find Casey. Maybe that was God's way of mending his own brokenness all along. Micah deepened the kiss, tugging Casey closer to him. God had taken his team, but maybe that team would look a little different in the days ahead. Just maybe.

Maybe his redemption looked like a small brunette with a fighter's heart. In that moment, Micah felt a tiny broken piece mend inside him. Not in response to everyone he'd lost, but this time, this time for what he had found in the arms of a beauty under the Texas stars.

∽

She climbed down from the rusty, red pick-up truck and waited for Micah to join her on the sidewalk. Her heart pounded as Micah's warm hand came to rest on her lower back as he walked her up the sidewalk to the front porch of her duplex. His boots scraped along the concrete, reminding her of the southern gentleman California couldn't beat out of him.

A low chuckle broke through the stillness and Casey swiveled to squint at Micah in the dim, Texas, suburban night. "Don't tell me our kiss earlier freaked you out."

"Who me?" She snorted and then silently groaned at the unladylike move. "Why would a kiss freak me out?"

They came to a stop on her front porch. It was as she feared. Only the sound of her racing, traitorous, longing heart greeted her. He took a step closer, his boots brushing against her shoes. "You tell me, tiger. Why would a kiss freak you out?"

"It didn't freak me out." She shrugged. "It was good. But it wasn't all that."

A slow smile spread across his handsome face, and she knew she'd just issued a challenge. And not just to any man. To a Navy SEAL, a warrior, and a man in full pursuit. That's what terrified her most. Her walls crumbling. He'd already tumbled one tonight, and the look in his eyes said he knew it.

His arm slipped around her waist and tugged her flush against his chest. She braced her hands on his arms. Safety like she hadn't known in a long time wrapped around her in the form of Micah Richards. And that scared her, too. She couldn't get hurt again.

"I'm calling your bluff. That was a heck of a kiss." His nose grazed her cheek. "You know it." His breath fanned against her ear. "I know it." His lips drifted over her cheek. Casey leaned in to Micah, wilting against the losing battle raging inside. "And honey, the whole neighborhood is about to know this one is ten times better."

And then his lips were on hers again, and Casey swore the kiss was strong enough to send the stars scampering across the Texas sky. She clutched his shirt and didn't fight him. For a moment, just this moment, she gave in. His lips moved over hers, strong, challenging, yet tender. A guy who knew what he wanted and knew how to treat her with care. Casey sank into his arms.

Too soon, his lips left hers. She forced her eyes open to a knowing smirk. "You can lie to yourself, gorgeous," his fingers drifted down her cheek, "but you can't lie to me."

Desperate to keep some version of her walls erect, she ignored his gaze, shoved her key in the lock, and turned. She threw the lights on in the entryway and froze. "Emery Renee Martinez, get off that couch right now!"

She felt Micah at her side before she rushed into the room. Emery and TJ lay sprawled on the couch in full lip-lock. TJ bolted off the couch and fell backward. His shirt lay on the floor, his teenage chest bare to the room. And her baby sister. Her fourteen-year-old baby sister that she was in charge of protecting cowered on the couch, her hair a mess and her shirt in a pile with TJ's on the floor.

Fury swept through Casey. Not again. Not tonight. TJ tried to rise to his feet. "You better stay on that floor unless you want to wind up back on it." Casey pointed to him and tossed him his shirt. She bent down and grabbed a blanket from where it slumped on the floor and tossed it at Emery. "Find your shirt and get dressed now."

"Casey." Micah's hand on her waist made her jerk backward.

"Don't touch me, Micah." She took a step away from him and eyed TJ on the floor, the whites of his eyes luminous in the shadows. They were kids. Kids. But all she could see was Tanner, and rage swept through her again. She took a step toward TJ. "How dare you..."

A hand gripped her and whirled her around. "Case, you need to calm down and take care of your sister. I'll take care of TJ." Casey shoved away from Micah, red tinting her gaze. But he refused to back down. With a gentle hand, he pushed her toward her sister again, now crying and trying to pull her shirt over her head in the corner, her back to the room. "Now, Casey. I'll take care of TJ." His voice was gentle, yet firm.

With a final look at the kid on the floor, Casey stalked to her sister.

"Up and outside, right now," Micah barked at TJ. She stared at her sister's back, the girl's arms wrapped around herself. Scrambling met her ears before the sound of boots, the door shutting, and then tears. Her sister's. Casey's from so long ago.

And just like that, her anger wilted. Replaced by grief. For the girl she'd been. The woman she'd wanted to be only moments before. That she and her sister had a mom who didn't care for them. And for the innocence that could so easily be lost by naïveté and one poor decision.

Casey approached her sister, but Emery whirled at her touch. "How could you?" Tear tracks stained her young face, just starting to lengthen and leave behind traces of childhood. "How could you embarrass me like that?"

"Excuse me?" Casey crossed her arms, compassion fleeing in light of the accusation. "You live under my roof. And you know the rules. No boys over when I'm not here, especially not TJ. And definitely no making out in your bra."

"You're such a hypocrite." Emery stalked the couch and plopped down. "You brought Micah home. And I thought you liked TJ!" she shrieked.

Casey towered over her sister. "For starters, missy, Micah was not going to stay. He was dropping me off. Have you ever seen me bring a boy over to spend the night any time you have ever come to visit me?"

Emery shrugged. "There's a first time for everything," she mumbled.

Yes, there was. But Casey wanted Emery to be ready for her first time with a boy. And not like this. Never like this. "Em, look at me."

In pure teenage form, she raised her eyes and fixed them on a point over Casey's shoulder. Casey sighed. Close enough. "I love TJ. But there is a reason I'm trying to help him so much. He's not ready for you. And honestly, missy, you aren't ready for what was about to happen."

"How would you know? Tanya in my class was bragging about her first time just last week. She said it was so romantic and sweet. And that we were losers and missing out. So I just thought . . ." She slumped down, her fingers twisting in knots in her lap. "TJ said he liked me. I figured, 'Why not?'"

Casey sank onto the couch with a groan. Emery's fight drained from her. Sobs shook her small frame, and she dropped her head in her hands. Casey pulled her sister into a hug, tugging her close, rocking her. The longing to protect overwhelmed Casey. She tightened her hold. The last thing she wanted for her sister was the life she'd lived as a teenager, the walls she built that had yet to topple, and the defenses she kept so close. Because pain ripped a hole that could rarely be mended. Even when stitched, scars prevailed. She wanted more for Emery than she saw of her mom with men. Casey wanted nothing more than to shield her sister from mistakes. Her own heart broke at her powerlessness.

"Ah, Em. Boys are going to come and go." She nudged her sisters face up and brushed away the tears. "You are gorgeous and strong and exquisite, and a guy who isn't willing to stick around isn't a guy worthy of you. Especially right now, Em. Not when you are just figuring out who you are."

She remembered a lesson from her small group leader, Mrs. Todd. She'd told the girls in Casey's group that God designed intimacy for marriage. She'd told them God wanted the best for them, which is why they should wait. Casey had messed that up two years later. Then everyone had abandoned her. Then it felt like God had abandoned her. But . . . maybe. Once upon a time, she'd wanted a marriage like Mrs. Todd's. Once upon a time, she'd seen that what Mrs. Todd said about a guy who loved you enough to wait for marriage was best. She'd definitely seen that doing it the opposite way led to disaster.

Feeling rusty, she dredged up the memory of Mrs. Todd's old words. If only she had listened. Maybe Emery would. "Wait for the guy who fights for you so much that he waits for marriage. The guy who won't ask you to take your clothes off. He won't push you. He'll fight for you and love you and won't mistreat you. Wait for that guy, and hold your head up until then. You choose yourself when no one else does. And you fight for your heart and your body."

From what she was learning, Micah sure did fit a lot on that list. Just maybe he was a guy worth opening up to. But Casey wasn't sure she was ready to tear down her walls. She didn't know if she would ever be, especially not for a wounded warrior still trying to find himself. What were the chances of him staying? How would she know she could trust him? With anything. With everything she guarded behind the walls.

"How will I know when the right guy comes along?"

Casey squeezed her little sister. "Well, you'll be thirty, and I won't want to kill him."

Emery giggled and shoved Casey away. "I don't want to be an old maid like you."

"I'm not an old maid." Casey attacked her sister's rib cage, fingers poking all the right buttons to make her sister a pile of giggles.

"Am I interrupting?"

His rich voice stilled her assault. Emery shoved up on the couch. "Please interrupt. I need to go to my room anyway."

Casey shuttered her feelings and faced her sister. "Phone?"

Emery paused mid-rise. "What?"

"Phone, please." Casey held out her hand.

"Just because he's in here, you want to go all parental on me?"

"Em, please don't make this harder on your sister," Micah pleaded from where he lounged in the entryway.

"Mind your own business," Emery sassed.

Casey gritted her teeth and braced for the tantrum. In a level voice, she repeated, "Emery, phone now, or the sentence will be longer."

Emery fumed and slapped her phone in Casey's hand. "I listened to you. Why are you still punishing me?"

Casey stood and faced her little sister, now almost taller than her. Stepdad number six had been tall, too. "Because you disobeyed the rules of the house, and as much as you listened, I don't trust you to not text TJ. So, until further notice, the phone is mine."

Emery squealed and stalked off. "I wish I still lived with mom!" she screamed, right before her door slammed, shaking the walls.

Casey dropped her head in her hands, too emotionally exhausted to run after Emery. "What happened with TJ?"

Micah unfolded from where he leaned against the wall and made his way to her, his boots booming on the wood floor. Casey shifted to the far end of the couch. She saw his desire to sit close to her, to comfort, but it was all too much. She couldn't reclaim what they'd had earlier. Not after what she'd shared. Not after what she'd just seen. Not with the memories racing too close to the surface.

"I stopped short of giving him a beat down and told him how a man treats a woman. It doesn't start by asking her for that." He motioned to the couch. Casey shifted. "I also threatened him if he did it again. So I wouldn't worry about it anymore." His voice lowered an octave, soothing her fraying nerves.

"Easy for you to say." Loud music blared from Emery's room. She would need to take her laptop, too.

"You don't have to be alone in this, Case. I want to help." He scooted closer and slipped his fingers through hers. She stared at their hands for a heartbeat before slipping off the couch. "Thanks for your help, but it's been a long night, and I think you should go."

Micah stood. "C'mon, Ace. Don't shut me out again."

"I've had enough for tonight, Micah, please." Memories of Tanner and curling up on her bed in the aftermath flashed. She took another step back.

"Casey." Micah now stood in front of her, his voice a mere whisper as his hands pulled her close. "TJ is not Tanner."

Every brick that had toppled immediately flew back into place, and she slammed the door on anything she'd felt earlier. She shoved away from Micah and rushed to the door, throwing it open. The night yawned like a gaping black hole beyond her, broken only by the pinprick of porch lights. "Out, Micah."

"Casey."

She held up her hand, steeling her voice. "I didn't tell you all that so you could use it against me." Against her bidding, tears pricked her eyes.

"Hun, I swear to God . . ."

"God?" This time she gave him the full force of her confusion, pain deeper than anything she'd felt earlier slashing through old wounds. Al's advice rang in her head but she pushed it away. She didn't know how to trust God again, to love and be loved. Her walls were safer. "Where was He when Tanner kept pushing? Where was He when my mom mocked me and abandoned me? Where was He when I had to stand up to my stepdads?" Her voice cracked. "And where was He when I lost my baby?" She spat. "He doesn't care about me. I don't think He ever did. He never fought for me."

Micah looked as if someone had slapped him. His face flushed in the dim lamplight. He nodded and walked out the door. "I'll call you tomorrow, Casey."

She shut the door, flipped the locks, and wilted against the wood. Less than an hour before, she'd felt free to get lost in Micah's arms. But just like usual, no one was safe. Casey wrapped her arms around her waist and sank to the floor. Not even the God she'd believed in as a kid. The one who promised to protect His creation, who made a beautiful marriage for Mrs. Todd, for Al and Ellie. Just not her.

CHAPTER 11

After the longest night on the planet with Micah calling and texting multiple times and Casey tossing and turning, Casey groaned and glared at her ringing phone in the dim morning light. Who dared call her this early on a Sunday? She flipped the phone over and blinked at the screen.

Teagan.

"Someone better be dying, Teag."

Her friends tinkling laugh rubbed against her nerves. "Well it sounds like you are. You have twenty minutes to look presentable before I show up with coffee."

After a rough end to the night with her sister and Micah, today, Casey didn't care about anything other than sleep.

"No way. Sunday mornings are sacred. I don't get out of bed before ten."

"Not this Sunday."

Casey heard a car door slam.

"You have nineteen minutes. Jeans and a cute sweater. No ball cap. No leggings. Chop, chop, missy."

"Teagan, I swear..."

"Your threats carry no weight with me. Now, Case."

It was futile to argue with Teagan when she got a new harebrained idea. That girl had a gypsy heart if Casey ever saw one. She didn't like plans, but she loved to drag her friends on adventures. Casey sat up and tossed her cream comforter off her legs.

"Fine. Fine. Where are we going?"

"That's a surprise," Teagan sang. "Eighteen minutes."

With a click, Casey was left in silence.

She groaned at the digits glaring at her from her phone. "8:07. Teagan, I'm going to strangle you."

With a groan, she stumbled into the hallway and flipped on the shower. Within minutes, she fought her way into skinny jeans, a burgundy knit sweater, and had added just enough product to her hair to add a little body wave. This would have to do.

The doorbell rang just as Casey forced her ankle boots on her feet. She toppled against the counter. A free-spirit Teagan might be, but when the girl wanted something, she was freakishly punctual.

She hurried into the living room where Emery sat on the couch eating a bowl of cereal and watching her latest Netflix obsession, something with mermaids and really cute teenage boys. No wonder she had a thing for TJ. And that other guy back home. Casey didn't want to think about how her mom had handled that indiscretion.

"I'm running out with Teagan. Do you need anything?"

Emery rolled her eyes. "I'm fourteen, not four." She saluted with her cereal bowl. "Go have fun."

"Teenagers," Casey grumbled under her breath. She grabbed her purse and keys from the hook near the door just as the doorbell sang again. She yanked on the door handle.

"Good morning, sunshine!" Teagan's bright smile and flowery shirt were much too chipper for this early on the weekend. She held out a coffee cup from Mudleaf. "Your favorite with that caramel stuff you like."

Casey accepted the offering and pulled the door closed behind her. "This better be good, Teag."

"Only the best." Her friend flashed a smile as she slipped behind the wheel of her sunny yellow bug. "Just close your eyes, enjoy your coffee, and we'll be there in a jiffy."

Casey sank into the charcoal gray leather seat and followed her friend's suggestion. The coffee warmed her throat before slipping into her belly. Shot one of morning juice. Only the rest of the cup to go. "Who says 'jiffy' anymore, Teag?"

"People who aren't so surly in the mornings."

The car pulled onto the freeway, reggae music blared from the speakers, and Casey regretted having a friend who was a morning person. "Just tell me when we get there." She slipped on her knock-off Ray Bans and closed her eyes.

Within ten minutes, the car came to a halt. A door closed but Casey wasn't ready to move. Until her door sprang open and Teagan tugged her hand.

"We're here!"

Casey opened her eyes and bit back a word she would have yelled at Emery for using. She might get struck by lightning just for using it, especially this close to Redeemer Community Church.

"Teagan, I really am going to kill you. This is your grand adventure?" Casey tugged her seatbelt to her chest and refused to budge. "I thought we were driving to Marble Falls for the day or maybe visiting a new brunch place you are obsessed with. I am not going in there; do you understand me?" Anger laced her voice but hidden deep within her was sheer panic. She hadn't been in a church since she was sixteen and her high school small group leader, Mrs. Anderson, had gone on about the cons of abortion instead of asking Casey what had happened to her baby. If only she'd still had Mrs. Todd when her life had fallen apart.

Teagan crouched by the passenger seat, her caramel brown eyes a little too understanding. Casey knew there would be no changing her mind. Good thing Casey was just as stubborn.

"Casey Stewart, do you not think I understand better than anyone why you wouldn't want to go in there?"

Casey swallowed another sip of coffee and refused to look at her best friend. Teagan did know better. So why had she dragged Casey here? Around them, people exited cars and flocked to the doors where ushers smiled and greeted them. Children skipped through the parking lot, eager to get inside, while parents yelled at them to watch for cars. A group of teenagers chatted outside the doors of what looked like a youth center, perfectly happy to be with their friends at church this early on a Sunday. Teenagers like she used to be. Before that night changed everything.

"Case, look at me."

Teagan's soft voice drew Casey from her memories. She took another swig of coffee, hoping to swallow away the urge to cry. She wouldn't shed any more tears for the girl she'd once been—the girl who had given her heart to a loving Father, who loved going to church as often as she could talk someone into taking her in her early teen years, who prayed and read her Bible, even when her mom made fun of her. And who'd been torn to shreds when she'd gotten pregnant and lost the baby and then been accused and blamed for the loss. She'd never been inside a church again.

"Case..."

Casey finally looked at her friend. "Why?"

"Because I've been coming the last few weeks with Mama Rosie."

Casey bolted upright. "Teag, you promised."

Teagan held up a hand. "Casey, I have more right to hate the church than you will ever know." Her green eyes were as hard as jewels. "You know I was beaten countless time by my foster dad who was a deacon at a local church."

Casey had known. She'd been the one Teagan had called to help her hide the bruises.

"But Mama Rosie has been talking to me a lot about people and about God."

Casey flinched, but Teagan reached for her hand and squeezed it.

"The God she talks about and the Christians she describes, the Christian she is, they aren't like the ones we experienced. And it makes me wonder if we are missing out on something we used to love and if the people who hurt us . . ." Teagan swallowed and shifted her eyes to the church doors. This time Casey squeezed her hand.

"Maybe . . . maybe they were as hurt and messed up as we were and don't deserve to be the thing we associate with God or believers."

Casey knew what was coming next. She wanted to withdraw, to run, to avoid the memories.

"Please, Casey. Come inside with me."

Music filtered through the open doors. Only a trickle of people still entered. She shifted her sunglasses on top of hair and met Teagan's begging stare.

"I know how much it hurt. We can't . . ." Teagan shook her head. "We're almost thirty, Casey. We can't keep letting it win. Letting them win. Just come inside with me. Please," she whispered.

Her heart stalled out. Teagan had stood by her through everything. Understanding, knowing, and yet she asked. Casey could do this one thing. Even if the memories hounded her. She fumbled with her seatbelt and slipped from the car.

If Teagan could do it, then so could she.

Teagan wound her arm through Casey's. She shivered, her

steps faltering, but Teagan's arm through hers didn't allow her to waver. Before she could blink they were past the smiling greeters, through the doors to the worship center, and occupying two cushioned seats on the back row.

Casey shrank back, expecting people to stare, to know she didn't belong. But the woman next to her smiled briefly and then turned to sing along with the band. Teagan began to sing next to her. Teagan. Her best friend. Church-hating, anti-organization Teagan. Singing. Worshipping. It had been a long time since Casey had thought of that word. But everyone worshipped something. Casey wondered if she'd been worshipping her pain for far too long.

She took in the room around her. A few hundred people stood in front of rows of chairs and faced the stage, coffee cups in hand, singing along. Two screens displayed art and lyrics on either side of a full band. Casey almost smiled. The guitarist and main singer had the hipster, longer hair—lightly greased and combed to one side—plaid shirt, skinny jeans, and Converse. At least he was predictable. But the way he sang, the way the base guitarist behind him held his hands high, it didn't feel fake. She studied the room again. Eyes closed, calm faces. A few curious glances, just like hers. But overall, the people were engaged. Something in here felt . . . real.

Casey turned her focus to the lyrics as a new song began. She listened, the words hitting the scars that marked her heart, lyrics about a good Father who loved her and defined her.

Teagan sang with abandon next to her. Something had changed in her friend. Her usually caustic attitude toward church had changed to one of peace, joy even. She studied her friend, her hand held high, eyes closed, and the gentlest expression on her face.

She believed what she was singing.

The refrain repeated about a good Father. That it was inherent to his character.

Casey had believed in a good Father once, too. But it hurt too much now. How could He allow Tanner to hurt her, people she trusted to turn their backs on her, her baby to die? She wrapped her arms around her chest and closed her eyes.

She heard Teagan sing about His ways being perfect.

Tears began to pour from Casey and she shrank into herself. How? How was He perfect in all of His ways? How was what had happened perfect?

The lyrics went on to claim His love was undeniable and His peace overwhelming.

The peace that Teagan felt. The peace Casey craved. Maybe Teagan was right. Maybe God had loved her, but she'd made bad decisions and people had handled her poorly. Maybe God loved her still.

She wanted that peace.

"As you call me deeper still into love, love, love."

Love hurt. That's why Casey built her walls. Teagan's arm wrapped around Casey's waist, and she sank into her friend's embrace. Something wet landed on her hand. Teagan was crying, too. Could it be that they had pushed God away? And not the other way around?

But He had still allowed their abuse. Their hurt.

"You're a good, good Father. It's who you are. And I'm loved by you. It's who I am."

Teagan's voice broke and something inside Casey broke, too. She so desperately wanted to believe in a good God, identify herself as His kid, know she was loved. Know she was protected by her Father.

Tears soaked her face but the sobs remained trapped inside. Teagan had never left her side despite her own abuse. Shawn had stood by both of them, another foster kid in the system, another hurt boy who had become a good man. He'd never stopped believing in God or loving his friends.

Mama Rosie. Mama Rosie was a saint. She loved Jesus with

abandon. Even though her husband had died. Even with all the violence and pain she had seen in the neighborhood. She accepted the good and bad as coming from or being allowed by a loving Father, and she loved with a courage Casey craved. Casey loved her kids that way, wanted the best for them, talked them through their hurt. And Micah. She didn't know what he had seen, but she knew he trusted God, believed He was good.

The crack inside her stretched until another wall crumbled. Next to her Teagan sang that God was perfect in all of His ways.

The rest of the crowd sang loudly and off-key. The band had stopped playing, but the room resounded with the cry, the confession, the acknowledgment.

And Casey claimed it. The words stumbled from her. Rusty and ringing with the teenager she'd once been. She'd thought no tears were left for that girl, but maybe these tears were for the woman she was now. The one who wanted what she'd once had and didn't know how to reclaim it—to belong to a loving Father, a role model she'd never had.

"I am loved by you." The music began to slow. "It's who I am." The sound tapered off, but something full lingered in the air.

Casey sucked it in.

I don't know how all that can be true. But you were once a loving Father to me. Help me . . . to believe it again, her heart cried as her tears continued to flow.

Four days. Micah hadn't heard from Casey in four days. And it had been four days of wondering. Four days of reliving. Four days of waiting.

He hurt people he loved. It was becoming a consistent theme in his life. He wasn't sure if Casey would ever want him around. He wasn't sure if he wanted to stay long-term.

But he was coming to love his Dallas neighborhood—cop cars, night raids, and all. He hadn't wanted another war. Still wasn't sure he could handle this. But these kids caught in the middle of bad cycles, they hadn't asked for one either.

He and Shawn sat across from Mama Rosie in her frilly kitchen for Tuesday night dinner. TJ and two other boys from the football team, Kason and Wilson, surrounded him, used to dinner nights with the neighborhood grandmother. Thankfully, kids who walked into Mama Rosie's were always on their best behavior, most likely because she wasn't afraid to love them and give them a whipping, sometimes at the same time.

"I saw Casey and Teagan at church on Sunday," Mama Rosie said, her shrewd gaze darting between Shawn and Micah. Micah wasn't sure who Shawn was interested in, but he suspected it was one of his longtime friends. Why he had never made a move on either of them, Micah would never know.

Shawn took a sip of his water and nodded. "Teagan told me she had been coming with you. She also told me she was going to take Casey this week."

Micah shot Shawn a look but remained quiet. He could feel Mama Rosie's maternal gaze on him.

"Well, I'm not sure how Teagan convinced Casey to go, but I've been praying she would. It's about time both of those girls went back to their roots."

"There's a lot of history there, Mama Rosie."

Micah noticed the boys glued to the conversation, clearly interested in what the adults were saying about their mentor and counselor.

"What have you got to say about all this, Micah?"

From the corner of his eye, he watched Shawn suppress a smirk. Micah twirled his fork, his meatloaf officially unappetizing.

"I don't think I have an opinion."

With a loud whack, Mama Rosie popped the back of his

head. Micah jerked away, rubbing the sore spot. "What was that for?" The boys fell over in their seats laughing. Shawn's deep chuckle joined theirs.

For such a small woman, she packed some force behind that slap.

"Boy, I got eyes in my head. You are smitten with that girl."

Shawn grinned next to him, and Micah glared.

"Don't get me started on you, Shawn Delgado."

The tall athlete next to him immediately sobered. "Yes, ma'am."

This time it was Micah's turn to smirk.

"Boy, you better fix whatever you did to that girl and fix it fast. Don't you dare hurt her, or I'll hurt you."

"She means it, Coach," TJ said. "I watched her wallop Bryan down the street when we tried to steal some beer money. He was walking funny for a week."

"That's because you shouldn't be stealing or drinking. That stuff is nasty and bad for your brain and your senses. You're too young, and even if you weren't too young, I'd still be giving you a lecture. Don't you do that again."

"Yes, ma'am." TJ shoveled another bite in his mouth. Micah smothered a smile until the full weight of Mama Rosie's all-seeing stare focused back on him.

"Well?"

He choked back a laugh. "I didn't do anything to her, Mama Rosie, and I have no intention of hurting her."

His phone buzzed in his pocket

Casey. Finally.

His hands grew slick.

"No cell phones at the table, or do you want me to pop the back of your head again?" The hint of a smile graced her brown, wrinkled face.

"It's Casey."

Her smile spread. "Well then go answer it." She nodded to

the hall. "But just this once, you hear? Meal times are for verbal conversation and quality time. Not electronics. Good for nothing devices." He heard her muttering behind him as he darted into the hall.

Micah opened the joint text between him, Shawn, and Casey. It's wasn't much, but at least it was acknowledgment.

I need a couple more coaches to help with the community basketball fundraiser. You two in?

Micah fired back a response.

Absolutely. When and where?

Her reply came within seconds.

Next Saturday. You'll play until your team is out.

I'm in. He shot back. He wasn't sure Old Faithful would get him from Dallas to Alabama to see his family, so he had decided to spend Thanksgiving in Dallas with Mama Rosie. Maybe he could even get some of the guys together for a pickup game. But he officially couldn't wait for the Saturday after Thanksgiving.

He waited a few minutes, pacing the hall. His phone buzzed again. This time a text just to him.

I know I've been distant. I just needed some space. But I really need your help on this.

You can count on me.

He slipped back in his chair to the raucous chorus coming from the boys as Mama Rosie dished out cherry pie. His team. These boys were his team. And Shawn and Mama Rosie. It was an interesting group, but the more time he spent with them, the more he wanted to sink roots into this new city.

He took a bite of his meatloaf, the taste exploding on his tongue. Home cooking. He'd missed it.

Micah didn't know what the coming months would hold. He didn't know what he would do after he said his final goodbye. But the more he stayed in this neighborhood, the more he felt the stirring of belonging. No matter what came next, he didn't want to let these people down.

CHAPTER 12

Bodies and helmets slapped and slammed on the grassy practice field after school on Wednesday afternoon, preparing for the playoff game the week after Thanksgiving. Most of them would trickle over to Ellie's Place after practice where Casey, Al, Teagan, and their team of mentors would help with homework, host the leadership class for a few, and support whatever else needed patching in the lives of these teens. But for now, nothing existed in their world besides their teammates, their coaches, and a football.

Sweat beaded under Micah's cap despite the cool temperature as he and Shawn called plays, broke up arguments, and shouted encouragement from opposite sidelines. The more Micah spent time with these boys, the more he was convinced that they needed a version of boot camp—discipline, team building, and the knowledge of how to fight for one another instead of with one another. Something like that could turn reluctant teammates into brothers. It would be perfect for off-season. Or perfect for an afterschool sports program as part of Ellie's. Maybe he could recommend it to the new coach, whenever Casey found one.

He wanted that for these kids. But that meant staying past his planned time. Christmas. He had to make his last visit by Christmas and close out this part of the journey. He needed to end the nightmares and the nagging that he hadn't finished paying for the death of his brothers. After that final goodbye, he didn't know where he would land next.

His phone buzzed. Mom.

If he ignored, she would just call back. She was persistent that way, and she'd taught them that family always came first. Something that had made his induction into the SEALs much easier.

"Hey, Mom. I'm kinda busy right now. Watch Zane, TJ!" he shouted, holding the phone away, his eyes glued to the field.

"Good, then I'll make this short. Pap bought you a ticket home tomorrow morning at 6:30 a.m. Seth has the weekend off from football, it's Gran's birthday, and it's Thanksgiving, so the whole family is coming in." Which meant Nick and Kaylan. He hadn't seen his best friend and sister since he'd left California, hadn't talked to Seth beyond a few texts to see how college and football season were going. He couldn't remember the last time he had checked in with David. Clearly, he wasn't doing great in the family-first category. Just one more way he failed the people in his life.

He shouted a few more instructions, the phone plastered between his shoulder and ear as he clapped. "Mom, I thought I told you I would just spend Thanksgiving at Mama Rosie's this year. You didn't have to buy a ticket."

"I know you did, Micah." He heard the weariness in her voice over the clash of pads and teens on the field. "But, we all want you to come home, Son. Time to be around your family. Just for the holiday weekend. You've been all over the place. Come home and let us be with you. Please. The ticket is already bought and paid for. You just need to be at the airport in the morning."

What she meant was that they all wanted to make sure he was okay. He rubbed a hand over his face, sweat streaking his palm. He wasn't used to being the family priority. He didn't like it.

He needed to get off the phone. Needed to focus. Needed to not feel like a project, although he knew he would never really be that to his family.

"Sounds good, Mom. I'll be at the airport in the morning. Just send the ticket to my email."

"Great! Pap already checked you into a Southwest flight out of Love Field. I can't wait to see you tomorrow."

She hung up before he could protest anymore. Truth was, he didn't want to. TJ sprinted down the field and scored a touchdown. Micah jumped up and down, yelling words of encouragement, and then shouting for the team to regroup and do it again.

Alabama didn't feel like home any more, even though most of his family lived there. But it would probably be his best place to start over . . . if he didn't stay in Dallas. He glanced at his watch. He'd be back where he grew up in less than twenty-four hours.

It was time. Maybe the time away from Dallas would help him decide what to do about Casey. He hadn't heard from her again after the text. Hadn't seen her at all since he left her house.

But he couldn't get their kiss out of his head, couldn't scrape away the image of her haunted eyes as they walked into her house or the shuttered look of a door closing as she'd kicked him out after a night that had left both of them breathless. She was running and he knew it. He understood but he didn't like it, wanted to stop it.

Shawn's team ran down the field for an answering touchdown and field goal.

Maybe he was still running. But if he were ever to decide

how he felt about Casey, or the SEALs, or even Dallas, he needed to go back home.

After all, his running really began his senior year of high school on a football field in Alabama. And it was time to face the memory.

The family lake house smelled like roses and vanilla the second he walked through the door. His dad slapped him on the back as he entered behind him. "Welcome home, Son."

"Thanks, Dad."

"I'll go drop your bag in your old room."

"I can do that."

His dad's soft smile, so like Micah's brother, David, ceased any argument. "I'm not that old that I can't handle a few stairs. Besides," his dad motioned to the kitchen where Micah could see the rest of the family laughing and milling around the island, "I think some other people want to say hello."

He didn't even make it down the two steps into the living room before arms wrapped around his neck and the faint scent of lavender tickled his nose. Kaylan. He dropped his backpack and picked her up, sinking into the hug he hadn't realized he'd been aching for. He'd missed her. She'd been his best friend growing up, the first person he'd ever wanted to protect. He'd tracked her down in Haiti after the earthquake shattered the country and her heart right along with it. He'd encouraged her in her love of Nick, chased after a terrorist stalking her. He'd held her when she'd cried, fought with her—often for her own good— and loved her fiercely.

The arms wrapped around him now were clearly returning the favor. He hadn't realized how broken he felt until his baby sister reminded him what home felt like.

"Happy Thanksgiving, and welcome back. I've missed you."

He dropped her back to her feet and squeezed her shoulders.

Her pale skin had the faintest hint of color from her days on a California beach. A few more freckles dotted her nose. Her auburn hair hung in layers to her shoulders, the slight wave making her look like she'd just come from a day at the beach. He'd missed life with her, her steadiness.

He kissed her forehead and dropped an arm over her shoulder, finally stepping from the entryway and into the family living room. "I've missed you, too. What did you fix me to eat?"

She rolled her eyes. "Gran and Mom did all the cooking before we got here. But they fixed your favorites."

"Basically they didn't want to let you near the kitchen."

She elbowed him in the gut. Hard.

He doubled over chuckling. "At least you still know how to get in a cheap shot."

She crossed her arms, leaning against the leather sectional taking up the center of the high-ceilinged room. "No joke. I grew up with three brothers, and I live with Nick."

"You taught her a little too well, Bulldog." Nick stepped next to his wife, twirling a strand of wavy hair around his finger absently. "In some places, what she can do is considered spousal abuse."

Micah grinned, knowing the two of them would never hurt one another. Not for the first time, he craved a relationship like his sister and brother-in-law shared. Kaylan teased him about finding a girl all the time, but truthfully, he'd never been ready to commit. Probably because he never found a girl who really turned his head. Until now.

"Very funny." She slipped onto her toes and gave him a quick peck on the cheek before darting away to the kitchen.

Micah rubbed his stomach and stood up straight. "Well I have definitely not missed how sickeningly cute you two are. Or your subtlety."

Nick smirked and took up his wife's place leaning on the sectional. "Never could get much past you."

"No, that was you, Hawk."

Quiet descended between the two. The quiet born of countless operations, late nights at home, early morning runs, and life-and-death experiences. Laughter still sounded from the kitchen, but Micah knew this moment would shape the rest of the weekend.

"You look good, Bulldog. More like your old fighting self again."

Micah crossed his arms, matching his friend's stance. He felt better than the last time he'd seen Nick. Something felt more put together in this moment than it had in a long time.

"Dallas has been good for me."

Nick nodded. "Kaylan has missed you. Logan and Kim's kids have been asking for you."

Just thinking about his old teammate and his family made longing bubble to the surface. His team had truly been a family. When Logan lost a leg after an op gone wrong, Micah and the team had swarmed Kim and the kids, taking care of them, helping out. He'd spent countless nights on the beach listening to them laugh around a firepit with the guys who cared for them, fought for them, loved their dad. He missed all of them—Colt, Jay, Titus, Logan—but especially Nick and Kaylan.

"C'mon, Hawk," Micah allowed some of the old teasing to drip into his voice. "Just say it."

"Say what?"

"You know . . . that thing you're dying to say." He cupped his ear and leaned in close to Nick.

"You're still a pain in the butt."

Micah choked back a laugh and grinned. Familiar. This moment felt familiar. He was in his childhood home with his family and his best friend, a man who had felt, seen, and experienced the same things he had.

Nick's steady gaze pierced right through him.

"I missed you, too, man." Nick gave him a quick hug, slapping his back, the emotions easing in the wake of brotherhood. Home. In more than one sense.

They fell into step, approaching the family kitchen where everyone else had now spotted him. Nick leaned in close before the vultures descended. "But if you tell anyone I said that, I will hurt you worse than your sister could."

Micah grinned. "Only if you are ready to get beat." He took a quick step out of reach. "Hey everyone, guess who just admitted he missed me!"

The family laughed as Nick crossed his arms and smirked. Challenge accepted.

For the first time in a while, Micah felt a little more whole.

CHAPTER 13

It was Saturday night. Thanksgiving had been delicious, and Gran's birthday celebration had been a blast. Their family gathered and played Catch Phrase, ironically her favorite. She claimed it was because it made everyone laugh and think all at the same time. Micah wasn't so sure about the second part, but he would do anything for his Gran. Anything.

Luckily, the University of Alabama had a bye week on Thanksgiving weekend this year, so Seth was home, but in normal Richards family fashion another football game blared on the television. Micah had heard rumors of his brother partying more and more. Scouts were on the hunt, and Micah was worried that if he didn't stay away from parties and on his game he might miss out on a great opportunity. So much potential. Such a slippery slope. Micah wanted it all for Seth.

He sat next to him on the couch in the living room, several guys from the University of Alabama piled around them munching on snacks. They loved Gran almost as much as the family and had crashed the party. His mom sure knew how to lay out a spread for big athletes. She'd made burgers, sandwiches, vegetable and fruit trays, cookies, and chips and salsa by the buckets.

David leaned over the couch between Micah and Seth, his gaze glued to the screen hanging over the fireplace. David was Micah's lighter alter ego. His loose comb over of chestnut brown hair varied from Micah's dark chocolate strands. His eyes were closer to their sister's green than Micah's deep brown. He was the eldest in the family, steadier than either Micah or Seth, and their rock in rough moments.

"How ya feeling about the end of the season and these scouts that are hovering?" David asked their younger brother.

The redheaded tight end didn't look at their oldest brother. "I'm really interested in Colorado, but I don't know. It seems surreal to be talking to professional scouts."

Kaylan shuffled across the room and squeezed her way between Micah and Seth on the couch. "You can't talk about scouts without me! What are you thinking?"

Seth lost some of the charm he usually had around his friends, and a hint of insecurity peeked through. "I feel like I have no clue what to do with my life if this falls through."

Micah knew the feeling. Micah was living the feeling.

"You find the next thing. You don't give up. I know God created you for big things, Seth," Micah assured, not quite claiming that truth for himself.

"God created me for football, Micah." He glanced around their sister, perched on top of both of them. "I don't know anything else."

David gripped Seth's shoulder. "God created you for more than football, Seth Richards."

"And if for some reason I don't get recruited?"

Micah watched his brothers and sister. The four of them each played a unique role in the dynamic. David the quiet leader, Micah the warrior protector, Kaylan the sweetheart and caregiver, and Seth the encourager joy-bringer. This is who they'd always been. A team, even when they were fighting with each other. In this role, with these people, the protector in him rose from slumber again. His inner fighter was doing that a lot lately.

"Then Bulldog and I will personally take out whichever idiots don't choose you for the NFL," Nick assured, bending over the couch next to David.

"And I'll help." Kaylan grinned, pounding her fist into her open hand.

"I think they may be more scared of you than Micah and Nick," Seth said, poking their sister in the ribs. She could definitely hold her own when she needed to. They just never put her in that situation.

"That is for sure." David kept watching the television. "I'll help with the cleanup."

They all looked at him. "Which might be the creepiest comment all night, big bro." Micah grinned at his brother. People thought David was silent and intense. Micah knew he might be the most loyal and fierce protector of them all.

"What about you, Micah? What's next?" Seth asked, immediately putting Micah in the hot seat as the eyes of all his siblings focused on him.

He squirmed next to Kaylan. "I guess I need to figure out a job. I've been helping out with coaching at a school in Dallas, and I love it more than expected. The kids are challenging, but it's so cool to watch them learn and excel, you know? And there's something about being a coach for a kid at that age. You can make a big impact. But . . ."

Kaylan nudged him in the ribs. "But what?"

Micah sighed and ran a hand through his dark hair. "I'm just not sure I can handle that responsibility right now. These kids need someone they can depend on, and I'm not sure I fit that bill."

"Bulldog, I think you have bought the lie that you are broken and a failure because of what happened earlier this year. You are one of the most dependable people I know. I never questioned or doubted you when we served together. You have got to move past this. It's destroying you, man, and it will destroy the future that lies ahead of you if you let it." Nick gave no room for argument, and while Micah bit back a defensive retort, the words also winged their way to the parts that had felt broken and questioning.

"It sounds like Dallas might just be the place you need to start over. And it sounds like those kids could use a guy like you, bro. A guy who knows what it feels like to have life kick him in the teeth and who still rises up anyway," David chimed in, squeezing Micah's shoulder in the process.

Seth's friends cheered for a touchdown on the screen, and attention was immediately pulled from Micah. Kaylan burrowed further between her brothers, looping her arm around Micah's. "I think the Lord may have provided Dallas as your next opportunity. The question is, are you ready to stop running?"

It was a question he still didn't know how to answer.

Micah didn't show and even worse, he hadn't let her know. She stood on the sidelines of the last game of the day, cheering her team on while Brad, her potential new coach, hollered on the other side of the court. It had been a successful day of fundraising, even better because the community showed up and participated. Big donors were always helpful and welcome, but there was something about the people in the community giving even a little to support the neighborhood kids.

"Shoot, shoot!" she yelled at TJ.

With a swish, the ball cleared the net and her team won the

tournament. Mama Rosie hooted and hollered from her seat on the front row of the bleachers.

Casey finished high-fiving her team and then wandered over to Emery and Bianca at the tables.

"Casey, look at all this money!" Emery fanned a full stack of green bills, marking the event as a success. "People keep buying food tickets and bounce house tickets for their kids. Maybe we can build two baseball fields."

"How about a cheerleading gym?" Bianca suggested.

"How about y'all quit waving that money around and put it back in the box for me?" she laughed, loving their enthusiasm for everything happening at Ellie's Place. She tapped the metal box on the table where they sat at the entryway and moved to check on Shawn who was cleaning up the pie-eating competition.

"Good competition?"

Shawn grimaced. "I may never eat pie again, but it was a great year. How is it that Leah Gonzalez weighs one hundred and thirty pounds soaking wet and yet manages to out-eat every large man here?"

Casey chuckled. "That is definitely a mystery." Raised voices made her turn her head, and her gaze landed on Coleman towering over Bianca, trying to take some dollar bills out of her hand. She stretched, keeping it out of his reach, her voice raising in a stream of Spanish Casey couldn't quite make out.

"Shawn." With one glance in the direction she pointed, they were both jogging toward the table, Coleman now yelling at Bianca. Emery sat next to Bianca, clutching the metal box containing the rest of the money in her lap.

"Bianca, just a couple bucks, Babe. Why you treating me like this?"

"You are loco. This is not your money. This is not my money. Coleman, stop!"

His hands almost swiped the dollar bills as he bent over her.

"Coleman, back up, man," Shawn boomed as they arrived at the table. Shawn quickly shoved his way in between Bianca and Coleman as Casey swiped the money from Bianca's hand and took the lock box from Emery. With a quick turn of a key, she unlocked the box, tossed the rest of the cash in there, and snapped the lid shut.

"Is that all of it?" Casey whispered to Emery as Coleman shouted at Shawn, his mouth only inches away from Shawn's face. Shawn held his ground, calm. Around Coleman, a group of guys began to gather. Some Casey recognized as high school dropouts from a few years back.

"That's it." Emery's rich brown eyes looked like saucers.

Casey nudged Emery and Bianca from their chairs. "Can you go find Al, please?" The girls took off at a run, and Casey turned to help Shawn, Brad arriving and standing nearby.

"Man, why y'all always up in my business? I just needed a few bucks. Wouldn'ta hurt nothing for her to give them to me."

"Coleman, you know why she didn't give them to you." Casey respected that Shawn didn't move, didn't budge, as the antsy teen now prowled back and forth in front of him. Baggy jeans, white t-shirts, tattoos on display even in the cold.

"Y'all aren't even from this hood, Coach." A few guys around him nodded. "Why are you causing trouble?"

"I'm not the one causing trouble, Coleman." Shawn took a step toward him, forcing Coleman to stumble back at the unexpected move. "Why don't y'all go ahead and leave? Don't ruin a good day."

Coleman's grin sent a chill down Casey's spine. She felt Al's hand on her shoulder and his gentle undertone, "Do I need to call the police?"

Before she could answer, Coleman lifted his baggy shirt, revealing a dull, silver gun tucked into his belt. "I run this neighborhood, Coach. Sooner or later, you'll understand that." With a quick pivot, he and his crew exited through the balloon arch marking the entrance to the field next to the basketball courts. With a quick jerk of his arm, balloons began popping, his laughter maniacal over the bursts. Casey approached the arch and lifted one of the destroyed balloons. Ragged edges. From a knife.

Soft steps approached behind her, and Casey turned to find her nervous prospective coach. "Casey, I thought I knew what I was doing with this job, but . . ." Brad feathered a hand through his short blond hair. "I don't know that I can handle this. Today was fun, but I think I'm going to have to pass up the position."

"I'm sorry to hear that." Casey gave a nod, resigned. If he couldn't handle this, she couldn't handle him here. "Best of luck."

"I'm truly sorry." With a nod, Brad turned toward the parking lot.

Casey groaned and dropped her head in her hands. Micah didn't show. She was down a coach. Coleman was escalating. Her excitement over the fundraiser dimmed.

"What's on your mind, Micah?"

Micah didn't even need to turn around. He'd been staring through the glass windows in the sunroom at the lake for fifteen minutes now, but only his image and the blackness beyond had stared back. He'd seen Pap watching over his shoulder for two minutes. But that was Pap. Never pushing. Always asking.

"I can't see anything out there." Micah didn't need to see the view to describe it. A wooden dock spanned from the back porch steps to the water beyond. A boat and two jet skis sat docked under the wooden roof. Micah and his brothers had spent one summer building every inch of it with their dad. They'd mowed lawns and done chores for neighbors over two summers to earn the jet skis. And they'd laughed and played for summers since.

On the other side of the lake sat a few more houses interspersed among climbing trees. When the sun broke over the tree line and spread over the lake in lemonade tones, it was truly a sight to behold. He'd spent many mornings with Kaylan watching from this very room. And many mornings with David getting an early start on the water. Of course, his siblings always had to bribe him with coffee first. Seth had always joined them later when he stumbled from bed.

But despite his memories and knowledge of the view, only a shadowed image of himself stared back. And blackness. Only blackness behind the windows with the faintest hint of moonlight.

Pap pushed off from the door jam, his cane tapping a rhythm on the cement floor. His minor heart attack a few years earlier had weakened him. Dave had whittled the cane as a gift—truly a work of art. Pap stopped next to Micah, his gaze fixed on the windows before him.

"Know what I see?"

Micah wasn't sure he wanted to know. Micah saw a man marked by age but standing tall, the confident, retired state judge still able to command a room and hold court. He could mete out justice to criminals and then come back and play dolls with his granddaughter or cheer his grandsons on at a game. His stature wasn't all that different from Micah's—broad shoulders, now slightly stooped with age. Tall. His thick white hair combed over and green eyes still sparkling. If Micah could be half the man his Pap and dad and Dave were when he got older, then he would count himself blessed. But right now, he just couldn't see it.

Finally, Micah answered. "What do you see, Pap?"

"I see the best quarterback I ever watched play." Micah rolled his eyes but Pap's gaze shifted to his and held in the glass. And Micah knew he was only getting started.

"I see a Navy SEAL who fought for his country. I see a brother, son, and grandson who makes this family complete. I see a friend who would do anything for others. I see a protector. I see a warrior."

Micah couldn't meet Pap's eyes.

A hand rested on his shoulder, and Pap turned them both away from the haunting glass images. "And I see my grandson who has lost confidence in himself. I want him to find it again."

"I messed up, Pap."

"You didn't mess up. It was just circumstances."

"You know it wasn't just that. If I hadn't been stupid in high school that night. If I hadn't injured myself."

"*If* can be a crippling word, Son." He turned them both back to the window, this time resting both of his hands on Micah's shoulders. "*If* can also be a powerful word. Look."

Micah glanced at the window, this time their images blurring together. The moon now peeked from behind the clouds, and a slice of moonlight danced on the lake, illuminating his silhouette in the window.

"Turn the *if* around, Micah. Tell me what you see."

"I have no idea what you are talking about, Pap."

His grandfather smirked, and in that turn of his lips Micah saw himself, his sister, his brothers, the spunk, the strength, the drive. The love.

"If you'd never injured yourself in high school . . ."

"I would probably have been in Seth's shoes," he started slowly. "I would have probably gone on to star at UCLA instead of sitting on the bench most of the time. I probably wouldn't have had the time to become friends with Nick. I might not have joined the SEALs."

Pap nodded. "Then what?"

"If I hadn't joined the SEALs, I wouldn't have fought for my country. I wouldn't have found a new team, a new brotherhood. Kaylan wouldn't have met Nick."

"Where would your sister be if that hadn't happened?"

More moonlight illuminated the water outside. Micah could now make out the outline of the dock. He shoved his hands in his pockets. He remembered finding his sister in Haiti, the light gone from her eyes and the people she had befriended and loved for weeks now dead, homes destroyed. Nick had been the driving force helping her heal once she returned home. "Kaylan probably wouldn't have healed as quickly after Haiti. They never would have fallen in love. Never would have gotten married. Probably never would have had the courage to go back to Haiti again." He frowned. "She also wouldn't have been hunted by a terrorist." He cringed remembering the arms dealer, Janus, who had taken a particular interest in their team, even making it personal and stalking their loved ones in California.

"Now you aren't God, so you don't control any of those outcomes. But the point is, bad can come with good, Micah. We live in a broken world. Keep going. What else?"

"If I hadn't joined the SEALs, Nick might be dead by now." He'd saved Nick's back, but Nick had saved Micah's too, on more than one occasion. It's what teammates did. He stopped. His heart felt heavy. "My friends also wouldn't have died, Pap. If I hadn't made a stupid decision in high school, gotten hurt, and then reinjured that weak muscle on an op, my friends wouldn't have died."

Pap squeezed his shoulders. His wise gaze never wavered from Micah. "They also wouldn't have traded serving with you, fighting alongside you. You aren't God, Micah Richards. You are just a man whom He chooses to use. We can 'what if' all day. The truth is, we can never fully understand God's plans. But we can't keep living in the regret and shadow of our past mistakes."

"They're still gone, Pap."

"And the timeline of each life is set by the good Lord long before we are ever born. Your friends were warriors. Don't dishonor their memory by wallowing in regret and blame. Do you know what I see?"

Micah remained silent. The television blared from the family room. He heard the musical trill of Kaylan's laughter and the murmur of Nick's response. He heard the voices of his parents and brothers, rising and falling, teasing, laughing. His team. A team that he never had to try to belong to. He just . . . belonged. But he'd always wanted, needed more. He needed to know he belonged to more than just a family who was required to love him, although he knew they didn't feel that way.

"Micah."

The moon had climbed well above the clouds, and Micah could clearly see his childhood playground, the place that had seen him through every victory and every defeat. It shone through every part of him, shining light on the pieces he loved and hated.

"You see a man who lost his way, his team, and his confidence."

"Wrong." Pap stepped next to him and put his arm over his shoulders. "I see Micah Richards, my grandson, a son of God, an incredible brother, son, hopefully father someday." He smiled. "An incredible friend. An honorable teammate. And a man who needs to remember exactly where his confidence lies."

Micah turned from his reflection and met the knowing gaze of his grandfather. Dread curled within him, but he knew his grandfather had issued a challenge. And a Richards never backed down from a challenge. Neither did a SEAL.

"How do I do that, Pap?"

"Well now, I think you may need to visit the place where this long root of *if* began. And I think you need to go now. If you hurry, you can make it before your flight."

Back to the scene of his first regret, the one that led to all the rest. And even to some of his greatest victories, sweetest memories, and best relationships. Maybe Pap had a point. Pap shoved car keys into his hands. "Take mine. And don't leave until you see what I see staring back. Your dad can take me to pick up my car at the airport in the morning."

With a quick nod, Micah left to face his demons.

"We did it, Case!" Teagan pranced into the storage room as Casey shuffled a tower of orange cones to the corner. The mentors and kids had helped clean up the campus, but the closet had seen better days. Casey tossed another cone on top of the stack with a plop before turning to face Teagan.

"Yeah, it was a good day, Teag." But she'd missed a very handsome, very absent someone.

Teagan danced in front of her, her red ponytail swinging behind her. "Okay, I really need you to get on my excitement level here."

Casey rolled her eyes at her friend but allowed a smile to peak through. "Not possible, Teag. But I'll try. Tell me again."

"Okay, here goes. Ready?"

Casey fought another eye roll, but she couldn't help the full grin that finally cracked her features. "Ready."

"We did it! We raised the rest of the money for the baseball field!" Teagan jumped up and down.

"Wait, what? That's incredible!" Casey joined her friend in a small jump. "But I am also back to the drawing board with a coach."

"Yeah, that's unfortunate." Teagan winced. "But the right guy or gal is going to show up. I just know it."

"I wish I had your confidence," Casey groaned.

Al appeared in the doorway, a smile on his sweaty, lined face.

Despite the chill of the day, he was in his classic, short-sleeve button-down and casual slacks complete with fedora. Jacket slung over his arm. "I'm calling the contractor tomorrow. We raised the money, and my company and a couple other contributors will match the rest."

"Wow, I can't believe it."

Al pulled them both into a hug. "And I couldn't have done it without my girls. You two did a great job planning all of this."

"If only we hadn't been short a coach. I'm sorry, Al."

Al squeezed Casey's shoulder. "I'm sure he had a very good reason. Give the boy a chance to explain. But you did a great job coaching, as always." He motioned to Teagan. "Can you help me wrap up a couple things in the office really quick while Casey finishes in here?"

"Sure thing. See ya, Case." The two left the small room, leaving Casey to her arranging and thoughts. It had been a good day. The kids had played hard; many from the neighborhood and other parts of Dallas had showed up. They had bounce houses for the kids, fair food for purchase, t-shirts, and more. The day had been perfect.

Except for Micah.

She hadn't seen him in a week. Hadn't heard from him all day. He hadn't shown. And she hadn't wanted to text him.

She tossed a basketball in the corner and caught it as it snapped back to her. Her hands stung from the impact of the rough rubber.

"Can I help with anything else before I leave, Case?"

Shawn hung from the doorframe to the equipment room as she wrestled with a few basketballs that had rolled from their rack.

"I don't think so. I'm about to head out." She shoved the balls into place, another bouncing off the end of the rack.

"He had a family thing, Casey."

"Who?" She slapped the ball back on the end of the rack and then began to count. All there.

"You know exactly who. That guy you are pretending not to be mad at. You always were terrible at charades."

"I hate charades. No point guessing when we can just say what we mean." Casey tossed her hands on her hips and faced her old friend. He looked every bit the Italian that she assumed his birth parents were. Olive-toned skin. Dark eyes. And beautiful, dark hair. A darker version of Micah. But she felt only brotherly affection toward Shawn.

Micah just made her mad. And maybe a little disappointed.

"Don't pretend you know me so well, Shawn Delgado."

Shawn crossed his arms over his broad chest. His backwards-facing cap made his intense stare more cute than intimidating. She knew that look all too well.

"Listen. I don't know why Micah didn't let you know he was going out of town. I know his family unexpectedly bought him a ticket for Thanksgiving and asked him to come home."

"Don't make excuses for him."

"Sister, I am not making excuses for that fool. He should have told you. But you also should give him the chance to explain. And you should also call him because it sounds like he actually handled the TJ thing well."

Casey tossed her hands in the air. "He told you?"

Shawn grinned. "He told me enough."

Casey blushed. She couldn't help it. It was weird for her stand-in-brother to know all the details of her date.

"All I'm saying is he is trying. And yes, he messed up. But stop damning him for everything else. Talk to him, Casey."

Casey made to squeeze past him, but Shawn tossed his heavy arm around her and drew her to a halt. "Talk to him, Little Sis, or I will lock you two in a room together until you make up or kill each other. Got it?"

He would, too. Casey returned his side hug. "Fine."

As betrayed as she felt, she really wanted to see Micah again. Ever since the service at church, her walls were weakening. She owed Micah an apology. He owed her one now, too. And he better make it good. But she would, at the very least, let him make it.

Beyond apologies, she also owed him an explanation. She'd told him she felt abandoned by God, but the truth was she had done a lot of the abandoning, and she was finding her way back. Al was right. She needed her Father—she just didn't know how to fully trust Him. But Micah seemed to. She didn't understand what had happened to him, but she knew Micah had held tightly to his faith.

Casey fiddled with her phone. Typing, deleting, and retyping. Trying to choose her words with care. Trying to fight the walls . . . just a little. Finally, she hit send and stared at the blue text bubble on her screen.

Even with Micah's forgetfulness, his persistence, care, concern, and strength drew her to him. And that made her nervous—and despite his failed commitment, she felt oddly hopeful.

The field had once been grass. Now AstroTurf greeted him at Memorial Stadium, home field of the Tuscaloosa Wildcats. The moon glinted off stands on either side of him, and the press box loomed large and as intimidating as always to his right. Yet somehow it didn't seem as big as it once had. In fact, the whole stadium felt a little smaller. Night air and the lingering scent of plastic and sweat greeted him as he came to a stop in the middle of the fifty-yard line.

He'd been a hero on this field. Crowds had cheered. And he'd been surrounded by his team. As their quarterback, he'd led them to victory and playoffs sophomore and junior year.

Then senior year came and with it a perfect season and a shot at state.

And he'd blown it.

He settled onto the white line in the center of the field. His knees pulled to his chest. The moon hung directly over the press box, and the light cast the field around him in shadows.

With a deep breath, he let himself fall back to the place and person he'd once been.

It was senior year, and they had made it to state. Micah was surrounded by all his buddies and friends from school. They gathered in his friend's backyard, the pool full of teenagers with red plastic cups. And Micah held his own red cup for the first time ever. He'd always been the good kid. The confident kid. The Christian kid. The kid who had never desired to drink, never needed to to have a good time. But tonight, under the haze of winning and the state game looming the next day, he decided to make an exception. He wanted to celebrate, to cut loose. Just this once.

He didn't know how many refills he'd gone through, pumped into his waiting hands by his buddies. They were dumb teenagers, not realizing how badly the alcohol would impact them in the game the next day. Or maybe just not caring. It was a curse of youth—thinking the future ahead was bright but never pausing to consider the choices of the present day.

Micah had felt like he was on cloud nine.

His buddy threw him a pass, and Micah dove after it. His feet hit slick cement. He slipped. Pain unlike any he had felt ripped up his leg just as his fingers wrapped around pigskin and he smashed into the water.

That had been it.

They'd lost state. Their star quarterback sidelined. All because he'd made a bad decision.

He'd been in physical therapy for months, and his scholarship to UCLA had turned into a second-string option for two years before he left the team.

And found Nick. And the SEALs.

And ten years later. That same injury, same weak muscle, had flared in the middle of running from an ambush. And he'd led their enemies right to his friends.

He'd held his buddies as they died. And they'd never known it was his fault, his weakness, his past mistake that led to their end.

Never would've blamed him.

But he'd left anyway. Because he hurt those on his team. Any team. And he couldn't stay.

He stretched out on the field, his arms folded behind his head and face toward the moonlit sky overhead.

He'd once been a star. A football player. A teammate. Not anymore. Maybe he defined himself too much by where and to whom he belonged. His world shattered and he faltered every time the Lord stripped those pieces away.

Maybe he cloaked himself so much in the identity of his team that he continually forgot his identity as just Micah. Like those stars he'd seen with Casey in the night sky only a week before. Together, they made a beautiful skyline, but individually, they still had a light and uniqueness all their own.

Maybe Micah needed to get there. He'd been the quarterback and played an important role. His role would be nothing without the team, but his identity was secure without it. He was a United States Navy SEAL. He was best with his brothers, but a role change didn't change the relationship. He was still a SEAL, they were still his team. Life just looked different.

He belonged to the Richards clan. But he wasn't the brother who was present every day to support David or protect and pick on Kaylan and Seth. But he was still their brother. Whether with them or apart.

And he was still a son of the God who painted the night sky

and knew every star by name. God might have created Seth to play football. But he had created Micah to be part of a team. Micah was beginning to realize that might look different in different seasons.

He was a leader. A teammate. And if that was how God had wired him, why wouldn't he want to use Micah to grow and build into the lives of others?

He was Micah Richards. Created in the image of the God who created unity and teamwork. But he wouldn't stand before the Lord someday as a teammate. He would stand before the Lord as himself, and he knew the Lord saw him just as he was and wanted him to be more than Micah dreamed he could be.

Micah was a warrior. And he belonged to God. Period. With or without a team.

And right now, for this season, he belonged in Dallas, coaching a team of hurting kids who needed someone to believe in them. He was meant to support and care for and learn from Shawn and Mama Rosie and Al and Teagan. And maybe, just maybe, he was there to learn to love a woman who had fought many of life's battles alone, who felt like she had to do everything by herself. Maybe it was Micah's job to show her how valuable and incredible she was to God and how he created people to team up and do life together.

After all, teamwork was Micah's specialty.

His phone dinged in the quiet, the screen glowing as he held it over his head to read the message.

Where were you?

Micah's sprang up. Was the fundraiser today? *This* Saturday? He scrolled to Casey's earlier text. Apparently when she said next Saturday, she'd meant today. He'd missed it. He kicked the turf, wishing he had something to throw. He was trying to get back in her good graces.

But he'd let Casey down, let the kids down. Despite his breakthrough, Micah cringed. He balled his hands into fists.

Somehow, he had to fix this. He had to let her know that he was a man of his word, that he hadn't let her down intentionally. He hurried toward the exit. Time to leave his past behind. Time to summon up the courage to remember who he was and fight for a future.

CHAPTER 14

Casey's door bumped open at 6:45 a.m. She bolted upright, reaching for the weighted bar she always left on her nightstand.

"Whoa there, killer. It's me, Emery."

Casey could only make out her sister's silhouette against the hall light.

"Emery, you have two seconds to explain why you woke me up before my alarm." She was supposed to meet Teagan for church, but that wasn't for another couple hours.

"I'm not allowed to explain. I'm only here to tell you that you need to get up now, and you need to make sure you are fully clothed when you leave this room. You've been warned."

With the click of her door closing, Casey once again sat in the dark, her foggy brain working overtime to decode her sister's message. The scent of coffee laced with syrup wafted beneath her door. And was that bacon?

She tossed her duvet to the side and ran fingers through her shoulder-length tangled hair. Grabbing her phone, she turned her alarm off. Fifteen minutes. She could have had fifteen more minutes of glorious sleep. She'd tossed and turned until two,

Shawn and Al's advice rattling in her head: Let Micah explain. Let him into what she held behind the walls.

She was more mad at Micah this morning. His gorgeous, charming smile, that last kiss, and his infuriating nicknames had all cost her sleep. That alone was grounds for banishment from her life. Come to think of it, she might just ground Emery for life, too. That is, if she could talk her mom into letting Emery stay in Dallas.

Casey tugged open her door and trudged into the living room, squinting against lamps and early morning light filtering past her paneled curtains. And then she stopped.

Six-foot-three inches of gorgeous, infuriating SEAL moved around her kitchen, laying out plates and silverware with her sister.

She did a quick check. Shorts, "Namaste in Bed" long sleeve top, crazy, mismatched knee-high socks. Toothbrush. She needed a toothbrush. Even though he wouldn't get anywhere near her lips again. But who didn't want to brush their teeth before they ate, you know? She tiptoed quietly backwards in her sock-covered feet, watching Micah laugh with her little sister while he dished scrambled eggs onto a plate.

Within two minutes Casey's mouth was minty fresh, her hair freshly combed, and her socks matching. All before 7:00 a.m. Winning.

She padded into the kitchen, her socks slipping slightly on the hardwood floor. She shuffled around the tiny island and stopped when she saw the fully laden, booth-style table tucked against the window overlooking the neighboring house.

"What's going on in here?"

"Micah made us breakfast." Her sister blushed. Clearly, Micah had a way with the women in this family.

"Correction." He slung a dish towel over one shoulder and offered his annoying, heart-stopping grin. "A little birdie told me you have an interesting craving for red velvet pancakes with vanilla chips in them. So naturally, that birdie helped me out with the recipe. And all the baking, too." He motioned to a covered platter on the table. A hint of red peeked through the translucent cover.

Casey's mouth watered. Curse him. He had cooked her favorite food, and he looked far too good in his faded jeans and navy, V-neck t-shirt. She fought the urge to comb her fingers through her hair. Again. She was not that girl.

"Is this your way of saying 'I'm sorry' for blowing off your commitment to the tournament fundraiser?" She crossed her arms. Her anger and the tinges of betrayal reared their ugly heads again. Good. She'd rather that than what her traitorous heart wanted at the moment—to fill a cup of coffee, lean in for a morning kiss, and laugh with him over breakfast.

Something in her panicked. She'd never wanted those things. Never imagined them possible. But with Micah, she saw what could be, and it terrified her.

He was here for three to four more weeks from what she knew. And Casey couldn't handle picking up pieces of her heart again.

Micah took a few tentative steps her way, his boots loud on the hardwood. Casey took a step back. He stopped. "Case, I am so sorry. I should have clarified the date with you. I thought you meant the Saturday the week following Thanksgiving. I was planning to be here, to be all in. And I would have been here this past Saturday, but my family unexpectedly bought me a ticket home for Thanksgiving. I didn't intentionally let you down, but I know I left you without a coach, and I'm so sorry. Please let me make it up to you?"

Her heart pattered a bit faster and she shuffled on her feet. The pancakes smelled so good. And he had a good reason, right?

What was going on? She was never this girl. He'd broken her trust. She should stay angry.

But he'd also consistently been there when he hadn't needed

to be. And Casey couldn't help but want to give him another chance. Just this once.

"C'mon, Sis. The food is getting cold. Look," Emery pointed to a dozen coral roses. "He even brought flowers. Please?" Emery clasped her hands and batted her eyes. Eyes that had on makeup before seven in the morning. Casey smirked. Dang, this guy was good. Emery was a nightmare to get up in the morning.

"Please?" Micah mimicked Emery.

Casey's choked back a laugh. "Fine. On two conditions."

"Name them."

"One. You hand me a cup of coffee within the next sixty seconds. It needs to have almond milk and a little honey in it."

Micah's brows rose, and the corners of his beautiful lips turned up. "That's specific."

She snatched her gaze from those lips and the memory of a couple weeks ago.

"Two, you never wake me up before my alarm again. I'm talking *ever*."

His grin grew. He turned to pour her coffee and made quick work of adding almond milk and honey. He sat her flowery mug in front of a waiting plate in the breakfast nook and motioned to the chair. "Your morning drug call, my lady. Am I forgiven?"

Emery giggled from across the table. Casey glared at her.

"One more thing." She took a step toward him. "Repeat after me: I'm a jerk for not calling the best woman to walk the earth, and as long as I am in Dallas, I will not bail on a commitment I make to her again."

She kept her eyes glued on Micah as she moved toward the open chair. But her socks betrayed her. With flailing arms, she slipped and pitched forward. Right into Micah's waiting arms.

Emery burst into laughter. Casey felt her face heat as every bit of blood in her body rushed to her cheeks. So much for her big power move.

She tried to pull away, but Micah shifted her and pulled her closer, his hands firmly anchored on her waist. "Casey, I'm a jerk for not calling the best and most beautiful woman I have ever met, and I will never even for a second bail on a commitment I make to her again, whether I'm in Dallas or not." His deep voice poured over her, making her traitorous legs jelly beneath her. She leaned a little more into his chest, his lips now a whisper away.

"Please forgive me?" He whispered. Despite the teasing tone, sincerity rang clear in his gaze.

"For goodness sakes, forgive the handsome man so we can eat."

Casey jerked away from Micah at her sister's exclamation and plopped down in her chair.

"Good grief, Casey. You are one of the most stubborn people I have ever met." Emery rolled her eyes and dished eggs onto her plate.

"I second that." Micah slipped into the chair next to Casey.

She ignored his stare and reached for her favorite breakfast food, loading two red pancakes on her plate. She couldn't help the groan as she took her first bite. "Oh my gosh, that little birdie outdid herself. Remind me to thank her later."

His chuckle reignited the flames in her cheeks. What the heck? *Die down, emotions and hormones. He's not* that *handsome and charming.*

Oh, who was she kidding?

His breath tickled her ear. "Guess that means I'm forgiven."

This time she forced herself to meet his challenging stare, a stare that promised to revisit this moment later. "Just this once."

As they passed pancakes and bacon around the table, Emery's phone vibrated, rattling the dishes.

"No phones at the table," Casey chirped, her spirits higher than normal for in the morning. Must be the coffee. Definitely the coffee.

"Yes, Mom." Emery rolled her eyes and turned her phone on

its face, but the vibrating continued every few seconds. She cast a quick glance at Casey.

"Go ahead. Check and see who it is." Casey muttered around a bite of red velvet goodness.

Emery flipped her phone over. As she scrolled her brown face drained of color.

"Em, who is it?"

"It's Mom." Emery turned the screen so Casey could see some of the texts, filled with expletives and threats. "And she's not happy."

Micah didn't know who to comfort or who to protect—Casey or Emery. Probably both. Casey paled, her tanned face now matching her sister's. Definitely both. The more time he spent around Casey, the more the warrior, the protector inside rose to the surface.

"Case, what's going on?"

"What?" She shook her head, her beautiful brown eyes focusing on him and growing into saucers. "Oh shoot. It's nothing. I can handle it. I got it."

"Case." He rested a hand on her knee. "You and Emery don't look so great. What's going on? How can I help?"

"Help?" She squeaked and cleared her throat. "I don't think you can help. Our mom is just upset about something."

"About..."

"It's noth..."

"Al hooked Casey up with a lawyer to talk about getting custody of me so I don't have to live with mom anymore, and mom found out and now's she mad and Casey will probably get a call and get cussed out in a couple minutes."

"Em!" Casey yelled.

Micah whistled low. "Okay. That's a lot."

Casey ignored him and turned to her sister. "Why and how?"

Emery grimaced. "I'm sorry." Her hands flew around her head like a swarm of mosquitoes. "You know I ramble when I get nervous, and mom makes me nervous when she gets mad, which is half the time, and I overhead you talking to the lawyer on the phone asking questions, and I think it's great because your house is so much calmer than home and you don't get mad at me like mom, and I'll miss my friends but I like my new ones here and . . ."

"Em, rambling." Casey smothered a strained laugh. Micah wasn't so successful. He shoved another pancake bite in his mouth.

"Well at least you don't ever have to worry about her keeping a secret," Micah offered Casey a smile.

She chuckled and then groaned, rubbing her hands over her face. "Ugh, there is that."

Emery only nodded, her cheeks now boasting a slight pink shade.

"So what are you going to do? How can I help?" Micah squeezed Casey's knee, taking it as a good sign that she hadn't jerked away. Either that or she was too preoccupied, but he preferred to think positively.

"Know anything about custody? I was just asking questions. I wasn't ready to do anything. But this might ruin everything." Her brow quirked. Micah thought it was the cutest look.

"Well I don't know a ton. Your mom is probably just surprised and lashing out. I'm sure she will calm down."

Casey and Emery both laughed. "Mom doesn't really calm down. She just escalates more," Emery chimed in.

Casey's phone rang on the table between them.

Micah tossed his head back in a laugh. "You have the purple emoji devil head next to your mom's name? I'm sensing some things you need to pray through."

The phone kept ringing.

"Baby steps, Genius. Baby steps."

"Genius, huh?"

She leaned in closer, picking his finger up and dropping his hand from her knee. "Don't make me call you the opposite."

"Feisty."

"Guys, hello! Not the time to flirt. Are we answering Mom or not?"

Micah knew the ringing would come to an end within seconds. Without pausing to consider the consequences, he grabbed the phone and lunged away from the table.

"Casey's phone, Micah speaking."

Silence. On the phone and from the women sitting at the table with their mouths hanging open.

"Hello?"

"I'm sorry, who is this?"

"My name is Micah, ma'am."

"Don't call me ma'am. I'm not old. My name is Mona. And don't listen to anything my daughters tell you about me. They are ungrateful little liars, and . . ."

"I'm going to have to stop you there. I happen to think both your daughters are pretty great."

Casey was out of her chair and on her toes reaching for the phone. Micah wrapped his arm around her waist and pulled her to his other side, keeping the phone just out of reach from her short arms.

"Well apparently, they have you fooled. Now I want to talk to my daughter. Now, Mathias."

"It's Micah. Your daughters aren't available, ma'am." She rattled a string of curse words in his ear. He wouldn't have handed over the phone if someone paid him. This lady was out of line.

Casey fumed and stretched, but Micah pinned her to his side. He held the phone away and turned his focus to Casey. "Do you mind? I'm trying to help you out."

"I don't want your help." She strained for the phone. Yelling continued to stutter through the speaker. Casey still fought for the phone. "She won't change, and this isn't your problem."

"Wrong, Case." Micah set the phone on the island, wrapped his arms around Casey, and pulled her flush to his chest. She stopped squirming, shock and frustration dancing through the flecks of caramel in her dark chocolate eyes. "I care about you so it is my problem. Plus, she ruined a completely good breakfast moment."

The shrieking reached a new pitch.

Casey gripped Micah's shirt, staring at the phone just to the side. "Micah, give me the phone. Please. This isn't your fight."

Keeping his gaze leveled with hers, he put the phone back to his ear. Using a voice better suited for his team in the middle of an operation, Micah stopped Mona's tirade. "I'm sorry, Mona, but Casey and Emery are unavailable right now. When you calm down and are able to talk to your daughters without mistreating them, you are welcome to call back. Have a good morning." With one quick move, he hung up.

For the second time that morning, Casey's mouth hung open. She stopped fighting, her body still wound tight in his arms.

With one finger, he tipped her chin up, closing her mouth. She swallowed, remained still. "What did you just do?" she whispered.

Micah slipped her phone back into her hand and turned her back to the table. "I might have just delayed the inevitable, but right now, in this moment when she is most angry, you don't need to talk to her. You don't have to talk to her." He guided her to her chair and placed her coffee mug in her hand, grinning at how docile she remained. He liked surprising her, even in the midst of unfortunate circumstances.

"Micah, this is a mess." Casey put her head in her hands.

Emery slipped next to her sister, curling into her side and wrapping her arms around Casey's neck.

"It's a mess you don't need to handle alone."

"Ellie's Place exists to be a home away from home for kids." New mentor orientation had begun. Teagan had led the first part of the presentation, laying out the duties, responsibilities, and expectations. But Casey had the best part of the presentation.

She shared the heart. She shoved away all thoughts of her mom and yesterday's call and focused on instilling a vision near and dear to her own heart. She prayed it fell on listening ears.

"We don't want our mentors to hang out with the kids, check our volunteer box, and go home. We want to see real change." She settled in to her favorite part of the presentation. In front of her sat nearly twenty young adults, parents, and grandparents from around Dallas. "Think back to a time in your life when you felt stuck, trapped by circumstances, emotions, or even people." Casey thought back to life with her mother and the endless cycle of verbal and emotional abuse by the men allowed in the house. "Most of you were blessed enough to have resources available to break free. Most of our kids do not. But they want to. And we show them how."

Just like Al and Ellie had shown Casey how to let go of pieces of her past when she stumbled her way to Dallas.

"You get to encourage them, challenge them, walk next to them. You get to show them that you are in their corner. It's why we vet you so seriously. We aren't just mentoring and helping with homework. We are mentoring and changing character, lives, the way they see and feel about themselves."

She clicked to the next slide showing the photo from the

community event the year before that had brought the community together.

"We are about transformation of this community with the goal of seeing a new generation succeed and break free from the status quo. There are a ton of kids out there who need to know they can make a difference, that they have talent and brains—they need to know they can accomplish big things. They need to know they are not alone, that you aren't coming down here to show up and leave. We want you to integrate into their lives. Meet their family and teachers. Know their schedule. Help them dream. Help them plan."

Casey paced in front of the group, making eye contact with each person. Tears pricked her own eyes. Once upon a time, someone had done this for her, and it had changed everything. "Let's show them they have a future. Let's give them something to hope for, shoot for. Welcome to Ellie's Place." The volunteers cheered, and Casey joined in their revelry.

In the back, holding a cup of coffee with a look Casey had seen in far too many romance movies, stood Micah Richards, whistling and cheering with the rest. She remembered the grin on his face as he handed her coffee yesterday morning in her kitchen, almost like he enjoyed being there. Like he belonged.

As Teagan ushered the volunteers out of the classroom for a tour of the center, Micah strode up to the front of the room. Twice in one day. She didn't know what to do with him.

"Coffee, m'lady." He offered the paper cup with a slight bow.

"Medieval Times called. They want their nickname back." Casey rolled her eyes but accepted the offering. He'd had her up before the alarm. It was only fair that he brought gifts.

"I'll just tell them I've put it to good use." He took a step into her personal bubble, and she immediately blocked with a hand, pushing back on his chest.

"Oh no you don't. That one is not sticking. Back to the drawing board, mister."

His warm chuckle made her cheeks flush in response. Or maybe it was steam from the coffee. She took a quick sip. Yep. Definitely the coffee.

"That was pretty great, you know?" He nodded to where the volunteers had sat moments before.

"That is one of my favorite things about this place—painting the vision for what could be for these kids. My job is earning their trust. Getting them to talk to me. Sharing their confusion, pain, anger, tears. We've literally seen kids of every color walk through these doors, and the same thing remains true—they want and need someone to fight for them, to love them, to tell them they can do big things. That kind of encouragement spans ethnicity, socioeconomic standards, religious backgrounds, and more. Al and Ellie," she motioned to the room around them, "they made all that possible."

He stepped into her bubble again, this time skimming his fingers down her arms before tangling his fingers with hers. His dark eyes held admiration and something else she couldn't pinpoint. Pride? Longing? Either way, he chipped further into her wall. "You, Casey Stewart, make all this possible. Your walls don't exist for these kids. You see the hurt and step into the fight." Another step closer. One hand slipped up and tucked a loose strand of hair behind her ear before slowly grazing her cheek. Her breath stalled.

His lips were an inch away, his fingers stroking her face with tenderness that punched holes through every foundation inside her. "Why won't you let anyone step into the fight for you?" he whispered.

"Case?"

Casey sprang away from Micah, bumping into a desk and stumbling over a chair before finally righting herself. His smirk told her enough. He knew he'd cracked another wall. And he was willing to let her retreat. For now.

"Case?"

"Yeah, Teag."

Teagan rounded the doorway and handed Casey her phone. "TJ just called. The police are at his house. He's asking if you can come."

Casey grabbed her phone and bolted from the room with Micah hot on her heels.

"Casey, Bianca is in your office." Emery stepped in front of her. Casey grabbed onto Emery's shoulders to avoid plowing her over.

"You almost hit the floor, little sis. I have to go. TJ needs me."

"But Bianca said she really needs to talk to you. She's crying, too. I told her you can help fix whatever it is. Can you go talk to her, please?"

Micah gripped her waist. His touch grounding her. "You take care of Bianca. I'll go to TJ."

Casey whirled around to study his face, her hand finding his and squeezing. "Are you sure? TJ's had it rough. If the police are at his house, then I may need to go."

"Casey, I'm sure. I know TJ. I coach TJ. And I can't talk to Bianca. Only you can. You can't do everything, Super Girl. How about tagging me in for this one?"

That smirk was back, which snapped Casey out of the cloud hanging over her. She couldn't be in two places at once. So far, she didn't have a body double, but she really needed to look into inventing that tool.

"Alright, you can be my sidekick this once. I'm not sure you are up to the task, but hey, we all have to start somewhere."

Micah took a step back, pulling his keys from his pocket. "Is that how you tell your mentors to encourage the kids? I think we may need to work on your affirmation skills there, Doc."

He was almost at the door.

"Casey, she's waiting." Emery tugged at her arm.

With a final look to Micah, she offered a small smile and a

small prayer that he could handle this. "Don't do anything I wouldn't do."

"Honey, I don't think you could keep up with my pace. I'm slowing down to meet yours."

Before she could protest, he was out the door.

CHAPTER 15

TJ's yard desperately required a lawn mower. Weeds clawed through the scraggly grass around a cracked sidewalk, evidence of the normal Texas heat and shifting clay foundation. Two police cars sat outside TJ's house, the door open to a dim interior. Micah stepped through and paused, his eyes adjusting to the shadows.

Voices sounded from the small living room up ahead where lamplight glowed, painting silhouettes that loomed large on white walls. TJ sat on the worn, plaid couch with two younger boys and a scowling teenage girl. An older woman marked by wrinkles rocked back and forth in a glider. Her hands worked knitting needles as she focused on the two officers in the room.

"Micah!"

The officers stopped talking as TJ bolted from the couch and stopped at Micah's side.

"I thought Casey would come."

Micah squeezed TJ's shoulder in greeting. "I decided to tag in for her. Is that okay?"

He nodded, the weight of the situation stooping his normally square shoulders. "They caught my mom down at the corner again," he whispered. "It's the second time in a month. She wasn't doing anything. This time." He averted his eyes. "They brought her home as a warning."

Micah noticed the woman standing before the officers wearing clothes that told a story of a terrible quest to provide for her family. It made his blood boil. No mother, no woman, should ever feel like this was her only option.

"And who are you, sir?" One of the officers approached Micah while the other continued a quiet conversation with TJ's mom.

"Micah Richards." He extended his hand to the officer, appreciating a man in uniform, even if this was probably a task he would prefer to avoid. "I'm a temp coach at the local high school, and I am helping out at Ellie's Place."

The officer's handshake was firm. "Are you the new guy staying at Mama Rosie's?"

"Does everyone in this part of Dallas know that woman?"

The officer chuckled. "Around here they do. More than once, we have picked up a kid who got into trouble and dropped them off at her place."

"Why hers?"

"Because she's a better option than our parents," TJ answered, drawing a small smile from the officer.

"And she tans their hide before sending them home. Most of Mama Rosie's kids don't end up in our car twice."

"That's because Mama Rosie is much scarier than you." TJ smirked and folded his arms.

"I am okay with that. Whatever works. Come to think of it, most of the kids who are really involved at Ellie's Place have cleaned up their act, too. Most of them," he emphasized as his partner walked up.

Micah could have sworn TJ muttered "Coleman" under his breath as the officers left the house, and Micah turned to face the room. He introduced himself to TJ's mom, grandma, two little brothers who appeared to be twins, and his cousin.

"You all live here?" He motioned to the house.

His mom lifted her chin high. "It isn't much. But we are all together under one room. It's home."

A team. TJ had a team, but they needed some help. TJ needed some help.

He clapped the kid on the back and nodded at his mom. "Ma'am, would you mind if I take TJ out for a bit?"

She wouldn't meet his eyes as she offered a quick nod and tugged at the hem of her dress. He stood his ground, giving her the respect and dignity she deserved in her own home.

"Just have him home before too late."

"Yes, ma'am."

Micah steered TJ out of the house and into his beat-up truck.

"She hasn't busted on you yet it looks like." TJ slammed the door and ran a hand over the dashboard.

Micah turned the engine, the old truck groaning before roaring to life. "You better find some wood to knock on. *Yet* is the operative word here." He pulled onto the road, the sun barely visible on the horizon.

"What are you hungry for?"

"Ugh man, y'all killed us at practice today. I could really go for some Taco Bell."

"Taco Bell?" Micah laughed. "I thought you were going to say a burger or a chicken finger basket or something."

"No, no, no. You don't understand. Their sauce is so good and tangy, and they have these supreme tacos that are the best. Dude, I'm starving just talking about it. We gotta go now. There's one just up the road."

"Well I wouldn't want you starving. We gotta keep our new varsity wide receiver happy."

"No way, really?" TJ rolled his window down and hollered at the passing houses. "I made varsity!"

Micah grinned. "I bet you'll be seeing a lot of W's next season."

TJ cheered all the way down the street.

The more time Micah spent in this neighborhood, the more he understood the war Casey fought on a daily basis. Circumstances were stacked against some of these kids. They needed to know they weren't bound or identified by them.

He swung the truck into the Taco Bell parking lot and followed TJ inside as the kid rattled off his order, filled his drink, and plopped down in his seat.

Micah slipped into a chair across from him, the legs scratching against the tile floor as he pulled close to the table.

TJ took his first bite and groaned. "Coach, this is so good. Perfect treat after a bad day." Pieces of lettuce and tomato dripped from the corners of his mouth.

"Easy there. Slow down. We're not in a rush, and the food isn't going anywhere."

"Sorry, Coach."

TJ had called him "Coach" several times in the last hour. He rolled the new title around in his head and liked how it sounded. It was a title he could stand behind, grow into.

"Want to tell me what happened back there?"

TJ's chewing slowed to a halt. He placed the taco back on the tray and reached for a napkin.

"I thought Casey would come. I didn't want you to see that."

Micah took a sip of Dr. Pepper, weighing his words. "Why don't you start with what happened with your brother and Coleman."

"Jeremy was five years older than me. Ellie's Place wasn't around until his senior year of school, and by then he had gone off the deep end big time. My dad leaving when we were kids really messed him up. He started working a job to help pay for things around the house. But then he got in with the wrong crew."

"Coleman," Micah said.

TJ nodded. "Coleman's brother was a little bit older than Jeremy. He got Jeremy running drugs. Just little things at first. Then it turned into more. It helped pay the bills, but Ma wanted him to stop. She said she would take care of it. That's when the cops started catching her and bringing her home."

"Coleman's brother gave Jeremy a hard time because he started to see mom around. I think his dad even got involved. He started to tell Jeremy he would make life hard for Ma if Jeremy didn't start running for him again."

TJ picked at his taco, his appetite clearly gone. Micah leaned forward. "Then what happened, TJ?"

"There was a fight one night. I'm not sure what happened. But next thing I knew, colored lights were flashing on my bedroom windows, Ma was wailing, and Jeremy didn't come home."

TJ looked up, his black eyes heavy with shadows. "It was Coleman's brother, and Coleman was there. I just know it." He took a long drag from his straw and then picked up his taco again, trying to carry on like he hadn't just shared the most life-altering information with Micah.

Micah could fill in the pieces from there, gathered that what happened tonight wasn't abnormal.

"I'm sorry about your brother."

"You wouldn't understand." TJ shrugged him off.

Micah gritted his teeth, his knuckles turning white where they squeezed together. "Unfortunately, I'm all too familiar. I lost a few of my . . . brothers about a year ago now."

"I guess you've seen a lot of war."

"It sounds like you have, too."

TJ only stared. "I want better. You put me on varsity, Coach. I won't let you down. Maybe I can get a scholarship. Casey says my grades are alright, and Teagan is helping me in the afternoons after practice. Maybe if I can do better, then Ma won't have to keep up what she's doing. My brothers won't know the neighborhood that Jeremy did. I can get us all out." A single tear tracked down his cheek.

"You don't have to be alone in that, you know."

TJ swallowed hard. "You're starting to sound like Casey."

Micah leaned forward and beckoned TJ to lean closer across the table. "Don't tell her I told you this, but she's pretty smart most of the time."

TJ started laughing uncontrollable. "Oh, Coach. I'm totally going to tell her. And I'm going to make sure both of us are there to see her reaction."

"Traitor."

TJ only grinned. "Thanks, Coach." He inhaled the rest of his dinner.

Micah sipped his Dr. Pepper and stared at the street lights outside the restaurant windows. Looking out at a neighborhood represented by one teen, Micah was reminded that all wars weren't on the streets. Sometimes the hardest battles were the silent struggles no one could see. He definitely had his own inner demons. To move on, to win the fight, he would have to keep focusing on the hardest place of all.

Himself.

"Can you tell me why you're crying, Bianca?"

The girl sniffed and swiped a tan hand across her nose. "I don't know what to do."

"It's okay, Bianca. Casey can help. Just tell her," Emery blurted.

Casey shot her little sister a look to remind her of her promise to stay quiet. Casey had agreed to let Emery shadow her at Ellie's Place, and Bianca had agreed to let her sit in. The two had become fast friends since Emery had begun spending every afternoon at Ellie's and had showed an interest in cheerleading.

"What don't you know how to do, B?"

"I want to go to college. I don't want to stay here. But my ma and Coleman both say it is unrealistic. That we can't afford it, that I shouldn't dream so big." She turned big brown eyes on Casey, filled with dying hope. "You and Mr. Al and Teagan and my mentor tell me all the time that I can do it. But the people who tell me they love me tell me I can't. I'm confused." Another tear wound down her cheek.

Emery hopped up and handed Bianca a tissue.

"It's good to dream, Bianca—to work hard, to know your potential, and reach for it."

She dabbed the tissue under her eye, the white marring with black mascara. "Coleman says it's stupid, that I should be happy to stay here with him."

Casey refrained from saying exactly what she thought of Coleman.

"I'm about to start my senior year. I have to take tests, apply for colleges. And I don't know what to do."

Casey bridged the gap on the couch and squeezed Bianca's hand. "I'll help. Your mentor will help. Teagan will help. We want to see you succeed."

"But how?"

"You made Varsity Cheer Captain, right?"

Bianca nodded, her face lighting up. Passion. Casey loved that look on her kids.

"Then let's look at some D2 and D3 colleges that you can apply for, maybe get a cheerleading scholarship."

"My grades are good, too."

Casey squeezed her hand. "You've been working so hard. With your grades, cheerleading, and your family's income level,

I bet we can get a lot of your school paid for. And a smaller school may not cost you quite as much as a big D1 school, so you will save money and won't rack up as many loans."

Bianca nodded again, her eyes beginning to brighten.

"You always tell us to make something of ourselves and then come back and help make our neighborhood better. What if I don't want to come back? What if my ma is mad? What if I don't want to date Coleman anymore?" She finished in a small voice.

Casey saw Emery sit taller in the corner, alert. Casey once again swallowed back her knee jerk response. Bianca was too good for a guy like Coleman who didn't want anything bigger for himself or those around him. She was too sweet to deserve his manipulation.

"B, we encourage y'all to come back to your own neighborhood because no one will be able to change your community quite like those of you who grew up in it. When one of you believes you can do more and you fight to accomplish it, that drive lets others know they can change, too. We talk about this all the time, remember?"

"One life touching one person can make a world of difference."

Casey smiled.

"Just like you are trying to make a difference with me."

Casey nodded. "You don't have to come back, B. We won't make you. That may not be what your future holds, and if not, that's okay." She scooted closer, reaching for Bianca's hand. "But if you do come back, we want you to come back ready to fight with us to make things better."

Bianca wiped another tear, this time smiling. "Even if I don't come back permanently, I won't forget what you've taught me. I want to be a teacher."

"And you'll make a great one. You already help some of the younger kids with their homework." Casey bit her lip, choosing her words carefully. "Can I ask you a question now?"

"Of course."

"You have big dreams, and you are trying to chase them." She paused. "Why are you with a guy like Coleman?"

This time Bianca dropped her eyes.

"Hey, B, you can talk to me. Is he hurting you?"

She shook her head. "He gets angry a lot. You've seen it." Bianca nodded to the basketball court visible out Casey's window where they could both hear the faint slap of the rubber ball hitting the concrete, a loud game in full swing lit by the court lights. "He yells. But he can also be sweet."

"A guy who is only sweet with you isn't really a sweet guy. You don't deserve that, Bianca. He's going to hold you back from where you want to go."

"But he says he loves me."

Casey bit back her rising anger. "Bianca, if I yelled at you all the time and threatened you in order to get my way, do you think that's very loving?"

She shook her head.

"If I told you your dreams were stupid and that you shouldn't chase them or even dream them, would you think I was supportive, that I cared about you?"

She shook her head again.

"Then if Coleman is willing to threaten you, yell at you, tell you what is most important to you is stupid, and is only kind when he wants something, do you think he really loves you?"

Casey froze, watching the battle rage on Bianca's face. She knew all too well the allure of a good-looking, charming guy paired with a massive personal insecurity. It was like lighting a match and throwing it on dynamite. It never ended well.

"No," she whispered. "I don't think he loves me. I don't think he knows what love is."

Casey suspected that Coleman had never experienced love without strings attached and didn't know any other way. Unfortunately, though he came to Ellie's, he never let anyone help him.

"So what are you going to do about it?" Casey squeezed Bianca's hand again, drawing the girl's gaze to hers. Iron solidified in her previously broken expression.

"I'm going to pursue going to school and becoming a teacher. I'm going to enjoy my senior year and work hard. And I . . . I'm going to end things with Coleman."

"Thatta girl." Casey grinned.

Bianca stood, her short skirt falling back around her thighs. She threw her arms around Casey. "Thank you," she whispered. "I told Mom I would be home to help cook before six so I better go."

She hurried out the door, significantly more hopefully than the crying girl who had entered less than an hour before.

"Wow, you're good." Emery stood from the arm chair in the corner.

"Your sis is more than just a looker," Casey teased, drawing a circle around her face with her finger. "I've got brain and skills to backup this pretty face."

"Yeah, but nothing can help you in the cool department," Emery snorted.

"Hey, I'm cool."

"No, you're helpful. Helpful and cool are not the same."

They walked to the door, and Casey switched the lights off behind her. She dropped an arm around her sister. "Seriously, though, what did you think?"

"I think that you helping Bianca chase her dreams is actually pretty great. And telling her to break up with that jerk Coleman is even better."

"Great. Better. Cool, even?"

Emery rolled her eyes as they stopped next to Casey's car in the small parking lot.

"Okay, okay, okay. This one time. It was cool. Just this once."

"I'll take it." Casey grinned then waved at Al and the guys playing on the court before crawling in her car. She couldn't be everywhere at once, but she had been right where she needed to be. Maybe Micah had been a small miracle, a gift from God today. And maybe, just maybe, Bianca would see what it took Casey a lot longer to see: that she was fully capable of changing her world, even if she had to fight uphill the whole way to make it happen.

CHAPTER 16

Casey wasn't so sure she liked Teagan's new workout obsession. Teagan was on a "remake Casey Stewart kick," and fortunately or unfortunately it was working. She was getting reacquainted with the church thing again after a couple weeks of going back, even started to look forward to it, although she hadn't told Teagan that. Casey had even thought about joining one of the home groups through the church.

Now Teagan had her running. Running. Casey liked kickboxing kind of workouts, but running around and around wasn't really her thing. While running untangled the mind, according to Teagan, Casey abhorred the time to think. Thoughts ran as rampant as her legs on a run. She much preferred punching bags. They kept her focused, her mind quiet.

So they'd compromised. Teagan had picked White Rock Lake at sunset, and Casey had agreed since she would have something pretty to look at, something calming.

"Teag, can we please stop?" Casey slowed, grabbing her side. "It hurts. Things hurt."

Teagan turned around, jogging in place, somehow making sweat look good while Casey dripped and struggled to bobby pin her layered dark hair out of her eyes. Despite her efforts it fell in jagged strands, sticking to her forehead, her neck.

Teagan smirked at Casey's struggle. "It's supposed to hurt. Feel the burn."

"I don't want to feel the burn. I want to feel the couch."

"No way, Lazy Bones. You can watch more episodes of NCIS later. Besides, where else would you rather be than out with your bestest of friends on a pretty cool evening?"

Casey sucked in a breath and glared. "Well I think you just covered that. At home. On my couch. Watching NCIS. And by the way . . ." she hunched, gripping the stitch in her side. Maybe she was out of shape.

"Is there any end to that sentence?" Teagan jogged in a circle around Casey, slapping her in the thigh on her way around.

Casey thought about unleashing her amateur kick-boxing skills in that moment. "Yes. There is." She sucked in another breath. "You have currently slipped down on the best friend scale. Shawn is in first place. By a large margin at the moment."

Teagan began another slow circle, prompting Casey to start jogging just to avoid feeling corralled. "Oh Casey, you can't fool either of us. Though you claim to have a point system, we know the truth. You're really just a softy."

Casey smirked. She couldn't argue there. Something in her was changing. Her walls were weakening. She almost felt . . . as if she didn't need them anymore. She wasn't sure if it was renewing her relationship with God, things at Ellie's Place, Emery living with her, or . . . Micah. Maybe a little of all. But something truly was changing. Brick was crumbling inside, more every day. The realization both terrified and thrilled her. Walls had felt safer.

"You can feel it, can't you?" Teasing fled Teagan's voice.

Casey focused on her breathing. The knowledge that her

best friend noticed the change too was unsettling. "Yeah, I can," she whispered. They jogged in rhythm, their breath puffing in the chilled air.

"It's a good look on you, Case. It's the look you used to have. Softer, more passionate and less angry with a cause. I've missed it."

Casey dared a quick look at her friend running next to her, in step the way she had been since childhood. "I think I've missed it, too." The acknowledgement caused a shudder through her walls. Maybe safety was overrated.

The sun splashed pastel pinks and oranges across the sky as they rounded the last bend. The colors bounced off the lake, drawing Casey's eye to the reflection. A slightly distorted mirror, but something of beauty all the same.

"Casey, look out!"

She jerked her gaze forward right as she face-planted into a broad chest, sending them both back a few steps.

"I'm so sorry." She untangled herself from the grip on her arms but the deep chuckle made her freeze.

She slowly looked up, feeling stuck in slow-motion. Her gaze collided on an all too familiar set of deep, earthy, brown eyes and lips set in a smirk. The lips that made her want to kiss or punch depending on the moment. Stupid, traitorous emotions.

Casey snapped into motion. She shoved away from Micah.

"What are you doing here?"

Shawn's snicker sent her focus whirling his direction, noticing her other best friend for the first time.

"What are you doing here?" She whirled on Teagan. "What are they doing here?"

Teagan only grinned, forcing Casey back to the guy still standing before her.

"And why does this," she gestured to Micah's chest, "keep getting in my way? Everywhere I go, it's right there."

This time, Teagan and Shawn both choked on laughter. Micah's eyes danced in the setting sunlight. "Maybe you're just attracted to me."

"You wish."

It only took a step and his lips were near her ear. "I know," he whispered.

She retreated. Space. She needed space. "Good grief, you are full of yourself."

He quirked his brows at her, all too handsome and cute for his own good. And hers. "And yet, you still keep coming back for more. Why is that, my Mona Lisa?"

Casey snorted. "Where in the world did that one come from?"

"Well, you have these small smiles sometimes, but you're right—I'm not feeling it." He tapped his chin and let his eyes wander up and down.

"Sport?"

"Apparently that's Teagan's new thing. Not mine."

"Juliet?"

"Too tragic, and you definitely aren't Romeo."

His grin curled her toes. "I never said I was, darlin'. But clearly it crossed your mind."

She rolled her eyes, propping her hands on her hips. "Let's get this out now while you have an audience to entertain. Continue."

Micah widened his stance and continued to tap his chin. "Doll?"

"Too cute."

"Temptress."

"Are you into extremes?"

"Kitten."

"That one will get you hurt if you try it again." She fought her growing urge to match his grin. Those moths in her stomach fluttered weakly. Or it was just the run. Definitely the run.

"Pumpkin."

"It's almost winter."

"So I can put that one on hold for next year?"

"Are we finished yet?"

"Not even close."

"Angel eyes."

"I am pretty angelic."

"Do I need to start recording you?"

"Then you wouldn't be a gentleman."

"Cookie."

"Only if you feed me chocolate chips."

"My suggestions all seem to be conditional."

Casey shook her head. "Sadly, I still think you are missing the mark, Sailor. Better luck next time."

"I'm a SEAL not a sailor."

"You say potato, I say po-ta-toe, Hotshot."

"So you admit you think I'm hot?"

Teagan burst into laughter. "Well that was fascinating. And on that note, it sounds like you two have some things to hash out still, so Shawn and I are going to exit stage right."

Casey rounded on her best friend. "I'm sorry, what?"

"Oh I'm pretty sure you heard me there, Kitten. Shawn and I are leaving you here with Micah and he is going to drive you home."

"Huh. It's almost like y'all planned this or something."

Shawn shrugged. "Or something. Later, Pumpkin." He snagged Teagan's arm and they jogged off before Casey truly began to fume.

"Well looks like you're stuck with me." Micah grinned.

She slowly pivoted to face Micah, chewing on her lip. "I'm guessing this is your idea?"

"Guilty."

"Well you could have at least asked me instead of giving Teagan the chance to try and kill me by running."

"And miss out on this opportunity to see you thrown off your game? Not a chance." He nodded to the lake behind him and sun making a slow descent in the sky. Purples and deep blues had joined the mix of red and coral. "Care to join me for the end of the show?"

"Best idea you've had all night."

He shrugged. "They happen occasionally."

He led them off the path and into the grass, right up to the bank's edge. They settled on the ground facing the water and the light show. A foot separated them, but Casey could feel Micah's presence as though he physically touched her. He had that kind of presence—full, commanding, comforting, vibrant. It made her want to lean in for a little more of what he exuded —life. Even in the midst of whatever brokenness he had experienced. He made her laugh. If she would actually give in.

"The colors are beautiful."

Micah nodded, bringing his arms to rest on his knees. "My sister prefers sunrises. She is an early bird if I ever met one." Casey grinned as his accent lengthened at the mention of his family. And in that moment, she realized she didn't know much about him. He had entered her world, but she hadn't really cared or dared to enter his.

"Are the two of you close?"

She could feel the warmth emanating from his smile without even looking. "She's my best friend. She's a couple years younger than me and as sweet as she can be. She's passionate and caring and tough, even when she thinks she isn't. She married my other best friend, Hawk. So it worked out well, having both my best friends in my family."

"Your sister married a guy named 'Hawk,' and that didn't set off any red flags for you?"

His laughter sent the moths fluttering again. Although she

was starting to wonder if the moths might be something different, something better. Micah didn't create holes in her. He filled them.

"His name is Nick Carmichael. He served with me, next to me, in front of me, behind me. No matter where or what, he had my back. Literally. He is a talented sniper, often in overwatch in the field. He was our eyes. He had the ability to see the smallest detail, assess, and respond before the rest of us could blink. So he earned his nickname. Kaylan couldn't have ended up with a better guy, although it took Nick a while to convince her of that. Years actually."

"Is she your only sister?"

"Only one." He shifted on the grass, reaching for a rock. "I have two brothers, as well. One older and one younger." He tossed the rock, skipping it three times before it dipped below the dimming surface of the lake.

"Are you close to them?"

"Yep. We are a pretty tight-knit group, although Kaylan and I are probably the closest since we have lived in the same city for the past few years. David is the oldest and is an accountant in Tuscaloosa. Seth plays football at the University of Alabama and will probably sign a professional contract in the next few months, so life will certainly change for him and our family soon."

"And your parents?"

Again she heard the smile in his voice. "I was definitely blessed in the role model department. My parents and one set of grandparents all live in Tuscaloosa. They're incredible. I wouldn't have stayed on a straight track without their guidance. They always encouraged us to discover how God had wired us. They never wanted us to be different than who we were, but they never let us settle for mediocre, either. I know that isn't everyone's story. I know that we don't get to choose our parents. But I thank God every day he chose to put me in the family he did. I used to take it for granted. I don't anymore."

Hearing him talk about his family, well, it reminded Casey of when she talked about her kids—with a mix of passion, longing, familiarity, even fight. He would do anything for his sister and brother-in-law. She liked that about him. Whatever he was doing in the moment, he gave one hundred percent of himself. She'd seen it in his coaching, in his time with her, and in the way he talked about his team and his family.

"How are you doing with the whole God thing these days? You don't shut down on me anymore when I mention faith," he said after several minutes of silence. The sun had slipped past the horizon and stars were beginning to appear in the growing twilight. The November air seeped through her jacket. She would need to find some heat soon. She shifted closer to Micah.

"God and I have been dealing with some things lately. Let's just say I'm not mad at him anymore, and I'm growing in relationship again." The admission felt foreign on her tongue. Life had taught her that vulnerability came at a high cost. Somehow, that lesson was no match for Micah. Something deep within her whispered one word: safe.

Micah picked up another rock and let it skip. Four skips this time.

"Why were you mad?"

Casey turned to look at Micah for the first time since they sat, the space between them seeming to shrink even more. "You're right. We can't all have families like yours. For better or worse, the Lord chose not to put me in a family that cares for me. I've had to fend for myself, protect myself and now Emery, and it makes me wonder how a good God could allow that kind of life for two kids."

Micah shifted on the grass, his knee brushing against hers as he turned to face her. "Did you get an answer?"

She thought back to her first church service, to the song

about God being a good Father and the way she had acknowledged God's perfection.

"I don't know that I will ever fully understand God's decisions or have an answer that makes my past make sense or my pain feel better. From what I can tell, the world is a mess, and from what I read in the Bible, that was never God's plan or desire for His creation. Maybe some of it is just that—mess. Man's choice despite God's plans. Man's sin attempting to mar God's perfection. And God's pursuit of fallen man with free will. He can't make us choose Him, make us love Him. But He says He still loves us." She shook her head, the thoughts just coming and taking root in her mind and heart as she voiced them. "Maybe the rest is the Lord trying to show me He is the dad I never had. I don't know, Micah."

He cocked his head at her. "You don't normally talk like this, Case. What's different?"

She cast a look at the Big Dipper, at the North Star, glowing faintly and nearly indistinguishable in the haze of city lights. "I guess there's just something about a starry, Texas sky that makes me wonder if anything is possible, that everything can be okay. Even if city lights sometimes hide their vibrancy." She smiled.

Micah settled back into the grass on his back. He patted the spot next to him. Casey lay next to him, her head nearly touching his and her body angled to the side.

"Did you ever wish on the stars?" he asked.

"Like that old Disney song from *Pinocchio*?"

He chuckled. "Yeah, like that."

"Teagan, Shawn, and I would wish sometimes. We'd lay on Shawn's trampoline in his backyard and look for shooting stars. We smelled like feet when we went inside." Casey wrinkled her nose and chuckled at the memory. "But those moments were worth it."

"There's something about the night sky that turns us all into dreamers." Micah held his thumb up to measure the moon. "What would you wish for right now if you could wish for anything?"

That he would stay.

The unasked-for thought pierced through her defenses, making her breath catch and her heart race. She didn't even know what life would look like, could look like, if he stayed. But wasn't that the purpose of dreaming? Casting a prayer for the impossible to the God who said nothing is impossible with Him?

She had another seemingly impossible wish. "I would wish for full custody of Emery so that we can build a different home than the one I grew up in."

Warm fingers slipped through hers, sending tingles dancing up her arms in the cooling fall night. She felt like a hot, sweaty mess, and yet one touch from Micah made her feel beautiful. Was that the same kind of weakness that got her in trouble in high school? Somehow, she doubted it. She felt safe, treasured—not chased.

"What would you wish for?" She turned to look at him.

His gaze held hers, sadness in his smile, his eyes hidden in shadows. "I would wish for a do-over. That this last visit I keep putting off, that it wasn't necessary."

In that moment, his hand locked in hers, Casey knew Micah Richards was struggling to crawl out of his past and into his future. And this moment, the two of them as a lifeline, felt like a taste of what could come.

Dreams had been cast under a Texas night sky. They stood to leave just as a shooting star flew to the earth behind Micah. And Casey prayed for Micah to find peace, to be all in, to find a new place to belong—but most of all, she wished he would stay and that she would have the courage to let him in.

CHAPTER 17

Helping kids get into college was no joke these days. Between Casey and Teagan, they had walked through a game plan to help Bianca choose colleges, figure out when to sign up for tests, identify scholarships to apply for, and determine a strategy for her senior year. The joy of seeing one of her kids "get it"—wanting more than staying in the neighborhood and struggling to make ends meet—almost made Casey want to go run a victory lap around White Rock Lake. Almost.

She whistled as she walked across the parking lot to her car, feeling lighter than she had in . . . years.

Born to be Wild sang from her pocket, and Casey freed her phone from its confines.

"Hey, Wild Man."

"I'm not sure how I feel about that one." A car door slammed on Micah's end of the line just as Casey opened her own door.

"I can't guarantee that you will like where I end this if we keep going with this nickname thing."

"Fair enough. I just got to your house bearing pizza, popcorn, and a Netflix password if needed."

"We've got the password covered. Why are we eating pizza and popcorn and having a movie night on a Wednesday?"

"That was a request from your baby sis."

"Emery is texting you now? What move did you pull on her, Casanova?"

"Well I don't have to fight to get her to admit she likes me."

Casey rolled her eyes and shifted her car into reverse and eased out of her spot. "I'll be there in a few minutes. I'm pulling out of Ellie's now."

"I'll try to save you a couple of pizza slices, but I make no promises."

"Your gentleman status is officially in question if you can't wait until I get there."

"Sugar, I have nothing against cold pizza, but it's best when it is fresh and warm and the cheese is gooey, and besides, you told me all about this Eno's place and I am dying to try it."

"I'll be there in five . . . Oh my gosh."

Casey slammed on her brakes. A silver, twenty-year-old Buick jerked to a stop in front of her car, parking parallel and blocking the empty side street right next to the clinic. The last person Casey wanted to see stepped from the front seat. Coleman Chapman unfolded from the car and slammed his door. His mouth set in a thin line, a muscle ticked in his jaw. Casey's brain went into overdrive. No way to retreat. She couldn't go around. Her hands grew clammy on the wheel.

"Casey, are you okay? What's going on? Did you have a wreck?"

Casey unbuckled slowly and stepped from the car, refusing to remain seated when Coleman approached. She had to face him head-on. Had to remove his attempt to intimidate. "Something came up. I need to take care of this real quick."

"Do you need help?" Micah persisted.

"I'll be home in a few. Maybe call me back in ten minutes if I'm not there . . . just in case."

"You are not making me feel better right now."

Coleman stopped in front of her, her open car door separating them. "I'll see you in a few, Micah." She hit the off button but kept the phone unlocked and loose in her hand.

"Man, why are you talking to Bianca, filling her head with all this junk?" Coleman spat.

Casey stood her ground, her legs slightly apart, ready to move. She'd wondered if this confrontation would happen, especially after Bianca informed her that she'd ended things with Coleman. She'd been scared, and that made Casey a little nervous.

"I don't need your permission, Coleman," she stated calmly, never breaking eye contact with the towering, angry teenager.

Casey eyed the hulking kid as he stepped closer. Coleman had never been easy. He was a kid who came but didn't participate. Knew the answers but didn't care to change behavior. He didn't want help. But he liked the benefits of Ellie's Place. And lately . . . lately he hadn't just been difficult. He'd become dangerous.

He took a step forward, almost touching the door separating them. "I said I don't like it." His nostrils flared and the faint scent of tobacco and something else set off Casey's internal alarms.

"Coleman, this isn't about what you like. This is about what's best for Bianca."

Only her open car door remained between the two of them. One quick step from Coleman sent it slamming into her chest. She stumbled. Straightened, fear now screaming at her to run.

"And what about what's best for you, Teach, huh?" His wide, wild eyes set Casey further on edge. More than nicotine was at play, and reasoning with an already volatile temper wouldn't get her anywhere. She shifted closer to her seat, preparing to slip inside and slam the door at a moment's notice.

"I think it may be best if you get in your car and leave before you say something we both regret." Steel edged her tone but panic pulsed. She ground her teeth and squeezed her trembling fingers into a fist.

In one swift move, he rounded the door. Casey's back smacked against her car, his hand anchoring her chest, his fingers digging so hard, she was sure she would discover bruises later. Casey met his even stare without flinching. She needed backup. She wanted Micah.

"You think you know what's best for us, for all of us." Spit flew from his taut lips, the white of his eyes glaring under the streetlights. "You think you're making a difference, but you're just creating false hope. Bianca was raised in this hood. She belongs here. But you're putting ideas in her head of something that can't happen. What if staying here with me is what's best for her, huh?" His pupils dilated more and this time Casey caught the whiff of alcohol on his breath, as well. What crazy drug and alcohol cocktail had this kid taken?

"Bianca is gifted and bright, Coleman." She fought against his hold, gripping his wrist in her hands she shoved his arm back, causing him to retreat a half step. The muscle in his jaw pulsed and his fingers tightened into fists. "If you care about her, you should want more for her. You should want more for yourself."

This time, he stepped toe-to-toe with her, his movements more erratic, more terrifying. "What I want," he spat, "is for you to leave her alone. Stop filling her head with stupid dreams." His voice lowered, his teeth bared. "Or you may not like what I do next."

He cocked his head to the side, a Cheshire grin crept over his features. His wild gaze scanned her body up and down, turning predatory. Casey inched toward the open door, her body trembling a bit. He cocked his head, studying her. "That sister of yours is real cute. And real gullible. It would be a shame if someone started filling her head with things you didn't like. Wouldn't it?"

Her calm veneer snapped, anger replacing her fear. "Leave my sister out of this."

He was so close his breath coated her, curling her stomach. "Leave Bianca alone, or I'll do what I want with your sister. It's Emery, right?"

"Don't do something you'll regret, Coleman. Going after Emery would be a mistake."

Wild Thing sang, cutting through the tension thickening the air. Casey answered the call but kept her hand lax against her side.

"Case?" Micah's faint voice twisted in the air right as Coleman leaned closer.

"Don't tempt me, Casey," he spat, his nose grazing her cheek.

She shuddered as he backed away, his teeth bared in a maniacal grin. Casey was starting to wonder just how far Coleman might go. What was this kid truly capable of?

"Casey!" Micah shouted. But she couldn't move. Not until Coleman sped away.

She lifted the phone to her ear, noticing the slight shake of her grip. "Micah?" She fell into her car seat, slamming the door and securing the lock.

"Casey, who was that?" Fire raged through the phone. Micah was two seconds away from showing up at Ellie's Place.

She took a shuddered breath, fighting back tears at her weakness, at the threats. At the possibilities. She forced calm into her voice. "I'll be home in a minute. I'll tell you then."

She ended the call, her nerves rattling, took a few deep breaths. Never before had she been afraid of one of her kids. But Coleman had never been one of hers, despite his presence. He'd threatened Emery, may have had something to do with TJ's brother. He was unstable. And she had no idea how to protect her sister.

. . .

Micah met Casey in the driveway and immediately swooped her into his arms. His gaze darted around the dark street. Someone had threatened her. He'd heard the rage sifting through the phone, boiling his blood as he realized he was too far away to do anything besides listen.

He tightened his hold, her small frame shaking but standing strong. "You can let go of me, Cave Man."

She'd let him hold her longer than normal. That was a step in the right direction. He released her but reached for her hand.

"I think I liked Wild Man better."

Her responding smile lacked the fire he had grown to love. He froze, that word bouncing through his brain as he filtered through his feelings.

"Can we go inside, or are you going to just stand there looking like an idiot and blocking the way to the door?"

Micah jumped out of the way and motioned her in front of him as they moved inside. He shook his head. Love. Is that what this was? He'd never been in love before. He'd always know it was driven by need to protect, defend, and honor—sometimes because of duty, but more often than not, because of a fierce love for who and what he fought for. This feeling inside of him felt similar to the drive he felt to protect his brothers and Kaylan. But a stronger current ran beneath it. Something he hadn't felt before. Couldn't quite identify.

"Micah?"

Casey stood holding the door, and Micah realized he'd halted on the welcome mat, lost in thought. He took her in. Lavender sweater, skinny jeans, and boots just wrapped the package. Dark hair fell in choppy, adorable layers to her shoulders, bangs swept to the side framing deep, dark eyes that he could get lost in because he clearly saw what lay beneath—a strong woman who looked up at the stars and dreamed on behalf of her kids. She fought for others, even when it meant fighting alone. And he wanted to fight for her.

Because he just might love her.

And that terrified him.

His past proved he only hurt those he loved. He couldn't hurt Casey. He wanted to be her greatest hero, not her heartbreak.

"Yo, Cave Man. Why are you staring at me? Do I have something on my face?" She ran fingers over her lips, wiping at phantom grime.

Micah shook off his stupor. He'd process later. Right now, he would focus on what he might be able to fix. He summoned a cocky grin that he knew drove her crazy. "Just looking at you, beautiful."

This time the smile he lo . . . liked, graced her face. "C'mon, Casanova. The pizza is getting cold."

"For the record. I'm a one woman kind of guy. That nickname doesn't apply." He stepped through the door and followed her into her cozy kitchen where Emery was already chowing down on her second slice.

"Too charming for your own good," she grumbled.

"So you admit I'm charming?"

There went that snort again as she smothered a laugh. Micah thought it was adorable.

"Trying to eat here," Emery mumbled around a mouth full of pizza. "You two are making me sick. Don't make me sit between you on the couch."

Casey dropped her arms around her sister. "Please do! Then I'll have someone to snuggle with."

Emery wrinkled her nose but kept eating. Casey grabbed a plate and passed another to Micah.

"Are we going to talk about what happened when I called you?"

Micah felt Emery's eyes on him, but he refused to back down and let Casey run behind her wall. She'd answered the phone when something bad was happening. That was progress.

This time, he was determined to plow through the brick blocking his path.

Casey darted a quick look at her sister and ignored him. "We can talk about it later. What are we in the mood to watch tonight?" She took a bite of pizza and looked to her sister.

"Anything but NCIS or the Fixer Upper reruns you are obsessed with."

"I am not obsessed."

"Please, look at your house! You are like a tanner, sassier version of Joanna." Emery rolled her eyes and took another bite of pizza. "Face it, Case. You are a closet interior designer in need of an intervention."

Casey grinned at her sister. "Are you saying I have good style?"

"I'm saying we are not watching that show."

"I didn't ask what we *weren't* watching. I asked what we *were* watching. Don't make me choose."

Micah grinned at the volley happening between the two siblings, a longing for his own family settling in. "You two are definitely related."

"Do you argue with your family, too?" Emery asked, turning to face him. He felt Casey's curiosity.

"My older brother, David, and I act a whole lot like you two. Seth is younger and our rare arguments are a little more heated."

"Must be an older sibling thing." Emery smirked.

"Must be."

"What about Kaylan?" Casey asked.

"Kaylan wins anytime we argue. Just don't tell her that. She really is always right."

"Well if I ever meet her, I can't promise that secret is safe."

"You two would be trouble together."

"Totally. I win every argument we have, too."

"That's what you think."

Casey grinned. "That's what I know."

Emery groaned. "Again with the feeling sick. We are not watching a romantic comedy tonight. You two dating is enough on that front."

"We aren't dating, Em."

Micah darted a quick look at Casey. It sure felt like it to him, but they hadn't actually had that conversation.

"What exactly would you call this then, Sis?"

"I kinda want to know, too." Micah chimed in. Casey shot him a look, but once again he refused to back down.

"Let's watch an older movie. *Italian Job*. It's got a little bit of everything." Casey left Emery and Micah in the kitchen and turned on the television in the living room, effectively ending the conversation. But Micah refused to let her win this round. If he had to fight for this, then ring the bell because round two had commenced.

Casey settled into a corner of her couch. Micah bent over the back, his lips grazing her ear. The faint scent of roses and vanilla filled his senses and he fought the urge to lean closer. "We aren't done with this conversation yet. And don't even try to argue about it."

Without waiting for her to respond, he rounded the couch, settled in right next to her, propped his feet up, and turned his attention to the opening scene. He'd won this round, but he had a lot to discuss with her before he left for the night.

If it hadn't been for the looming conversation Micah knew he would initiate after the movie, he would have been relaxed as a cat. He'd sat next to Casey the whole movie with the exception of a break to fix popcorn. And he hadn't touched her. Hadn't reached for her hand, hadn't pulled her into his side. Nothing. Because until he made his intentions clear, he didn't need to take another step. He'd already kissed her, already held her strong hand in his. But he wouldn't take another step until they talked. Emery had been right. They'd spent time together but never really gone on an official date. Never talked about more than that since he had originally planned to leave within a few weeks.

But now? He needed to know how she felt. He needed to know where she was with the Lord. He wanted to go all in.

The flickering of candles from the kitchen, entryway, and coffee table made out of old crates in front of him provided dim light and cast shadows across Casey's face. Emery had gone to her room, and Micah and Casey sat in silence, the quiet peaceful. So naturally, Micah decided to break it. He was tired of living an in-between life.

"Casey, I think it's time to talk about what happened earlier tonight."

"Uh oh. No nickname. This must be serious." She shifted to face him, her knees brushing his as they curled toward her.

"You deflect by flirting when you don't want to talk about something. I'm not sure whether to think it's cute or be offended."

She shrugged. "Maybe a little bit of both."

"So talk to me."

"It's fine. I've got it handled."

"See, that's the other thing you do. You give me the Heisman and retreat."

He felt her tense a bit. "Did you want to talk or fight?"

Micah held his hands up in surrender. "Talk to me, please."

She shrugged. Her gaze shifting to the blanket on her lap. She picked at a tassel. "No big deal. Coleman stopped me when I was leaving the center. He was upset."

Micah nodded. He really didn't like that kid. "How upset?"

"Nothing I couldn't handle." She shifted her stare to the flickering candle casting shadows on the ceiling.

"Casey. Retreating."

She turned the full weight of her gorgeous stare on him. For the first time in the conversation, Micah discerned fear. "Fine. I think he was on something. A couple things. And he didn't like how I encouraged his girlfriend to pursue a college education and break up with him. Happy?"

Micah stamped down his urge to assume the worst. "And why did you sound scared and get off the phone so quickly the first time?"

"Because he pulled his car out in front of me, blocked the road, and I almost hit him." Emotion no longer danced across her face, but her eyes. Those eyes told a different story, and he knew her well enough by now to know the emotions she had bottled behind her wall and buried deep inside. Control. She stayed in control to deal with the crazy situations that came her way. But who helped her deal and unwind when she got home?

"Okay." He fought the urge to track Coleman down and scare the kid into better behavior. A round of Navy SEAL Hell Week might do the trick. "And why did you sound terrified when you finally answered me?" He'd heard the threat, but he wanted to hear it from her.

Her lips pursed. She flexed her fingers. She looked everywhere but at him. And then finally she spoke, "Because he threatened Emery. And I'm not sure how serious he is or if he will act on it."

Micah stuffed his growing anger toward Coleman and reached for calm and focus that he had learned to seize in the middle of a fight. Emotions drove his desire to protect, but they couldn't drive his reaction. He doubted Emery was the only person Coleman had threatened.

"What did he say about Emery, Casey?"

"He basically hinted that he would do something I didn't like if I didn't stop encouraging Bianca." She shook her head. "I can't stop encouraging her, but I can't put my sister at risk either."

She wrapped her arms around her stomach and curled tighter on the couch. "I'm not sure what to do."

Her fear, her uncertainty, broke his heart. He grabbed her legs and gently unfolded them, draping them across his lap, then slipped his fingers through hers. He could feel the pulse pounding in her wrist, but she didn't offer a snarky comment or pull away. She gripped tighter.

"What if I told you that I'm staying in Dallas? What if I said that I want to be here to help with this and whatever else comes your way?"

She stared him down. "I guess that depends, Micah. Are you staying in Dallas? Are you ready to handle whatever comes my way?"

Micah bit back his own growing fear, the fear that he might love this woman and hurt her, the fear that setting down roots might lead to rejection, that he might be forcing a place for himself instead of actually belonging. He was tired of his past rearing its ugly head and crushing his hope for a life, a new team, a new home, a new future . . . with Casey. It was time to stop living in the in-between.

Micah squeezed her hand, tugging her closer. "I want to stay in Dallas and see what the future holds. I want to help TJ and the other kids at Ellie's Place and on the football team. I want to set roots down here." He leaned into her space, making sure she heard and received every word. "I want to date you, Case. I want those roots to be with you."

"Micah, you have no idea what you're saying." She tried to pull her hand away, but he held firm.

"Retreating, Case."

"Thin ice, Micah."

He released her hands, cradling her face. His touch tender, his mouth inches from hers. "I'm willing to risk it, Ice Queen."

"Micah," she warned.

"Casey."

Brown on brown, their eyes remained locked. The stare-off one for the books, but his determination only increased. He'd met his match, and he was up for the challenge.

He saw the moment the fight left her. She pulled away carefully and snuggled back into the couch, but her eyes never left him. He didn't back down. Finally, she whispered a single word. "Why?"

"Why what, beautiful?" He reached for a strand of her hair and wrapped it around his finger, the strand soft and strong. He'd seen Nick make this move with Kaylan countless times and now understood the appeal.

"Why stay when you have no reason to? Why date me, Micah? I haven't done this really ever. It's not like I'm good at it. You'll only get frustrated if you stay because of me. And then you'll wish you never stayed in Dallas, and I don't want to feel guilty about that."

He squeezed her hand. "Case, you're pushing away."

"I don't know anything different, Micah. If you want me, this is what you get. A girl who struggles to let people in, who is rediscovering a God who loves me for the first time in years, who is taking care of her teenage sister, who counsels and works with other messed up teens for very little money, and who doesn't know how to date." She shook her head. "No, I'm not doing that to you, Micah. You need to go wherever you were headed next. You don't need to get tied down here." She tried to pull away, tried to remove her legs from his lap, her body from resting against his, but Micah held firm.

"Casey, what are you afraid of?" he demanded.

"You!" She finally exploded. "I'm afraid of you. Are you happy?"

Ever so slowly Micah leaned in until the faint scent of roses wrapped around him. His finger traced a slow track down her cheek. He tipped her chin to meet his gaze, her skin smooth and silky to his touch. Her breath caught. She trembled but met his gaze. Micah could sense her desire to bolt from the couch. He knew her internal struggle. But he waited. No more running. Something tonight had snapped inside him, settling and holding firm. This was right.

His thumb ran over her chin, holding her steady. His own face inches from hers. "Casey, it takes more courage to let someone see every part of you, let them close enough to possibly hurt you, than it does to build a wall and hide behind it in the name of protection. That's not strength and courage, Casey. It's cowardice, and it's not a good look on you."

She jerked away from him. "Did you seriously just call me a coward, Micah?"

"What I just did, Casey, is what someone who cares about you does. It's what Teagan and Shawn do. It's what Mama Rosie and Al do. They challenge you. They see the broken parts and love you anyway. And they push you."

She froze. "What are you saying, Micah?"

He bit back his words. Now wasn't the time. He needed to be sure. He reached for her fingers, threading their hands together. "Exactly what I said earlier. I'm here, Case. I'm staying if you let me. You aren't the only reason. But you are a big reason. I want to see where this thing between us goes. I want to stick it out. But you need to know that I am not going to tell you that your walls are okay. If we do this, I'm going to shatter every foundation because I want the Casey that lives behind that wall to be the Casey that everyone sees, who isn't afraid to love and be loved by the right people because she knows the right people are going to love her just as fiercely in return."

He released her hand and stood. "Ball is in your court, Case. I want to take you out this weekend. And I want it to be a date—not just for fun but as my girlfriend. I don't want you to answer now."

She didn't move from the couch. Didn't stop looking at him. Simply nodded.

He kissed her forehead. "Thanks for a good night. I'll call you tomorrow evening after you've had time to think."

In a few steps, he was at the door and pulling it open. "Come lock it behind me?"

She still hadn't said anything but slowly rose and approached him. He could see the battle raging in her eyes but for some reason, he felt peace.

"Night, gorgeous." He exited and moved to his car.

"Micah? That courage thing. It goes both ways."

He stopped in his tracks and turned, her silhouette visible in the flickering candlelight behind her. Touché.

With a nod, he climbed into the truck. It roared to life with the twist of the keys.

Once again, his match. He'd challenged her. But she'd pushed right back. For as much as she still had her walls in place, Micah still hadn't shared the darkest part of his story. And it was time to make good on the courage he was asking of her.

He only hoped he wouldn't lose her after the dust settled.

CHAPTER 18

The basketball court felt like an appropriate place for Casey to think. To dream for the kids playing on the court in front of her. Every slap of the ball, laugh, or competitive jab made her wish that all of life was as easy for them as it was when they played basketball. The game made them play as a team, believe they could win, root for one another. Off the court, life too often pitted them against one another.

For Lance, she prayed he would pass junior year with flying colors. She wanted him to get a basketball scholarship and maybe go on to coach. He was the encourager on and off the court, but sometimes he didn't believe in himself.

Bianca had some of the local cheerleaders studying on the bleachers. For her, Casey wanted a cheer scholarship and a teaching degree. She wanted Bianca to find her confidence in Christ instead of boys, something Casey wished she had grasped at her age.

For Anton, she wanted a medical degree of some sort. He excelled at science and anatomy when he actually studied. He was always hanging around when someone got hurt, eager to learn how to help.

Rachelle shot and scored for her team. For that girl, Casey wanted a full ride to school for basketball and a degree in physical therapy. She loved sports and hanging with the boys. For goodness sakes, she looked up health and fitness tips in her free time.

TJ stalked across the court, noticeably absent from the game. For him, Casey wanted big things. She also wanted him away from her sister, but Micah had taken care of that. TJ's gaze darted around the court, clearly searching for someone. He clenched and unclenched his fists, his search becoming more frantic. Casey followed his trail until Coleman noticed him. TJ stiffened, gave a nod, and then darted out the chain link fence. Odd. He never turned down a game.

Casey slipped off the bleachers and hurried after him, giving Bianca a high-five as she darted past. She loved all of her kids equally but some held a special place in her heart. Like TJ. And she didn't love it when something felt off. She rounded Ellie's Place and saw TJ beelining for the parking lot.

"Yo, kiddo."

TJ sped up.

"Hey, freeze, mister."

His steps faltered a second before resuming their frantic pace.

"TJ Sellers, do not make me call Mama Rosie or stalk you all the way home."

He came to a halt.

Casey popped her hands on her hips and stood her ground near the front door. "Back up a few steps."

Without turning around, TJ took a few steps backward and stopped.

Casey sighed and rolled her eyes. Teenagers. So literal when they didn't want to do something. Sometimes in the middle of the mess, she had to go to them. She stalked across the parking lot, her tennis shoes pounding the concrete. TJ flinched at her approach but didn't move. His head hung low. Casey rounded on him, her hands still propped on her hips.

TJ stood several inches taller than her. He would be a giant when he hit another growth spurt, but compared to most of the seniors he spent time with, he was still small, a kid growing into his body and his potential. And he had bucket loads of that.

Up close, sweat dotted his brow. His eyes had fixed on a dried piece of gum visible right above his left, high-top shoe. His hands still balled into fists at his side.

"TJ, look at me."

He slowly lifted his stare, which wasn't far given his height.

"Bud, is there a reason you are acting weird right now?"

He shrugged. "No reason. Just your typical teenage mood swing I guess. Gotta go." He tried to step around her, but Casey blocked his way.

"Kid, subtlety is not your strong suit. Talk to me. You know that's why I'm here, right?"

He wouldn't meet her eyes again. "I know that, Casey."

"So . . . start talking."

"Sure is a nice sunny day out, isn't it? Cool enough where you won't get too hot when you take a walk."

Casey chuckled. "Alright. I'll play. Yes, TJ, it is such a beautiful almost-winter day that it makes me wonder why you aren't playing a pickup game on the court right now." She held up a finger. "It also makes me wonder why I saw you dart onto the court for two seconds and then leave, when you always hang out here until dinner." She held up another finger. "It also makes me wonder why on this beautiful cold day you decided to play nice and silently communicate with your archnemesis, Coleman, all of a sudden." She held up three fingers, waggling them in front of his eyes before folding her arms over her chest.

"I mean, not that I'm complaining or anything. It would

223

make my year if you two could get along, bury the past, and if Coleman would quit bullying people for no reason." She shrugged, watching TJ shift and squirm more and more as she talked. "But since I know for a fact that Coleman hasn't hung up his bullying cap, I'm going to assume the nerves and nod I just observed on the court actually have something to do with, oh I don't know, Coleman possibly bullying you. Which again makes me wonder what exactly would have you running home right this second, missing one of your favorite things, and consorting with your nemesis."

TJ whistled low. "Man, Casey, you sure do talk a lot."

"Well if I remember correctly, I asked you to talk."

"Well whatever just happened was torture and a bit dramatic."

Casey choked on her laugh. A teenager calling her dramatic. That was unsettling.

"Well I guess you now know the consequences of not talking next time."

"Do they teach you all that in counseling school?"

"No, they teach us to listen. But I work with teenagers, so I had to adapt my listening skills to include torture by talking. Should I keep going?"

He held his hands up in surrender. "Okay, okay, okay."

Silence stretched. An engine backfired down the street. TJ jumped.

"Alright, TJ, seriously start talking, bud. Do you want to go to my office?"

"No!" He practically shouted, then darted his eyes back to Ellie's Place, searching for anyone out front.

"Listen, I don't want to get you in trouble. I can't tell you anything." TJ turned to leave, but Casey stopped him with a hand on his arm.

"TJ, I'm not worried about me getting in trouble. I'm worried about *you* getting in trouble. You are doing too well with too much to lose right now. Talk to me. What you say won't leave the two of us."

"Promise?"

"Promise."

He darted one more quick glance to the building and then took a step closer to Casey. "My mom got into some trouble with her . . . boss. Since my brother is gone, I needed to step in to help. Her boss is Coleman's uncle."

TJ swallowed hard, his eyes large in his face as he continued to scan the neighborhood, never quite looking at her. Casey squeezed him, not loving the direction of his story. If Coleman or his family were involved, it wasn't good.

"He said if I did one job for him, he and my mom would be square. Just one thing." His shoulders wilted and emotions cracked. "But I can't do it, Casey, I just can't. You and Al and my grandma and Mama Rosie and Coach Delgado and Coach Richards keep talking to me about how God has good plans for me. And you keep telling me to work hard, that I can do it, that I can catch the ball, and go to school and maybe own my own mechanic shop someday. And some days I believe you. I believe that God is going to help me get there, help my mom and my brothers. But then stuff like this happens, and I don't think I will ever get out."

He wiped a dark hand across his face, tears escaping. "But I still couldn't do it."

Casey grabbed TJ's hand and squeezed, now wishing she hadn't promised not to say anything. "Bud, I need you to tell me what you couldn't do."

He cast another anxious look around and leaned in close again. "I couldn't make the drop, Casey. I couldn't pass off the . . . drugs. Those things are the reason I don't have my brother around, why Coleman's family and mine are so messed up. I can't do it, Casey. I just can't. But I have to do something. If not, I'm in big trouble."

"TJ, I want you to listen to me. We can figure something out. We can get help. You don't have to do this alone. We can call the police."

"No!" He shouted again, before lowering his voice. "No police, Casey. You promised not to tell. No police. They'll take my mom, maybe even Coleman's uncle, and they'll take me because I know where the drugs are. And then no one will be around to take care of my family. I'm all they have right now."

"That's a heavy burden for a fifteen-year-old."

"But it's my burden. Coach Richards says we look out for our families, for our brothers, and for our team."

"TJ, I need you to tell me where the drugs are."

He backed up a step. "You can't call the cops. Coleman's family will come after mine if their product goes missing. We can't lose another family member."

"TJ, I won't call the police. But I need you to tell me where the drugs are."

"Coach Richards is always talking about our team." He placed his hands on Casey's shoulders. "You're my team, Casey. I can't let them hurt you either."

He pulled away from her and started jogging toward the neighborhood across the street. "I'll figure it out, Casey. I'll figure it out," he hollered.

"TJ!" she called.

"Problem?"

Casey jumped at the booming voice behind her, the voice that sent a shot of fear racing down her spine.

She turned slowly to meet Coleman's leering stare.

"No problem. Just trying to finish up a conversation."

Coleman's gaze shifted past her to where she hoped TJ had disappeared in the direction of his house a few blocks away. It gave her a second to study the hardened teen in front of her. Coleman's pale, lean chest was pockmarked with scars, a few of which looked like he had served as an ash tray for someone. A faint, yellowish mark under his right eye resembled a healing bruise, and his knuckles were raw and scratched. Casey knew he bullied because he was bullied, but she had a hard time with compassion where he was concerned. He never showed an ounce of remorse or desire for anything different.

Coleman spat on the concrete and focused on her, tucking a basketball closer to his side. "Don't forget what I said Casey. That conversation now includes TJ, too."

Casey strutted past him, determined to gain an ounce of control. "Coleman, don't forget you don't get to dictate things around here. I'll talk to whomever wants to whenever they want to."

"Well like you tell us all the time, Teach. You can choose your actions, but you can't choose your consequences." He shouldered past her, making his way back to the court.

"And here I thought you never listened," she called after him.

"Only when it benefits me, Teach. It would benefit you to listen this time." He disappeared around the corner, leaving a growing sense of unease.

Where were the drugs TJ hid? Did Coleman think she knew something she shouldn't? And would he follow through on his constant threats? She could call the police. She could talk to Micah or Shawn. But none of that would help TJ if he thought she betrayed his trust. And it very well might land him in jail with more people hurt.

No, things in this neighborhood weren't black and white when it came to dealing with these situations. She needed to tread with discernment, with caution.

Her phone rang. Mom. She ignored the call for the fourth time. One problem at a time.

She really needed to figure out her options. She really needed to help TJ. She really was starting to think she needed some help.

"Oh, Lord, help." She muttered, walking back to the school

to help the students wrap up and get home for the day. One prayer. One step. One struggling kid at a time.

Casey's backyard wasn't much to look at, but an old oak grew in the corner, its branches stretching well above her roof and into the Texas night sky. She'd tried to do a little something on her porch. She'd hunted down deals in the ritzier parts of Dallas and landed some pretty nice, used patio furniture, perfect for cooler nights when she needed the quiet and a mug of hot chocolate. Tonight's temperatures would dip into the forties, but it wasn't quite cold enough yet to miss out on enjoying the quiet outdoors.

Her mind slowly unwound, charting a path back to sanity after several difficult conversations to end the day at Ellie's and then a fight with Emery when she got home. She'd warmed up day-old pizza, taken a few slices to Emery, who had locked herself in her room, and then retreated outside to think, to pray —something she was growing used to again. It felt easier in the quiet and stillness.

The same starry sky that had once urged her to dream now urged her to awaken some of those secret dreams and share with them with a Father who had been waiting for the prodigal daughter to come home. She was learning how to operate on His strength and not hers, but she was so used to operating on her own.

"God," she tried, feeling dumb talking into the stillness, but Mama Rosie told her to just start talking until it felt comfortable.

"You say to just come to You. Well, here I am. Sipping hot chocolate on my porch and wondering how to iron out the mess that surrounds me. TJ needs help, and I don't know what to do. Bianca needs help, and I don't know what to do. All those other kids need help, and I don't know what to do. It all seems . . . impossible."

She took a sip, swirling the melting marshmallows in her mug. "And then there's Micah. What am I supposed to do with him? I never wanted to like someone else. Well," she bit her lip and watched the candle flicker in front of her, "I guess I did. Way deep down. In places probably only You can see. I don't think I even saw them. And now he wants something more, and . . . I don't think I can give it to him. Where do I even start with trusting him in a relationship?"

"Maybe just start with a yes?"

Casey bolted from her seat, turned, and ran smack into Micah's chest. Again.

"Seriously?" She shoved away from him. "What are you doing here, and why is that in my face?" She pointed at his chest.

"Well to answer your first question, your sister let me in and told me you were back here."

"Remind me to ground her later," she grumbled. "And the second answer?"

He shoved his hands in his pockets and rocked back on his heels, his grin evident even in the light of the candle sitting on the black iron table. "And my chest is always there because you are really cute when I invade your personal space, and no offense, but you are really short."

"Listen, mister . . ."

He threw his hands up. "Adorably, perfectly short. But short."

She slugged his arm, and he had the decency to look slightly hurt. She plopped back down on the wicker sofa lounger, covered with outdoor pillows in ivory and rose. She motioned to the spot next to her. "Be my guest. Do you want something to drink?"

"Sure." The wicker creaked as he sat. "But I'd much rather share yours." He swiped her mug and took a sip.

She shook her head. "Do you have any manners?"

"I have the best southern manners this side of the Mississippi and don't let my gran, mother, or sister hear you say any different." His drawl stretched in the evening air.

Casey grinned. "Good grief, that accent is strong."

He handed her mug back. "I tamed it a bit when I was in California, but you should hear all of us when we go home. Our accents somehow know we've reentered the south, and they attack with a vengeance."

He offered her the mug. "It needs a little more chocolate." He smacked his lips. "Gran make the best hot chocolate from scratch. She has it down to a science really."

She accepted the cup and took a sip. "So let me make sure I understand this. You show up here uninvited, take my drink, and then insult my hot-chocolate-making skills?"

"I would never insult you."

Casey rolled her eyes. "Well, in all fairness, this was just a packet of hot chocolate. I'm sure hers is much better." She sank into the cushions, burrowing under the blanket, her mind and body relaxing into their pre-Micah state.

"Are we going to talk about what I overheard?"

Casey stiffened. She was trying to get this praying thing down. Then had been praying about Micah. Then speak of the devil, and he appears.

"I guess that all depends on how much you heard."

"Only the last part."

She rotated to face him. "Well I guess we can talk about that if you can tell me why you are here tonight."

He took the mug out of her hand and took another sip. "Probably for the same reason you were praying. I thought you would chicken out if I called or texted, so I showed up in person."

Casey smirked.

"And you can wipe that smirk off your face. This is not one

of those situations where you can decline just because I showed up uninvited looking for a yes. The only way we both win in this is if you say yes. Every other way one or both of us loses."

"Your logic is making me dizzy, and I think my brain is broken from today."

Micah grew quiet. "Tough day?"

"A little."

"Well I like your remedy." He took another sip and then followed her into the silence, sinking next to her until their shoulders rested against one another.

A week ago, Casey would have pulled away, put space between them. Tonight, she found the presence of someone next to her comforting. She didn't have to be alone. She motioned to the tree. "You really only have two patio seasons in Texas. Spring and fall. It's starting to get too cold even now. December is working its magic." She shivered a bit. "The fireflies really love that tree over there in the spring. I love to sit out here and just watch them."

"My siblings and I used to chase fireflies in the woods across from our house." Micah rested his arm over the back of the lounger. "We called them lightning bugs. We used to catch them and put them in mason jars. We'd use Moms' sharp knives to punch holes in the top of the jars. It dulled the knives and drove her crazy." He smiled at the memory. "Then we would collect leaves and twigs and stick them in the jar. Seth was always upset when his firefly died. I tried to help him keep it alive as long as possible, but creatures like that weren't made to be contained."

Casey felt Micah's eyes on her and turned to meet his stare, his face inches from her own. "They are meant to fly wild and free," he whispered.

"Sounds like you have some good memories from childhood."

Creases lined his brow in the flickering candlelight. "Tell me about your childhood, Firefly."

She rolled her eyes. "There's not much to tell. I lived with my mom in a small house in Austin."

"You know," he leaned in closer. "For someone who has a license to counsel, you aren't very good at this sharing thing."

"You are on point with the insults tonight, Soldier."

He flinched. There was something about that word... "I was just challenging you, but I might insult your cocoa again if you call me that one more time."

"So now you admit you did insult my drink?"

He shrugged and turned to study their fireflies. "My Gran just makes it better. It's not your fault."

"Well I'll catch up with her someday. She's had a few more years on me."

This time his grin sent fireflies dancing in her stomach. "That's the spirit. Now tell me about your childhood."

Casey didn't want to talk about her mom, or the men, or the bars, or her teenage years. "Micah, there really isn't much to tell."

"Maybe you're focusing on the wrong memories."

"How do you figure?"

"Well, I know Teagan and Shawn have been in your life quite a while and they're pretty great. I'm assuming you've at least got one or two good stories there."

At their names, a flood of memories swarmed Casey, making her smile. It was hard to look at her childhood and see anything carefree, but Teagan and Shawn had been her silver lining. Her saving grace.

Maybe it was time she focused on some of those memories.

"Earth to Casey."

She elbowed him, jostling their drink. But his prompting had awoken something she'd long since buried, memories of laughter and fun and games and playing. It hadn't been just supporting one another in low moments of lacking parental figures, school bullies, and bad relationships.

"There was this one night. It was Shawn's fourteenth birthday, I think. Teagan and I are a couple years younger, but we were the only ones he wanted to spend his birthday with. It was February down in Austin, so not too cold, but Shawn wanted a campfire and s'mores instead of a cake and candles. So, his foster dad set up a firepit in their backyard, and the three of us sat out there around the fire, ate s'mores until our stomachs hurt, and told ghost stories. Teagan spent the night with me afterward, and we were up all night jumping at every creak of the floorboards." She traced the droplets condensing on her glass. "That's probably one of my favorite memories with the two of them."

"That sounds like a good one."

He took the mug out of her hand and took another sip. "So about that conversation we had."

"You mean the one where you told me you want to be my boyfriend and then left?"

"Yeah, that one."

"What about it?"

He sat up and turned to face her in the dimness. Candlelight fluttered on his face. "You seriously don't make things easy, do you?"

"Consider this my way of making you squirm."

"Oh, I'm not squirming. I'm calling you a pain in the rear end, woman."

She sat up straight and narrowed her eyes. "Call me that one more time."

"Which one?" He leaned in close, his grin dangerous. "A pain? Or woman?"

"Both. But fair warning, if either come from your mouth again, this drink will end up in your lap."

"Harsh."

"Fair."

She settled back into the cushions, quieting her racing mind.

She'd been praying about how to answer him. She wanted to say yes. But she'd never thought she would actually be someone's girlfriend.

"You're starting to shake my confidence in this a little, Case. Do you want to talk about it?"

She took a sip, cooling her singing nerves. "Micah, I . . ."

"Casey, I need you." Bianca burst onto the back porch, tears streaming down her face, Emery hot on her trail.

"I tried to help her, Case, but she just wanted you."

"It's okay, Em. Why don't you let me handle this and you go back inside?"

Her sister nodded and closed the screen door, casting an anxious look at her friend.

"Do you want me to . . . ?"

"No." She stopped Micah's rise from the cushions. "Please stay." Casey had a feeling she knew what this was about and it might be good to have Micah around for a guy's perspective. Besides, she wanted to see what he would do under pressure with her kids.

"B, come sit." She gentled her voice and patted the seat next to her. Bianca sank into the seats. "Is it okay if Coach Richards stays?"

The girl only nodded and wiped her eyes. "I'm sorry it's so late, but I had to talk to you."

"What happened?"

"Coleman told me that he has plans for us and they don't include me leaving for college. He laughed when I told him I want to teach and work with kids like you and Teagan do. He said it was stupid and that I should stop letting you fill my head with stupid things. So of course, I told him he couldn't tell me what to do." She sniffed and wiped her eyes again.

"Then I got mad and told him to leave me alone for good, and then I needed to see you, so I called Emery and came straight over. And I interrupted, and I'm sorry." She burst into tears again, rattling off sentences in Spanish. Casey bit back a laugh at the girl's slightly dramatic response.

"It's okay, you aren't interrupting anything." Except the answer she would need to give Micah at the end of the night.

"Bianca, how did Coleman take it when you broke up with him?" Micah asked her, his tone a whole new level of gentle.

"He was pretty mad. He told me I would regret it, that he was the best thing that would happen to me. And then he stormed out of the house. The glass door cracked because of how hard he slammed it. Now my ma's not happy."

Micah grimaced. "I can imagine. Did he hurt you in any way?"

Casey straightened, scanning the girl in what little light flickered from the candle. She couldn't see any visible bruises on the girl's bare arms or on her legs.

Bianca shook her head. "He scared me. He didn't hurt me. But I won't let him bully me anymore. I'm going to go to college and cheer and study and then teach. Right, Casey?"

Casey's heart hurt hearing the waffling in Bianca's tone. She took Bianca's hands in hers. "You are going to be the best teacher, and you can do whatever you set your mind to if you work hard and give it all you got."

"And you're still going to help me, right?"

"Of course I am." She squeezed her hands. "Why wouldn't I?"

The girl looked down at her knees. "Because Coleman is scary when he's angry, and I don't think he is going to be too happy with you tomorrow."

Casey's pulse skipped a beat. Coleman definitely made her nervous, even more so now that he suspected TJ had talked to her.

Micah's hand came to rest on her back, his presence bolstering her courage. "He may not be happy, but he can't dictate what we choose to do. Do you want to stop applying for colleges just because he's mad?"

235

"Of course not."

"Then I'm not going to stop helping you because he's mad either."

"But what if he does something? He's into some bad stuff, Casey."

"You two let me handle Coleman," Micah chimed in. "Guys like that are below you, Bianca. They are little boys who haven't learned how to be young men who value the young ladies in their lives."

"But he said he loved me, Coach Richards. What if he is the only guy who ever likes me? What if he really is the best I have?" Another tear tracked down her sweet face, and Casey's heart broke, hearing her own long ago fears echoed in Bianca's words.

Micah leaned forward, invading Casey's space as he spoke to Bianca. "Bianca, any guy who does not value you like the treasure you are is never the best you will ever have."

She sniffed. "Really?"

"Really." Casey could feel Micah's smile without seeing it. It swept through his voice reassuring, restoring. "If God has a guy for you out there, he's going to be a man who adores you, puts you first, supports your dreams. And if and when he fails to do those things well, he will work to get better at them so he can love you the way you deserve. Don't settle for less, B. You hear me? Coleman is far from the best the Lord has in store for you."

Bianca began crying again, but this time a smile broke through as she nodded. Her shoulders straightened, her courage and hope seeming to return. Micah hadn't told Bianca anything new, but coming from him, it meant something different, something stronger. Casey felt like they were actually a couple giving one of her kids counseling and help after a long day. For the first time, she saw what it could look like to be supported while she did what she loved. She knew exactly what she would tell Micah at the end of the night.

And she was beginning to wonder if she just might be on her way to the "l" word with Micah Richards.

Casey made Bianca stay and hang out with Emery until her mom arrived to pick her up. No more walking on dark streets for the next little while, not until they determined if Coleman was just a loose cannon or bent on revenge.

As the screen door closed and Micah and Casey were once more left alone in the quiet of her backyard under a midnight Texas sky, Casey knew she couldn't hold back anymore.

"Yes."

Micah froze in midair between sitting and standing. "Yes, what?"

She giggled. "C'mon, Captain America, don't make me spell it out for you."

He straightened and spun her to face him, wrapping his arms around her waist. "What do you think about Iron Man instead?"

Casey reminded herself to relax, to stay in his arms instead of pulling away. But it didn't take much convincing. Her traitorous body and mind somehow sank into the security and laughter Micah provided in his nearness.

"That is something to consider. You might be a match for him on the annoying scale."

"He is not annoying. He is brilliant."

"Fine line there, Captain. Fine line."

"For a second, I actually thought you were being nice to me. But nope."

She placed her hands on his chest. "And here I thought you were anxiously awaiting my yes."

Even in the dim light, she could see the heat filling his gaze. His growing affection didn't frighten her as much as it used to.

"Casey Stewart, are you saying yes to being my girlfriend?"

"That's such a . . . strong word."

"From you, Case, I just want a commitment to try."

She licked her dry lips, stalling for time until she noticed his eyes drift and focus there. "Then how about we start with Saturday night?"

Ever so slowly he bent down and brushed a feather light kiss on her cheek.

"Deal," he whispered, his breath on her ear sending shivers down her spine.

He took a step back and winked. "I'll say goodnight before you change your mind. Sweet dreams, Case."

Casey plopped back down on the cushions and stared out at her tree long after Micah had left. Thinking, praying, and dreaming in ways she hadn't since she was a child all under the glow of her favorite Texas sky.

Fairy lights twinkled overhead, lining the path of the Bishop Arts District. The silhouette of trees formed a canopy over the sidewalk, and couples, quirky characters, and small families meandered around, enjoying the fall Texas evening. Despite the temperature dipping into the 50s, Micah wiped sweaty palms against his jeans when Casey turned to study a display window.

Dinner had been full of laughter at Billman's, a restaurant purely Dallas with the feel of the city and faux trappings of a cabin—chandeliers juxtaposed with distressed wood and antlers. Antlers everywhere. But the truffle popcorn had made Casey groan, the dinner had satisfied, and the conversation made him feel lighter than he had in months. A creeping shiver stole up his spine.

Next to her, watching the relaxed smile, her confident stance, and the way the lights danced off her earthy eyes, Micah thought only one word appropriate: home. He'd found home. And it wasn't the location, the Texas sky above him, romantic setting around him, or even the dinner they'd shared.

It was the woman before him, the woman he wanted on his team. Maybe even for life.

He wiped his palms against rough denim again.

"I saw that, Soldier."

Except that nickname. That he could do without.

He reached for her hand and wound her fingers through his, pleasure curling in his stomach at how easy she now made it to touch her, be close to her. "Have I told you I hate that nickname? Soldier is so . . ." he searched for the right word, "just wrong."

She turned the weight of those brown eyes his way. Her fingers brushed his forearm causing goosebumps to dance. "Okay, I'll humor you. Why is it wrong?"

Micah steered them to Emporium Pies, a cute shop around the corner crafted from the bones of an old house. The line wound outside the door and down the sidewalk. Couples and groups of friends congregated around chairs on the wraparound porch and in the yard, enjoying the largest pieces of pie he'd ever seen aside from his gran's. He had strong doubts that this would rival hers, but he would give it a shot. They paused at the back of the line, Micah quickly taking an assessment of the crowd around him. Habit. No longer a SEAL but he still wanted intimate knowledge of his surroundings.

A slight tug on his hand sent his gaze skittering back to Casey's oval, tan face and slight upturned pixy nose. Something twisted inside him. He matched her grin and tossed his arm around her shoulder, needing her closer.

"Micah Richards, stop staring at my mouth and finish your explanation." The guy in front of him choked on his chuckle.

Micah smirked. "A soldier follows orders without question because he's been trained to listen, respond, and obey."

"Okay," she drew out the last syllable. "And that's different from your time in the military how?"

Micah just smiled. "Oh you naive, little thing."

"Veto 'little thing.' That nickname better not stick."

"As long as you stop using 'soldier.'"

"As long as you finish explaining. And make it good." Her grin, turned full force his way, only made him tug her closer to his side. This time he couldn't help but focus on her lips, pink against her tan skin. Her arm wrapped around his waist and settled on his hips, and he gave a quick squeeze in return.

"Are you ready to listen and quit being so sassy?" He laughed as she tried to sock him in the ribs. "Apparently not. Minx."

She narrowed her eyes. He chuckled and guided them forward to the bottom of the porch step leading into the pie shop. "Fine. I'll continue. A solider takes orders. A warrior is trained to move, operate, and make wise calls as he goes. He knows his leader, and he operates in the freedom given by his training, his instinct, his team, and most of all love and conviction for what he is fighting for. Some men and women in the military are merely soldiers. Their service is no less honorable, no less appreciated. But others, others have a warrior's heart. You can find them in every branch. They love what's behind them and therefore focus all their passion on making a difference by fighting what's before them. It's not just a job to them. It's a duty, a calling. And they do it—sometimes to their own detriment, sometimes in defiance of well-intentioned orders—because they have one sole focus: Protect and serve what they are fighting for, no matter the cost. At least . . . that's how I see it."

This time her eyes bored holes into him. "Micah, why did you leave?"

They were almost in the door. He could smell the spicy hint of cinnamon, the rich, earthy scent of chocolate, and sweet blueberry mingling in the air. Soft laughter surrounded him. He wanted to tell her. But now wasn't the time. Not for all of it. Not for the ugliest part.

"Have you ever heard 'be sure your sins will find you out?'"

She nodded. "It's from the Bible, right?"

"It is." He kept his grip light, thankful she hadn't squirmed away from him at the mention of the Bible. He loved that she responded with openness, her guard down toward the things of God. Maybe He was working in Casey's heart, just like He was in Micah's. After all, He was in the business of making all things new, even two hurt and broken believers finding their way back home. "Let's just say my sins found me out and it cost my brothers."

A crease formed between her brows. He smoothed it with his thumb then rested his forehead on hers, a sigh heavy and deep escaping him. They were through the door now, and he cast around for something, anything else to focus on besides the empathy pouring into him from her side pressed into his. He accepted the menu from the girl in front of him and ignored her lingering eyes as he removed his arm from around Casey. A case displayed pies of all kinds. Tables and chairs crowded the small space of what had once been the smallest living room. A counter manned by three teens waited a few feet away. His mouth watered at the overwhelming scents and warmth of the cozy room.

"What do you want, doll face?"

"I want you to finish your story." One hand pushed the paper down, crinkling the eggshell cardstock. The other brushed his jaw, angling his face toward hers. "I want the apple pie because it's the best. You're going to order the chocolate so I can try it, too. And absolutely no complaining about how this treat doesn't measure up to your grandmother's. Just enjoy." A smile tugged at her lips, but her gaze remained firm. "And then, Micah Richards, you are going to finish your story."

"Yes, ma'am." He was used to direct Casey but not a Casey who wanted to dig inside his soul and disrupt the pieces. He wasn't sure he could handle the disgust that would fill her eyes once she knew.

He barely noticed that she'd slipped her hand in his and then stood on tiptoe to give their orders to the blond teenager behind the glass display. The girl nodded and began slicing massive pieces from the pies laid out behind her. Micah slid sideways and offered the second, freckle-faced teen his credit card.

Her brown braid hung over her shoulder, dusting the top of her apron. She looked back and forth between Micah and Casey, a blush dusting her cheeks.

"I've just got to tell y'all this," she whispered, leaning over the register, her Texas accent hanging thick in the heated, little shop. "Y'all are the cutest couple I've seen all night."

Micah knew Casey fought an eye roll next to him. He took the two slices of pie from the hands of the first blonde and turned once more to the girl behind the register. "Well, I only look good because of her. Thanks for the pie." He offered a wink and another grin, and then steered Casey outside.

"You know, I'm starting to think that Casanova name is going to stick after all." She led them to a high-top table surrounded by two stools at the back corner of the front porch.

"Not a chance, cupcake. I have to be more charming to make up for the surly retorts happening in your head all the time." He poked her in the side as they settled onto the stools. The evening was quickly dipping into the forties again, bringing in the chill of Texas winter and the coming Christmas holidays, but he was growing accustomed to the unpredictable Dallas weather, growing accustomed to a lot of Dallas things. But he didn't think he would ever grow accustomed to Casey Stewart. He wanted to know her more. The "l" word pushed to the edge of his focus again, but he shoved it away. He wasn't ready to use it . . . yet. But soon he would need to tell her.

"Time to finish, Warrior."

He grinned and took a bite of his chocolate pie. He groaned. "Good grief, this is incredible."

"Told you." She offered a smug smile. "The apple pie might even rival your grandmother's."

He covered her mouth with his hand and leaned close. "Don't ever speak such blasphemy again. Lightening might strike."

She scooped a bite of chocolatey goodness from his saucer. "Strike away. I know where I'm going."

Micah stilled. "You haven't talked about it much. God. Your relationship. The last time I brought it up you got mad."

"Who says I'm not going to get mad this time?" She took a bite of the apple pie and Micah followed suit.

"Okay, this might be about one point below Gran's on the tasty scale. I might need to tell her to step up her game."

"I win this round."

"You win no round. I said it was slightly below Gran's. Not equal to. But you were close so I'll give you that."

"Competitive, aren't ya?"

"Think you can keep up?"

Casey leaned forward, her cinnamon eyes glowing in the dim twilight of the porch. "I think the better question, Sailor, is can you?"

Micah matched her pose, leaning across the small round table to close the remaining distance between them. "I think I'm up for the challenge if you are."

Casey's gaze drifted to his mouth

"My eyes are up here, gorgeous."

"Oh, Micah, if you can't realize that I'm not concerned with your eyes right now I'm really not sure you can keep up."

"Smarty pants."

"Micah."

"Casey."

"How about you shut up and kiss me already?"

"Happy to," he whispered. He closed the remaining distance between them, brushing his lips over the corner of her mouth before sealing their lips together. She tasted like apple pie and hope. Walls were down tonight. He prayed they stayed that way.

Someone wolf whistled nearby and they broke apart with a laugh, noticing the crowd huddled in coats waiting for pie for the first time in minutes, but Micah felt no shame. He was proud of this girl. His girl. She was softening. And he loved it.

That word. It was about time to say it. But not until things were perfect. Not until he'd told her the whole story.

"Was it that bad?"

Her sassy crack snapped him from his thoughts. He shoveled another bite of pie in his mouth. "It's just getting better and better. When we first started this kissing thing, it was a little rusty, but I have got to say, you're a quick learner, Casey Stewart."

Her fist connected with his bicep. He winced. She might be tiny but she was fierce. "I'm kidding, I'm kidding. You're incredible, Sunshine."

"That's a little better." She scooped a forkful of apple pie and held it out for him. This Casey, the kind who didn't think before she acted with him, didn't shield before she responded to him—this Casey, he loved. He loved every version of her. But this is the Casey he wanted to see freely living in every moment of every day.

"Want to tell me what has you so quiet?"

Micah set his spoon down with his half-eaten pie. Time to lower his walls, too. "I never answered why I left."

She nodded and set her fork down. "Are you ready to tell me?"

He chuckled and ran a hand through his hair. "If you're ready to listen to the gory details."

Casey bridged the gap between their hands and wound her fingers through his. She'd never initiated contact like she had tonight. He hoped what he shared next didn't ruin the trend. "Gory details don't scare me."

He nodded. "We were on assignment overseas. We'd been deployed for a few months with our whole team. I was on a special team that took assignments here and there with Nick and a few others, but for this particular job I was with a group from my larger team." He paused, sifting through details in his head, knowing he couldn't share all but he could share his part.

"We were in a country that shared a coastline with a few others. One of our ships waited farther out and we were to meet a transport for rendezvous and debrief onboard. We thought we had completed the operation and began to move to the rendezvous. That's when everything went wrong." He brushed over the details and military terms. She'd learn them eventually. For now . . . he just had to get this out.

She squeezed his hand but remained silent. His heart ratcheted into his throat as the details burned in his memory, leaving behind the taste of dust and saltwater.

"Our ride to our boats was compromised so we had to run a bit over land. That became a disaster. An ambush lay in wait and we engaged in the fight of our lives." He fell farther into the memory. Gun shots. Pounding feet. Yelling. Desperation and determination dripping with every breath. "We'd almost made it back. I was the last to pull out, covering our flank until the team got away. I thought we were in the clear. I turned to run and twisted an old injury on a rock in my hurry. The pain," he shook his head. "I hadn't felt anything like it in years, but I kept running anyway. It slowed me down. My friends were swimming out to the boats by the time I dove into the water but it was too late. The enemy had followed me and caught up. They fired into the water. They had less than thirty seconds before a helo showed up, but by then we were sitting ducks. Five of my teammates . . . they went down." Micah paused and swallowed hard, remembering holding Harrison, remembering the last visit he needed to make.

"Four of them died. And it was my fault. If I hadn't been

clumsy, gotten hurt, been too slow, we might have all made it out." He rested his head on his fist, weary like he hadn't been in a while, the memory heavy and casting shadows on the night out with Casey.

A small hand pulled his arm down and nudged his chin up to meet the most determined, beautiful set of brown eyes. "Might is an awfully noncommittal word to stake so much guilt on, Micah. It wasn't your fault."

"Case, you don't get it. I got that injury because I was stupid in high school. Be sure your sins will find you out? That verse feels cruel. It's true, and it cost my friends their lives. It cost their families. That's a debt I can never repay."

"That's why you left."

Micah only nodded.

"Micah, look at me." Her featherlight touch brushed over his cheek, forcing his eyes to meet hers. He let her see it all—the guilt, the ache, the grief . . . the overwhelming, all-consuming grief. It had changed him.

"The night Tanner took advantage of me and my mom blamed me for not being able to handle my liquor or my men changed my world. Do you think the fact that he took advantage of me in my drunken state was my fault for drinking?"

Rage filled Micah at the very idea. "Should you have been drinking? No. Was it your fault that the guy was a jerk and took advantage? Not in a million years, Case. How could you ever think that? I wish I could hurt him on your behalf." He removed her hand from his cheek, gripping it between his fingers. "If you have his number, I'll make it happen."

Casey laughed softly. "I don't think it's my fault. I blamed Tanner, my mom, my stupidity, God, church people, but never did I think it was my fault. My hurt stemmed from people blaming and isolating me instead of comforting and loving me."

"Ok, I don't understand where you are going with this."

She cupped his face with her hands again, incredibly gentle, no rejection in her touch. "The way you feel about Tanner is the way I feel about the men who chased you, who killed your friends, who hurt innocent people. Your friends signed up to go to war. They never wanted to die, but they were willing. You were willing. Not one of them was indestructible or a machine. You are not a machine. You became a SEAL with a history, preferences, opinions, medical needs, all of which are part of you being an imperfect man who signed up to do a big job. You are not God, Micah. And your weakness did not kill your friends. Your past sins did not kill your friends. Bad men did. Men who set up an ambush. Men who wouldn't stop until they took a life."

Her thumb chased the tear that had escaped, the first tear that had escaped in over a year since his loss.

"You are not at fault, Micah. I'm relearning that I have to give the Lord the guilt, shame, and blame I carry. I think you need to, too. It's a heavy burden to bear."

Micah threaded his fingers through Casey's hair, the short layers winding around each digit. Sharing with Casey made the weight lighter, abated the loneliness. "When did you become an expert on God?"

"I've known Him for a long time, Micah. But that retreating thing? I did it with Him, too. I think I'm tired of retreating. I want something with Him that lasts, even when it's hard."

"Just with Him?"

She shrugged and shifted back, picking up her fork and restoring some of the lightness of moments earlier. "I may be open to negotiations with the right person." She took another bite of her apple pie.

"Well the right person better be the one sitting in front of you."

"Baby steps, Micah. Baby steps. You know a lot about me and vice versa, but we don't know everything, and I still never thought I would date. I don't know how to do this."

"Casey, we will never finish learning all we need to. Being on the same team starts by trusting one another to have the other's back. I just shared the darkest moment of my life, and you didn't run. I think you are going to be better at this than you think."

Casey stood, abandoning her now empty plate. "Oh, Micah. You have only scratched the surface."

CHAPTER 19

Nights under a star-studded sky, even one dimmed by city lights, had become their time, a time full of possibilities. With Micah's hand in hers, she saw possibilities. They cruised down her street in Micah's beat-up truck, but just like the truck had been given a second chance at life, it seemed God was giving her and Micah that chance, as well. A future and a hope. She was beginning to understand that verse in new ways.

Micah pulled to a stop behind an unfamiliar car parked in front of her home.

"Friend of yours?"

Casey shook her head. "Must be a neighbor."

Micah killed the engine and looked her way, the dashboard lighting his handsome features and five o'clock shadow. She ran her fingers over the scruff, in awe of how easy it felt with him. How safe. How unlike the past. His eyes warmed and the moths in her stomach fluttered to life. She was seriously starting to doubt they were moths. Maybe they had transformed into butterflies. Or maybe they had been all along and had just been dormant for a while.

"I like when you look at me like that." His deep voice sent them flying.

"Like what?"

"Open. Like I'm no longer on the other side of the wall."

She chuckled. "Baby steps, Micah."

"I'm not very good at baby steps."

"Is that a SEAL thing?"

He shrugged. "It's a SEAL thing. It's a Richards thing. It's a Micah thing. When I decide to be all in, I'm all in."

The butterflies gave a nervous flap in her stomach. She hoped she didn't mess this up, hoped she could let him in. There were just a few things she wasn't ready for yet.

"Does that scare you?" He nuzzled into her hand still resting on his face, tracing lazy circles with her thumb.

She tried for the open thing. "A bit."

"Try again, Pinocchio."

"I definitely don't like that one."

He chuckled. "I don't either. But I don't want you to be afraid of telling me the hard stuff."

She nodded. "I'm terrified I can't do this relationship thing."

"I'm terrified I can't either. But I'm tired of that feeling. We'll figure it out. One day at a time."

She loved that about him. He pushed her but never too far. Never to breaking. Micah was the guy she'd secretly dreamed of and never dared to hope would appear. She didn't know how to be on a team like this, but Micah was showing her it might be possible.

He placed a gentle kiss on her palm, sending every butterfly inside her in a wild flurry. That one act felt more special than any kiss so far. She felt . . . cherished. She didn't know that was possible.

"Let's get you inside, Ace."

He circled the truck and opened the door for her. "M'lady." He extended his hand.

A laugh escaped her. "Remind me to thank your mother if I ever meet her."

"*When* you meet her, she's going to love you. My mom is incredible. Y'all will get along great."

Casey doubted that. She didn't have a great track record with mothers.

"Speaking of mothers."

The voice laced with years of chain smoking and hard living froze her to the driveway. No.

"Hello, Casey-girl." Mona Rodriguez stepped from the shadows of her front porch. In the darkness, she reminded Casey of something evil from her nightmares.

Micah immediately took a step in front of Casey, pulling her behind him in one move. His chest swelled, the tension radiating off him, his shoulders stiff in front of her. She wouldn't let him stand in the line of fire. She stepped to his side, ignoring his iron hold on her hand.

"What are you doing here, Mom?"

"You haven't answered my calls." She took a step into the driveway, the streetlights finally illuminating her. She'd dressed in tight black jeans and a draping leopard print tank top from the junior's section, possibly from Emery's closet back home, complete with a faux fur black coat. Good to know she hadn't changed.

"So you just showed up?"

"Well this is one way to force you to talk to me." She turned her attention to Micah. "Hello, handsome. You must be Micah. You're much more attractive than your voice sounded over the phone. I'm Casey's mother, Mona. Enjoying my daughter?" Her simpering tone made Casey's toes curl.

Micah straightened next to her and took another subtle step between them. He extended his hand, despite the stiffness in his shoulders. "Micah, ma'am."

"Such good manners, but I told you not to call me that." Her mouth turned down at the corners. "Is it not a pleasure to meet me?"

"It might have been under different circumstances."

Casey smothered a small smile. Maybe Micah could handle her mom.

"I would agree if you hadn't turned my daughters against me." Mona sneered and turned her attention back to Casey. "I'm here for Emery. This lawyer stuff has got to stop. This was just temporary. She's had enough of a timeout with you, and I don't want to give you any more time to fill her head with nonsense about me."

"I don't think she needs help in that department, Mom."

Mona's gaze darted between Casey and Micah. "I see." She motioned between the two of them. "Like sister, like sister, I take it. What a poor example for her, bringing your latest fling home, Casey. No wonder I can't keep her under control. She's heard the embarrassing tales of your younger years."

Casey took a step forward, yanking her hand from Micah's. "If she is following in anyone's footsteps, Mother, it's yours. You kept a constant parade of men coming in and out of our house when I was growing up. Own up to your own lifestyle choices."

"At least I can handle my men, Casey. You never quite mastered that." She nodded at Micah. "He'll get tired of you soon enough."

Casey stood ramrod straight, ignoring Micah's presence at her back. Her mother's words weaseled into the parts of her heart that whispered the same. He would get tired of her. Casey knew it. Her mom knew it. It would be Tanner all over again and she would be left with an aching heart, the laughing stock of her friends. She couldn't do it again.

She took another step away from Micah, needing distance from the deceiving shelter of his presence. She knew a safety blanket could just as easily smother her as it could provide security.

"It's late. Emery is probably asleep, and you can't take her, Mom. We talked about this. You said she could stay indefinitely. I want full custody. She's still your daughter. But I need the legal ability to make decisions for her since she will be living with me."

"Excuse me?"

Micah's presence was at her back again. She took another step away.

"That's why I got a lawyer involved. You don't really want her in your way, and I don't want her growing up like I did."

"You ungrateful little brat." Her mother sneered. "Open the door right now, or I will call the cops. I'm her mother." Her voice approached a pitch that reminded Casey all too much of nights when some trinket or dish broke in their home in her mother's hysteria.

Micah stepped between them. "Mona, I'm sure we can talk this out. Why don't you come back in the morning, and we can figure out what to do with Emery?"

"So this little thing," she motioned between the two of them, "it's a *we* now?"

"No," Casey ground out smothering Micah's affirmative response. She felt Micah's eyes, but the last few minutes had reminded her that she had to handle this alone. She had to fight for Emery, and Micah couldn't help because she wouldn't be able to handle the fallout when Micah realized the full weight of what it meant to be in her family.

Mona's gaze sharpened. "So she still can't handle her men, huh, love?" She took a few steps forward, fixated on Micah. "Only now it looks like she is the heartbreaker." Her leering gaze swung toward Casey, who now felt sick. She fought the urge to curl in on herself.

"Break hearts first before yours gets broken. Love 'em and leave 'em and move on to the next one, eh, Casey-girl?"

She stopped next to Casey and lowered her voice. "I guess

you did learn something from me after all." She patted Casey's cheek twice and then strolled down the driveway to the foreign car parked in front of her house. Damage trailed in her wake.

"Have Emery ready first thing in the morning. I'll be back for her, and I don't want to wait," she yelled over her shoulder.

The car door slammed. Tires screeched. Then silence on the empty street. Shadows lurked in every lawn.

"Casey."

"Don't, Micah." She kept her back to him.

"Retreating, Case."

Acid built in her body, shutting down the butterflies, the hopes, the possibility that had been hers only moments before until her mother reminded her. What had she been thinking? She couldn't do this. She was better off alone. Emery needed her. And Micah would eventually get bored and leave her.

"Over, Micah."

His warm hand wrapped around her arm and she reluctantly turned to face him, steeling herself against the feelings she had felt only minutes before.

"Don't run from me, Casey."

She yanked back. "Don't you get it, Micah? She's right! This can never work!"

"Don't listen to your mom, Case. She doesn't know what she is talking about. This is working. It can work."

"No, Micah, it can't. Because eventually you'll leave, and I can't handle that again."

"I told you I wouldn't do that."

"Yes, you will! Because it's what you do." She yelled. "You run. It's what you've been doing since you left the SEALs."

She might as well have slapped him. He took a step away from her.

"You don't mean that."

"I mean it, Micah." She died a little inside at the hurt flashing across his face, the face that only hours before had held her captive, kissed her, maybe even loved her. But he would only hurt her. She couldn't let him in. She fortified the wall that had been crumbling inside her.

"Just leave, Micah," she whispered. "You would have anyway. Let's just make it happen tonight."

He reached for her, but she yanked away from his grip, backing up toward the house. "You don't belong in my life, Micah. Your family is good. Mine is a mess. You're a free spirit. And my world is here. I'm about to take custody, hopefully, of my teenage sister, and I don't think you're ready for that. You'll get tired and restless . . . and you'll break my heart."

"Casey Stewart, you are insane if you think I will do that." He ignored her struggle, and pulled her to him, his hands the gentlest iron around her arms. She felt a part of her heart shatter. It had already begun. He was already hurting her.

"Why won't you listen to me? You make me so mad!"

"Mad?" Micah laughed, but no warmth filled the sound. "You must mean interested. Although you would never say that because it would mean letting someone past that carefully crafted wall you hide behind."

"I'm not hiding!" Casey shouted.

"Yes, you are, Case. Because only two people on the planet have survived the test of time with you. When are you going to realize that I want to protect you, care for you, give you the moon?" He gripped her shoulders, pulling her toe to toe with him. "Casey, I love you. With everything in me. Do you hear me? I love you. Why won't you let me?"

The cracking Casey felt was the rest of her heart shattering behind the wall that stacked higher by the minute. But the wall couldn't protect from the pain now. And in that moment Casey realized that this time it wasn't Micah running from her, she was running from him, and she didn't know how to stop.

"Leave, Micah." Emotion fled. Numbness set in. She couldn't think. Could only pray to get inside, shut the door, and let the numbness wash her away. "Go away. Leave Dallas. And don't come back." With every word, she watched the warmth in his gaze fracture. He stiffened. Took a step back. Then another. Then turned and walked away.

The engine started. The truck pulled away from the curb. And what remained of her heart fell to the dust, the final brick in her wall back in place. She crumpled on the driveway, wrapping her arms around herself. He'd loved her. Something she'd thought impossible.

But he'd run. Just like she feared he would.

Only this time, she had made him.

CHAPTER 20

Casey woke the next morning feeling like a truck had run over her. Her eyes ached from crying, her head pounded, and something like jagged pieces of glass dug into her chest, aching with each beat, with each moment that propelled her further from last night and further from Micah.

But she didn't have time to give in to the pain, to curl up in her bed and forget the way his arms had felt safe and strong and the way his touch and every action had made her feel cherished for the first time in her life, like she had a partner who could defend her. But no one could fight her battles for her or shelter her from her past, from her present. The present she needed to address now. Or she would lose her sister.

She needed to call Al's lawyer friend back. Tell him that they needed to figure something out. Tell him she definitely wanted custody of her sister. Today, her mom still had custody. Her only option was to convince her mom to let Emery stay with her for the whole school year. Maybe she could remind her mother how much she hated living with teenagers. She could convince her and then worry about custody later.

"God, I know I'm still figuring you out again. I still sometimes feel like You didn't protect me as a kid. But I know that's not true. Could you maybe provide a miracle so that I can protect Emery? Maybe give her something better than what I experienced?"

No one answered her but she hadn't expected it. She summoned the energy to crawl from bed. She needed to find her sister. She needed to deal with her mother. And she needed to trust that God was a good Father, even though her world was crashing around her.

She opened her bedroom door and padded into the living room, noticing Emery's door slightly ajar. "Em? You up? We need to talk."

Casey stopped in the living room, taking in her small house. No Emery watching Netflix and eating a bowl of cereal. No Emery in the bathroom doing her makeup. No loud music blaring from her room. She stalked over to Emery's door, knocking before entering the shadows. "Em? You awake?"

The feather gray, down comforter drooped haphazardly. No Emery in sight. Responsibility one over the holidays: teach Emery to make her bed and help with chores around the house.

Casey came to a standstill in the living room again. She wasn't here. She padded into the kitchen for coffee. Needing a shot of caffeine before she fully panicked. Emery might have walked down to Mama Rosie's or met up with Bianca to practice cheerleading. She probably had a text waiting on her phone. Coffee brewing, she hurried back to her room.

Dead. She'd been too preoccupied to plug in her phone last night. She plugged it into the charger and returned for coffee while she waited for an initial charge. A folded white sheet of paper caught her eye underneath the kitchen table. She scooped it off the floor and unfolded the note.

I heard Mom last night, and I can't go home with her, Case. Please just make her leave.
I need to stay away until she's gone. I'll call you later. Em

"Oh, Emery, where did you go?" Casey groaned. If her mom found out she didn't know the whereabouts of her little sister, she would use it against her. Even if their mother never knew where Emery was half the time either.

Casey ran back into her room. Three percent charge. She could work with that. She plopped down on her floor and dialed her sister.

No answer.

"C'mon, Em."

She dialed again.

Straight to voicemail.

She shot off a text. *Em, you need to call and tell me where you are. Right now!*

No answer. Casey wanted to pace but she couldn't unplug her phone. She chewed her nail, her eyes glued to her screen. She was sure everything was fine. Emery was just being dramatic. Casey was overreacting.

She wished she could call Micah. Wished he would tell her everything was okay and help her find Emery. But that wasn't his job. And he was probably long gone by now.

He hadn't even tried to contact her.

A text came through. But not from Emery.

I'm leaving my hotel and will be at your house in ten minutes. Have Emery ready. I want to get on the road.

Casey groaned. There was no way her mother would listen to reason, not since she drove all the way to Dallas just to get Emery.

Emery, please text me back.

Within seconds, a text came through. *Help. Ellie's.*

What in the world? Casey ran around her room, throwing

clothes on. She glanced at her phone. Twenty percent battery. It would have to be enough.

She grabbed her keys and her wallet and darted out the door, Coleman's threats pounding like a drum in her mind.

Coleman wouldn't have acted on his threats, would he? Not at Ellie's Place. Not right now.

But a gnawing feeling in her stomach sent her speeding down the street. If Coleman was at Ellie's and was upset and high again, there's no telling what he would do.

And Emery might just be in the crosshairs.

The pain spreading through Micah's chest with every mile he drove felt worse than any pain he'd experienced at Hell Week, worse than any bullet. And he was only five miles out. The emptiness grew and with it an ache as if a core piece of his person had been ripped from him.

He'd told her he loved her.

She'd sent him away.

True to pattern. He hurt those on his team. The one thing he wanted most he could never have. Micah moved another inch in the bumper-to-bumper traffic. Another wreck clogging the Dallas highways, probably from another idiot on his cell phone. Micah rested his head on his fist. Temperatures had dropped over night, and the heater in Old Faithful worked over time to keep him warm.

Another inch. Another inch toward his last goodbye to his buddy, Juan Tanehill. Juan always said his name was a tribute to both sides of his heritage—his first name unabashedly claiming his Mexican roots and his last name a nod to his staunchly British father. Juan had just been himself—quirky, strong, and totally in love with his wife, Whitney.

Micah wished Juan had been around to meet his baby girl.

He'd been so excited, and he was gone before he ever met her. Though Micah was trying to remember Juan's death wasn't his fault, the grief still weighed heavy.

That's one thing he looked forward to about heaven. No more mistakes or pain.

And no more goodbyes.

He longed for that one more—no goodbyes. Ever again. Forever with his Father, family, and team, at least those who had trusted Christ so far. He and Nick were still working on the rest. Well, Nick was now. Micah didn't feel like he belonged anymore, even though Jay, Colt, and Titus had all tried to call him, as well as other buddies from SEAL Team 2.

He thought of Casey again and scooted another inch, his gigantic steel bumper threatening to slaughter the Volkswagen bug in front of him.

Silence.

He couldn't handle it anymore. He punched the dial to his newly replaced radio. 96.3 KSCS country smothered the quiet, the morning talk show hosts cutting up over some segment called "Second Date Update." He settled into the pending train wreck as the hosts talked with a girl who refused to go on a second date with some guy, all over a misunderstanding. Micah felt the guy's pain. Few things in life messed with a man more than the rejection of a girl he cared enough to try for.

He thought he'd found in Casey someone he would die for.

Now he'd never see her again. At some point, he had to take the hint and stop fighting for something she clearly didn't want. She kept trying to tell him. But he just hadn't listened. He would respect her this time. It was time to go.

His phone rang and his sister's name flashed on the screen. He debated not answering, but she would just keep calling, something she'd made a hobby since he'd left California. Run. He'd run from California. Like he was running again, even though he'd wanted to stay.

"Hey, Kayles. I'm fine. Everything's fine. Texas is fine."

"Well hello to you, too. I didn't ask any of those things. Maybe I was calling to tell you that Sandy caught another crab."

"Did he get pinched again?"

"Yeah... that's not why I'm calling. But he did catch another crab and he didn't get pinched this time, so maybe he's learning."

Kaylan had found her mutt on a morning run several years back and adopted him. The guy loved the sand, and crabs were his weakness. Micah smirked and propped his arm on the windowsill. Traffic finally broke. Rubberneckers slowing down over a minor fender bender.

"Why'd you call, Kayles?"

She ignored him. "Where ya headed?"

"Does Nick have you doing surveillance right now? I told you marrying a Navy SEAL was dangerous. I really should have talked you out of it."

"You were the number one person talking me into it. And you are hedging. Spill, Micah Matthew Richards. Where are you headed?"

"How do you know I'm headed anywhere?"

His sister fell quiet. Sandy barked in the background. He heard Nick shushing the animal. Of course, his best friend was nearby. "Kayles..."

"I know you are headed somewhere because I can hear it in your voice. You're running. Again." Her silence descended before she blurted, "And I stalked you on Find-a-Friend."

"I'm deleting that app as soon as we hang up." Micah groaned and sped around a black Mercedes. Dallasites had money, that was for sure. Just not where Casey chose to make her home.

"Where are you headed, Micah?"

He knew he couldn't dodge her anymore. He exited the highway and pulled into a Love's gas station. Mama Rosie's truck guzzled gas, and he didn't want the almost empty truck to die on the way to Fort Worth. No more breakdowns and no more reasons to prolong the inevitable any longer. He would return the truck after this trip and catch a plane to Alabama. He would figure life out from there. Maybe coaching. He'd enjoyed that.

"I'm on my way to see Whitney." He pulled under the awning and threw his truck into park.

"Micah."

"It's the last one, Sis." He turned the key and leaned against the wheel.

"Don't do this, Micah. Don't go alone."

"I need to go."

"No, you don't."

"Yes, I do." He snapped.

"Why?"

Trust her to match him step for step. She'd been doing it since they were little. "You know why, Kayles."

"It wasn't your fault, Micah."

"If I hadn't irritated that old injury. If I hadn't . . ." No matter how much people told him it wasn't his fault, it still felt like it.

"That's enough, Bulldog."

Micah straightened as his best friend's voice came on the line, commanding and leaving no room for argument.

"This is not your burden to bear alone. Let us do it with you, Bulldog. We fight together. We die together. We grieve together. We keep fighting."

"I'm not one of you anymore, Nick." Micah didn't belong anywhere anymore. Not even in Dallas.

"You will always belong, Micah. Always a SEAL, remember? You've told guys that before."

"Micah, please. Nick and I can fly down and go with you if you really feel like you need to do this. Please."

"Sis, I . . ."

His phone beeped, signaling anther call. "My Girl." He'd changed her name on his phone three nights ago. Why was she calling? She'd made her feelings for him clear. But maybe she'd changed her mind?

"Micah?"

He was running out of time. He couldn't hurt Casey anymore if he didn't answer. He didn't want to hurt anymore, either. But that name. Her face. The wall crumbling and possibility shining in those big brown eyes.

"Sis, I'll call you back."

He punched the button at the last second. "Casey."

Nothing.

Did she chicken out?

"Casey?"

He waited and counted to ten.

"I'm hanging up . . ."

"Coleman, just put the gun down and let's talk about this." Casey's voice sounded far away. Micah froze.

Casey was in trouble. And he wasn't there to help.

CHAPTER 21

Casey whipped into the parking lot of Ellie's Place, her heart rate climbing to unhealthy levels. Coleman's car sat front and center, along with TJ's and Casey's bikes, which she was sure Emery had borrowed. She relaxed slightly. Despite their past make-out session, TJ wouldn't let anything happen to Emery. But she wondered why he'd come back to Ellie's Place so early on a Sunday. Why would Emery send a text for help if she was with TJ? Unless this had to do with what TJ had said the other day. Unless Coleman...

A longing for Micah swept through her as she sprinted from the car to the front door. He would be by her side if she hadn't pushed him away.

It was too late now. He was probably far from Dallas and happy to be out of her life by now. But the look on his face as he'd walked away last night. She'd taken his story and thrown it back in his face. She hadn't had his back. She'd stabbed it. And accused him of hurting her in the process. She'd only hurt herself. All because she couldn't let people in.

Casey slowed as she neared the front door and tested the handle. Unlocked.

She held onto the door until it closed softly behind her. Elevated voices carried down the hall.

"TJ, stop it." Emery.

A harsh tone silenced her. Coleman.

Casey's heart rate took off at a gallop. Something wasn't right.

She padded down the hallway, forcing herself to walk on tiptoes. She didn't know why. She was the adult. She should be able to barge in and take care of the situation. But something warned her to proceed with caution. This wasn't a situation to charge into.

The yelling grew louder behind her closed office door halfway down the hall. Casey hugged the wall and crept closer, mindful of the window allowing people to see in from the hallway. Normally she kept the blinds pulled if she was having a serious conversation, but today they were open, giving her a view of the room. She kept her back flat. Deep breaths. No time to panic.

TJ stood in front of the couch where Emery sat, a gun pointed at her. His hand shook and she'd never seen his eyes so big. He shifted back and forth on his feet, casting quick glances over his shoulder every few seconds. He didn't look angry.

He looked scared.

Casey shifted to study her sister, careful to keep her back to the wall and remain out of sight. Mascara ran in tracks down Emery's face. Her chin quivered. She sat in a ball on the couch, hugging her legs, her eyes glued to the gun rattling in TJ's hand. Anger flooded Casey. What was TJ doing? She'd thought she heard...

Coleman came into view as he stalked to the bookshelf tucked next to the couch. Books and frames scattered to the floor as he dug around and behind them. Searching for something.

"Where are they, TJ? Where did you hide them?"

With a sinking feeling, the dots connected. TJ's anxiety. His nod to Coleman on the court. His quick exit. Coleman's search. Emery's tear-stained face. TJ had been running drugs for Coleman. When he had decided he couldn't fulfill his task, he'd hidden them. Most likely at Ellie's—the one place he deemed safe.

And Coleman thought Casey had them.

One more reason in a string of reasons for him to hate Casey. And one more reason Casey knew she could no longer handle this on her own. She could call the police but TJ might go to jail. She should call the police. She fumbled for her phone, removing it from her pocket with shaky fingers.

Her hands rattled and sweat slicked her palms. "C'mon, unlock." She managed to punch in her code and pull up her keypad. She took a deep breath, trying to quell the shaking. Emery screamed. Coleman stood over her, leering, a fistful of her hair gripped in his hand. Tears ran thick down her face.

The phone slipped from her hand and rattled across the tile floor. Casey dove for it, but too late.

The office door swung open, crashing into the wall with a bang just as her hand wrapped around her phone.

"Well, what do we have here?"

Her fingers flew, and she redialed the last call she'd made and prayed it went through. Micah. Need for him swept through her. He would know what to do. But after the way she'd treated him, she had no idea if he would come.

A hand gripped the back of her neck and yanked her to her feet. The cold press of metal ground into her temple. She sucked in a breath and prayed.

Coleman had a gun, too.

"Casey, talk to me," Micah ground out.

"You don't have to do this. Just put the gun down, Coleman."

"And why would I do that? I warned you to leave well enough alone." Coleman's voice sounded all too close to the receiver.

Micah smashed the phone against his ear. "Tell me where you are, Case. Give me a clue," he muttered.

"Just let TJ and Emery go. I'll give you what you want. But it's not in my office. I can't hide that stuff at Ellie's." Micah heard Casey plead, her voice muffled.

"Casey, don't tell him that. He'll kill you."

TJ's voice.

What was TJ doing there?

Micah hit speaker and dropped the phone in his lap. He had less than a quarter tank left but he could get back to Ellie's Place. The engine roared to life, surging and waiting for his command.

He could text Shawn. Have him meet him at Ellie's. But what if Shawn got hurt? What if Casey or TJ got hurt because Micah went in to try and help and just messed everything up?

"Stop talking to her!" Micah heard Coleman shout.

Something slapped hard next to the phone. Casey groaned.

He heard shuffling. Then, "Well what do we have here? Who's this?" Coleman. His words slurred, his tone dripped with venom. Micah didn't answer, hoping the kid was too high to figure it out.

"No cops, or I shoot them all."

The line went dead.

The engine roared. The tires squealed as he sped from the parking lot and back onto the access road. With no traffic going that direction, he could be at Ellie's in five minutes.

A lot could happen in five minutes. A lot could happen when he got there. But he was their only option. He wouldn't risk calling the police until he arrived, wouldn't risk Casey. He only prayed that he could save her before it was too late.

Four minutes out. The ache in his chest began to seal as he closed the miles.

He'd never been the guy to sit on the sidelines. He couldn't leave the woman he loved in harm's way without doing something, and he wouldn't let someone else have the job of protecting her.

That was his job. And it was time to fight for that role in her life.

"I'm coming, Casey. Hang on."

He shot a text to Shawn and sped around traffic.

He refused to think about the last time an enemy had him in their sights.

He had more to lose this time, and he was finished saying goodbye to people he loved.

CHAPTER 22

Casey's phone was gone, and she had no idea if help was on the way. She should have called 911, no matter what. But Micah had been the first person a phone call away.

He was the only one she trusted to help her out of this. And now he might not even come.

It was up to her to get them out alive.

She just had to figure something out. Anything.

The grip on her neck intensified, pain shooting down to her spine, Coleman's grip tightening as he muscled her across the room. She winced.

"Next to your sister, Teach." Coleman tossed her down on the couch. Her head cracked into Emery's shoulder. She righted herself and ignored her pounding headache.

Coleman leered over them, his gun pointed at TJ now. Without moving his eyes from Casey, he slurred at TJ. "Raise your gun and point it at Teach's sister here. You're all going to do exactly what I say."

Casey squeezed her sister's hand and remained silent, her mind racing. She could rush Coleman, hopefully knock his grip on the gun, but it might fire and hit TJ. TJ would never hold a gun on Emery without Coleman's prompting. But there was no way she could take Coleman out. He was nearly twice her size and hard living made him scrappier. She'd only get someone shot. Even high, he was still pretty steady on his feet.

She'd have to outsmart him.

"Where's my package?" He swung his gun wildly around the wrecked office. One of the shelves hung off the wall attached only by one side, glass littering the floor near the bookcase and her desk. Supplies lay strewn across the rug between the couch and chairs. One bookshelf lay broken on its side. He'd searched thoroughly.

"Did you hear me, Teach?" His swung the gun wildly in her direction. "I said, where's my package?" Spit flew from his mouth and his eyes grew wide, highlighting a deepening bruise beneath his right eye and spreading to his cheek.

High. Angry. And most likely scared for his own life. His voice rose, motions grew more erratic as he paced in front of them, eyes darting around the room.

"I don't have it, Coleman."

She tried to catch TJ's eye, but the teenager was frozen, his eyes blinking wildly at Coleman, the gun shaking in his hand the only movement. Casey worried he would accidentally pull the trigger if startled.

"Then where is it?" Coleman screamed. His hand pointing the gun punctuated every word. Casey feared he would lose control and squeeze the trigger.

"She doesn't have it, Coleman. I told you that."

"You stay quiet, you little thief." Coleman pressed the barrel against TJ's forehead. "I saw you talking to her the other day. I know you told her."

"I swear, I didn't tell her nothing." TJ's chest pumped air in and out.

"Liar!" He ground the gun in. TJ cringed, nearly dropping his own gun.

"Did I say you could stop holding the gun on your little girlfriend?" Coleman jerked TJ's arm level with Emery. Casey darted up from the couch and stepped in front of her baby sister.

"Sit back down, Teach." Coleman swung to face her. Casey tensed.

"Just let us go. You don't want to do this, Coleman."

"I have to do this! You, he, both of you took something that doesn't belong to you. I need it back. Now."

"She doesn't have it, C." TJ trembled, his gun now fixed on Casey. Emery huddled behind Casey's back on the couch. Her silent whimper drawing Coleman's attention.

Casey lurched forward. "But I know where it is."

The whites of TJ's eyes widened. Coleman spun around, and TJ began shaking his head.

Casey willed him to be quiet, but he ignored her. "We don't know. It's gone. We don't know. She doesn't know. Let them go, Coleman. Let them go."

Shut up, TJ. She had to get Coleman out of the room, out of a place he controlled, away from TJ so that he and Emery could get away and call the police.

"Someone better start talking now!" he roared.

"I took it, and hid it. It's not in here, Coleman." She held out her hands. "TJ didn't know. He never knew. You can let them go. I'm the only one who knows where your package is."

Coleman advanced on Casey, the barrel of the gun smashing into her chest and grinding into the skin over her heart. He towered over her, his voice a deadly whisper, "You have thirty seconds to tell me where, or I tell TJ to shoot your sister, and I doubt he's a good shot. The clock starts now. One . . ."

Micah screeched into the parking lot, his wheels spinning and truck bed swinging before snapping into line with his trajectory. He slammed the brakes next to Shawn's car and hopped out of the truck. The calm of battle wrapped around him, but inside, panic clawed at the calm. The last time he'd walked out of a war zone, his friends hadn't gone home with him. This time, he wasn't chasing after his friends.

This was the woman he loved.

Micah was prepared to die for her, but terror told him that this attempt to rescue would fail, and she wouldn't walk out of the school today.

"What's going on?" Shawn appeared at his side the moment the truck stopped.

Micah threw open the back door and stretched under the seat for his hand gun and a clip. He quickly popped the clip in, switched off the safety, and turned to face Shawn.

"Whoa, Micah, what's going on?"

"I need you to call the police. Tell them we have a potential hostage situation with at least one minor and the center counselor."

"Whoa, slow down. What?"

Micah shot Shawn a look. "I can't answer everything. I have to get in there. Tell them to come with sirens silent or people will die. Tell them a Navy SEAL is inside and armed. You got it?"

Shawn paused for a beat before grabbing his phone and punching buttons.

Micah heard two short rings before the operator took the call. Satisfied, he moved to the end of the truck bed, using the steel as a shield while he surveyed the building. Shawn rattled off details behind him and ended the call as Micah began to move in a silent jog toward the building.

The crunch of gravel behind him told him Shawn was hot on

his heels. Micah crouched behind a trash can near the door and motioned Shawn behind him.

"You need to stay out here."

"There is no way. I'm going in with you."

Micah surveyed the front door. Quiet. Everything was quiet. Too quiet. He hoped he wasn't too late. He wasn't exactly sure who was armed and how many were inside. He knew at least Coleman, TJ, and Casey from the little he picked up on the phone. But either way, he would need help. He needed a team. But one more person with him meant the potential of one more person hurt.

"You can't do this alone, man."

Micah didn't have time to debate. Didn't have time to figure out ten scenarios. He had minutes. Time was too precious. Casey was too precious.

He nodded at Shawn. "At least one person has a gun. Let me handle that. I need you to make sure Casey, TJ, and anyone else in there are safe."

Micah could see a thousand questions churning in Shawn's eyes, but he stayed quiet. Micah's respect for the coach rose.

"I'll follow your lead. Let's get them out."

With a quick nod, Micah moved to the front door, tested the handle, and slipped through silently, Shawn right behind them.

Casey's office. He took a quick turn down the first hall, pistol ready, heart pounding, but calm had finally descended. He wasn't alone. And this wasn't his last op. He would get Casey out.

Familiar rhythms took over as he assessed every way out of the building. The window in Casey's office overlooking the basketball court, an emergency door at the end of the hallway. But his biggest focus was how to stop a drugged teenager from hurting several other people.

His heart beat in his ears as he neared Casey's door, the only place he heard voices in the quiet halls.

"Twenty!" Coleman shouted. "I'm starting to think you may be lying, too, Teach."

Through the window, Micah could see the back of Coleman's head as he towered over Casey. Her mouth was set in a grim line, her face pale but determined. TJ hunched next to Coleman, a gun shaking in his hands, the barrel now angling to the floor.

"Two guns," he whispered back to Shawn, his soft voice sounding loud in the tiled hallway. He shifted closer to the door. Casey's eye flashed toward him. She stiffened, immediately swinging her focus back to Coleman.

"It's outside," he heard her say.

"I need a location, Teach. No more excuses. Twenty-five."

Casey raised her hands higher. Micah could tell she was fighting panic. He prepared to go into the room. He didn't want to shoot Coleman. He didn't want to shoot anyone ever again, but to protect someone he loved, Micah wouldn't hesitate.

"I swear, Coleman. It's in the mentor's lounge. I hid it in the back of one of the cabinets."

"And you expect me to believe that?" He shoved the gun harder into her chest, right over her heart. "Someone would have found it. Twenty-seven."

"No." Her voice was near frantic. "It's on a top shelf over the fridge in the very back corner in an old tin. No one stores anything up there. It's too hard to reach."

"You better not be lying."

The counting had stopped. Micah didn't know what that was all about, but he didn't want to wait around for the magic number.

"Here's the plan, Teach."

Micah strained to hear, his eyes fixed on Casey as he hugged the wall. TJ stood frozen taking it all in while Emery cowered behind Casey.

"You and I are going to walk out of here. Ladies first, of

course." Micah could hear the sneer in his voice masking the slight slur. "We're going to this lounge. You are going to give me what I want. If we aren't back here in three minutes, TJ here is going to shoot your sister, or I'm going to make sure I shoot him the next time I see him. And if he runs, I know where his family lives." Coleman swung around to eye TJ, his gun still leveled on Casey, hand shaking.

TJ only nodded. Micah heard Emery's squeal as Coleman grabbed Casey's arm and yanked her in front of his large body. "Walk, Teach."

Micah had seconds. He pushed into Shawn, the two of them silently backing up a few steps. He prayed Shawn wouldn't respond, that he would focus on the plan and get Casey out of the way. Micah had one shot to take Coleman down and limited mobility in the small hallway built for elementary age children. He crouched, counting the footsteps edging closer to the door. Casey's face appeared, her eyes darting and landing on him. Micah nodded to his left just as Coleman appeared in the doorframe.

Coleman yelled and swung his gun. Casey dove to the side, crashing into the wall as Micah knocked into Coleman in one swift move. With steady hands, he shoved the gun to the ceiling. It fired, plaster raining down on them and a sprinkler head bursting.

Micah wrestled Coleman to the ground, twisting his wrist and tossing the gun. It skittered down the hall and lay still. Micah knelt over Coleman, gun drawn and steady, pointed at his heaving chest. Water rained down as alarms blared.

Coleman had almost shot Casey.

Rage pulsed through Micah. He couldn't move. Couldn't speak. Could only stare at the teenager sprawled beneath him, hands held in surrender, defeat wilting his once angry features.

"Don't shoot, Coach. Don't shoot. I never would have hurt them, just don't shoot."

"Micah."

Casey wrapped a hand around his arm, still holding steady on Coleman. "Micah, he's just a kid. Don't hurt him."

Just a kid.

A teenager with a bruised eye, drugs in his system, and refusal to listen to anyone telling him he had other options. A kid who had bought the lie of the war he lived in, thinking he would never find a way out, didn't want a way out. A kid who hurt others because he had been hurt. A kid making bad choices. A kid stuck in a bad cycle.

A kid like the teenager who had pulled the trigger and killed his friends.

Micah lowered his arm, his chest still heaving. He could see it. The teenager, hauling the launcher on his shoulder, an older man yelling at his side. More yelling. And then fire.

A kid.

Micah hadn't killed his friends. Someone had. And it had been a kid just like Coleman, being pushed by an adult who didn't give him another option.

"Micah."

Micah slowly pushed to his feet, moving back a few steps, his eyes never leaving Coleman. His memory saw a different moment, one that could be different if someone helped kids caught in war zones not of their own making know there was a better way.

"Police!" a man shouted, and the sound of boots on tile echoed down the hall.

Micah placed his gun on the floor, wrapped his arm around Casey, and held his other high.

An officer appeared at his side, taking in Coleman on the floor, Shawn now standing with TJ, and a crying Emery rushing to Casey's side. "Are you the SEAL?"

"Yes, sir."

"What happened here?"

"Casey can fill you in." Micah rubbed the back of his neck and looked down at Casey, her body leaning into his all the reassurance he needed that things were okay and that he would handle this however she chose. "We'll make sure we get you all the details."

Casey shot a look to the officer taking the gun from TJ and asking him questions and then down to Coleman now being hauled up and handcuffed by another officer.

Micah rubbed circles on her back, offering a smile at Emery over Casey's head. She was okay. Everyone was okay.

Casey was safe, and Micah didn't plan to let her go.

CHAPTER 23

Sirens flashed and a few neighbors gathered behind the yellow police tape as police moved from Micah to Shawn to Casey to Emery and TJ asking questions and recording answers. Through it all, Casey kept her arm firmly around her sister, scanning the crowd for the moment her mother would appear, truly see her as unfit, and take Emery away.

Forever.

"I'm glad you came," Emery mumbled into Casey's shoulder. Casey squeezed her tighter.

"Always, Em. You hear me?" She gently nudged her sister so she could see her face. "Always."

Casey hated the tear tracks, but she would take them any day over her sister lying in one of the ambulances. Or TJ. Or even Coleman. Everyone got out safe.

Thanks to Micah. Thanks to her warrior.

To think she'd almost let her pride push Micah out of her life for good.

Micah sauntered up to the bench where Casey and Emery sat just outside the doors of Ellie's Place and bent down on eye level. He did a quick scan of Casey, and she offered him a small smile. He slipped his fingers in her free hand and turned to her sister, resting a hand on Emery's arm. "How ya doing there, Champ?"

"I'm thinking you've got to be insane to choose a job that involves facing bad guys with guns." She shuddered. "But I'm also thinking you're pretty brave. I could never do what you did. Thank you."

"Sure you could, Em. And I'll tell you a secret." He wagged a finger her way, motioning her closer. Casey grinned and leaned in with her sister.

"I was terrified," he whispered.

"You're joking."

"Not even a little bit."

"How come I couldn't tell?"

"Here's the secret, Emery. It's not really about bravery. It's about the people you have at your side, your back, and in front of you. And you . . ." his brown eyes drifted to Casey and that smirk she loved so much lit up his face. "You, kid, have a pretty incredible team."

Casey tightened her hold on Micah's hand, tears pricking her eyes. For the first time, she saw total peace in his gaze. And he'd reminded her of something, too. She needed people next to her, behind her, and before her, too. And she had that. She just didn't always let them play the part. Something she would be fixing in the days ahead, starting with the man in front of her.

"Yeah, Casey's pretty great. Too bad . . ."

"Casey Stewart, there was a gun pointed at my baby? A gun?" Mona Rodriguez came charging across the parking lot, tripping over cracks in her stilettos and flowing, leopard print dress, complete with dramatic coat.

Teagan and Shawn left their post talking to TJ's mom and grandma and rushed to Casey, TJ quickly following. A couple of officers turned to acknowledge her mother. Across the parking lot, Al's focus shifted to Casey and her tornado of a family reunion. He ended his conversation with an officer, his long legs eating up the concrete as he approached. "What's the problem, Mona?"

"Don't Mona me, you child stealer. You probably started her on this crusade." She came to a stop in front of their gathered group, all huddled around Casey. Her team. Micah slowly rose and stood next to her, her hand still firmly clasped in his. Their team.

"Mona, calm down. I didn't steal Casey from you, and she isn't trying to steal Emery or put her in harm's way. This was just an unfortunate situation." Al tried to place a soothing hand on Mona's arm, but she jerked away.

"She rescued Emery, Mrs. Rodriguez. She's taking great care of Emery." Teagan chimed in, resting her hand on Casey's shoulder.

"How is this taking good care of her? There are police all around." She reached for Emery. "Come on, Emery. We're going home."

"I don't want to go home, Mom. I really want to stay with Casey." Emery peaked from behind her sister.

"Look what you've done to her. Officer," Mona motioned over the nearest man in blue. "I demand you arrest my daughter. She almost got my baby shot and now she's trying to steal her from me."

Officer Donal's gaze volleyed from their group to Mona. "Are you talking about Casey here? Ma'am, she's one of the few people that makes this neighborhood better. She didn't almost get your daughter shot. Another fool kid did that." Officer Donal smiled in Casey's direction. "In my opinion, Emery has some of the best people looking out for her in this part of Texas, ma'am."

"Ugh. Do not call me ma'am." Mona pinched the bridge of

her nose. "How do I know she's going to be okay here? You've never raised a child before, Casey."

Al stepped forward, tucking his hands in his pockets and cutting off any reply Casey could have made. "With all due respect, Mona. In the short time Emery has been here, my understanding is that her grades are up, she is making friends, she is helping her friends, and she is helping around the house."

Casey smirked at Emery's grimace. They were still working on that last one. But everything else Al said was true. Emery had changed from a sullen teenager to an eager learner, a compassionate friend, and a sweet, if not a little sassy, young lady.

Clearly, they had experienced a few hiccups. She cast a quick glance at TJ. He stood with his hand on Emery's shoulder. He'd apologized profusely as soon as Coleman was in handcuffs, begging Casey and Emery to forgive him and not hate him.

"Emery is thriving here, Mrs. Rodriguez." Shawn stepped next to Micah, crossing his arms over his chest. Casey knew it took a lot for him to be respectful with her mother.

But it was Micah who took another step toward a now dumbfounded Mona. "Your daughter is incredible, Mona. Both of them are. But Casey is a protector, defender. She is kind and passionate, even if a little feisty at times." Casey dug her nails into his hand from a step behind him.

Micah chuckled and shot her a wink before turning to face her mother again. "She loves Emery, and she only got a lawyer involved so she can understand the legal ramifications of not having full custody of Emery should she need to make a decision on her behalf."

"But," Mona's voice sounded weak even to Casey, "Emery's my daughter."

"Mom." Casey stepped to Micah's side, wrapping her free hand around his arm. "I love my sister. I'm going to take good care of her. But we both know you don't like having teenagers around. Why not let her stay with me? I don't want to fight you for her."

Mona's gaze darted person to person surrounding Casey. Casey was overwhelmed by the love she felt from this group. Behind her, beside her, and before her. Just like Micah said. And it was their support that finally convinced Mona to cave.

"She can stay." She shuffled a step back, her shoe unsteady on the broken concrete. "She can stay as long as you acknowledge I'm still her mother. And I want her to come home every once in a while."

This time, Casey stepped forward and made herself reach for her mom's hand. She couldn't remember the last time her mother had touched her. But she could do this for Emery. For herself. "You will always be her—our—mother. I'll send her home for some of the holidays. Maybe I'll even come for a few days."

Mona offered a twisted smile. "Well I do think you should come home. You haven't seen all the changes I've made to the bar."

Casey bit back a groan. She would never have a mother who truly parented. But she could still love her mother. God hadn't given up on Casey after years of pushing Him away. Casey could figure out how to fight for the woman before her. "You're right, Mom. I haven't been home in a while. It's past time."

Mona pulled her hand back and took a few more steps before turning to walk away. She cast one more look over her shoulder. "You're different, Casey-girl." Her eyes roamed over Casey's friends again. Her family. "You sure have made a home for yourself."

Casey took her place next to Micah, slipping her hand into his. "It's Emery's too. As long as she wants it, and as long as you are okay with it." She would deal with custody if she needed to. Right now, she would count Emery staying as a win. It might be better to have peace and later conversations with her mother than push too hard right now.

With a nod, her mother turned and hurried to her car. Her friends and family erupted in conversation, pulling Emery into hugs, checking on TJ. But Casey had eyes only for the man who had pulled her into his arms.

"You really have let this God thing change you, beautiful. You handled your mother with more kindness and respect than she has earned."

Casey bounced onto her toes and slipped her arms around Micah's neck. "I think we need to stop calling it *this God thing*. He is a good Father who gives good gifts to His children. And sometimes," she ruffled her fingers through the hair brushing Micah's neck, "when the hard things hit, He brings good through those, too. Even when it's more difficult to spot."

Micah placed a feather-light kiss on her nose. "Nailed it, Ace. Does this mean, you and I are okay? You don't want me to leave?"

Her grip around his neck tightened. "I'm so sorry, Micah. I didn't mean it. I want you to stay more than anything."

He kissed her cheek. "Good. This thing we have here . . ." He kissed her other cheek. "Is pretty good, too."

Without waiting for him, Casey met his lips with hers. Micah Richards was a gift. The people around her were a gift. And a God who gave second chances to children who doubted His character, that was a pretty big gift, too.

Casey tugged the blanket tighter around her shoulders and curled her cold fingers around her coffee mug. She loved the warmth of Mama Rosie's kitchen. More than anything, she loved the people around her. Micah sat next to her, his body relaxed, one hand on her leg and the other nursing his own coffee mug. She liked him like this. Confident in his surroundings, any lingering traces of doubt gone.

Mama Rosie sat a plate of chocolate chip cookies fresh from the oven in the middle of the table and then sat down across from Casey, Emery and TJ on either side of her. She cupped Emery's cheek saying something in Spanish to soothe the girl before resting a hand on TJ's back. "My babies are all safe and home now. Don't scare me like that again."

They all nodded. Micah passed out the cookies, offering one to Casey last with a smile that held a thousand promises. After all her running and retreating, pushing him away, and then calling him in her worst moment, he'd showed up.

And he'd been willing to jump in-between her and a gun.

She couldn't, wouldn't lose this man. She didn't know how to be in a relationship like this, but she wanted to learn. Micah slipped his fingers through hers. "Don't you ever do that to *me* again. I think that is one of the worst phone calls I've ever received."

"You've had worse than knowing your girlfriend was on the other end of a gun?" TJ asked, chomping down on a cookie.

Micah's eyes landed on Casey. "That one was probably the worst but only by a little." The butterflies took flight. They were definitely butterflies, and they loved Micah.

She loved Micah.

The acknowledgement warmed every part of her.

"What ranked next?" TJ continued.

"Probably the phone call we got that my sister was in the Haiti earthquake and we couldn't get ahold of her."

"Your sister was in the earthquake?" Emery's eyes bugged out of her head. "Did she make it?"

Micah nodded. "She made it. My best friend and I went in to find her. Then we got a phone call that a terrorist was stalking her."

"You what?" Emery choked on her cookie.

"No way. What'd you do?" TJ gawked.

"I've got mad skills." Micah winked at TJ and Emery. Casey planned to ask him for details later.

"Did you kill him?"

His smile bore the weight of a secret. "Not exactly. But Kaylan is no longer being stalked. She is safe, happy, and now married to my best friend."

Emery sighed, a sappy look on her face. The same sappy look she'd had since Casey had kissed Micah in front of Ellie's Place. Casey was learning that her sister just might be a closet romantic, too.

"Well I never want a day like that ever again. It is not good for my heart. And you, young man . . ." Mama Rosie pointed at TJ. "If you ever resort to running drugs before you ask for help again and I find out about it, I will personally lock you in my basement and throw away the key. Understand?"

TJ sat up straight. "Mama Rosie, you don't have a basement." But there was a question in his tone.

"That's what you think. I got skills, too."

He gulped and Casey bit her lip. TJ might be safer in prison than if Mama Rosie got hold of him again. Mama Rosie had shown up at the school as the police finished interviewing TJ. Coleman had been taken into custody. The police had found drugs in his car. After searching the exterior of Ellie's, the police found TJ's package in a different location than he originally thought. Under pressure, it seemed TJ had forgotten and looked in the wrong place. Casey was thankful her mom had left before the big drug reveal.

"You just remember that we're your family." Mama Rosie gripped TJ's chin in her weathered, brown hand. "That means we help one another. If you hurt, we hurt. No more doing things on your own, sí?"

"Sí, Mama Rosie." He nodded.

Her gnarled fingers smoothed his dark brow, and her smile

split her face into a million wrinkles—a sign of moments spent smiling and days spent in the sun with her kids.

Casey leaned into Micah, seeking his touch. She hadn't grown up here, but the Lord knew what He was doing when she'd met Al during college. He'd introduced her to Mama Rosie, introduced her to Ellie's. She'd found a home, a purpose.

A family.

Micah placed a gentle kiss against her hair. She curled closer into him, watching Mama Rosie fuss and fawn over her little sister.

And God had brought her Micah, too. He was everything she'd never admitted she wanted and more.

"I'm glad you're staying."

His fingers traced lazy circles on her arms, but his silence hung heavy.

She twisted in his arms so she could get a good look at his face. Despite his relaxed demeanor, she could still see something lingering in his dark eyes, something unresolved.

"You are leaving."

She began to pull away from him, but he held her still. Micah wound fingers through her hair, playing with the tangled strands while Mama Rosie shooed TJ and Emery into her living room for a movie.

"About that. It seems we both have a dilemma on our hands. If I'm staying, then I need a job. And I believe you're looking for a coach. I think we may just be able to solve one another's problems."

Casey tapped her chin. "Well it doesn't pay much, and your kids may be a little rough around the edges, but you will have excellent coworkers." She scanned him up and down. "It's official. You're hired!"

Micah chuckled. "I look forward to working with you, Boss."

"I like that nickname."

"Don't get used to it." His smile dimmed a bit, and he grew quiet.

"Micah, what is it?"

"I was on my way to Fort Worth today when I got your call."

Casey nodded, slipping her fingers over his chest, the texture of his t-shirt cool against her palms. "Your last goodbye."

"The last one."

"When are you going now?"

"Next Saturday. I texted Whitney when we got to Mama Rosie's to make sure." His fingers wound through her hair, but Casey could tell his mind stared at a different day, one that had been coming since before he set foot in Dallas.

"I realized probably for the first time today that I wasn't responsible for their deaths, but I was still slow, still hurt, still not all I needed to be in that moment. And what I don't understand is why God didn't take me instead of them."

"Micah..."

"It's not survivor's guilt, Case. I just miss my friends. I wish I could have done more." He closed his eyes and rested his forehead on hers, their breath mingling in a slow rhythm.

Since childhood, Casey had understood how to shoulder the burden of someone else. She'd been the responsible one in her house, taking care of her mom and then Emery. She'd been a few houses away to care for Shawn and Teagan when something bad happened. But she'd never fully understood what it would feel like to care for someone she loved this completely. It was different than the love she felt for others. Deeper even.

She was still figuring out how to let people love her, how to let them in, how to need them and want them. It would probably be a lifelong process, but she wanted to try. She wanted to experience that with Micah. She could feel his sadness weighing heavy, the pain of losing a part of himself hanging like an anvil around his neck.

She kissed his forehead and raked her fingers over his scruff. "Can I go with you?"

"Case, no. This is something I need to do alone."

"Why?"

"Because..."

"Because you are still bearing responsibility that isn't yours to bear."

His smile didn't quite reach his eyes. "Baby steps, Casey. I may not have been the one to pull the trigger, but something I was responsible for cost us precious time. And Whitney, she's part of my family. My old family," he quickly corrected.

"They are still your family, Micah. You claimed them today. You donned the title at the core of who you are and ran into a building despite your fear. So let me be clear. I'm not asking if I can go with you. I'm telling you I am going with you. I don't know how to do this well, but you are the one who told me that a team has each other's backs. And you are honoring your teammate, even in death. I love that about you. I want to have your back like you had mine today."

He stroked her cheek. "Is that all you love?"

"Of course not." She snorted, that unladylike sound that he somehow drew out of her. "I love puppies, the stars, bluebonnets in the spring, watching *Fixer Upper*, the scent of roses, my sister, Teagan and Shawn, the color of fall." She rolled her eyes. "And a few other things I'm probably forgetting about right now."

"You're forgetting, huh?" He tugged her closer, her chair scraping the linoleum floor.

"There is one more thing that I could never forget." Casey turned so that she could see him and took his face in her hands. "I love you, Micah Richards. I don't know when it happened or why it happened." She grinned at his smirk. "But I want to do this thing with you. I want to figure it out. I don't really know how to do this team thing, but I want to learn."

His lips found hers, promising, adoring. Once again, she felt cherished. Micah Richards had shattered every wall and had become her pillar of strength.

"Casey?"

"Yeah?" She pulled away from him, her head swimming a little.

"Would you come with me on Saturday to Fort Worth?"

"You couldn't keep me away." She wrapped her arms around him, laying her hand on his chest right over his heart. "We'll do this last goodbye the right way. Together."

CHAPTER 24

Micah pulled in front of Casey's house and threw Old Faithful into park. Hard to believe he hadn't wanted this hunk of metal, hadn't wanted to stay in Dallas. Okay, it wasn't that hard to believe, but a woman like Casey could make any man with sense change his mind. And Casey was a keeper. He still couldn't believe she wanted to go with him to Fort Worth today.

He stepped from the truck and slammed the door, noting more cars on her street than normal. Someone must have family in town.

Casey was part of his new life. She hadn't been present with the deployments, the wondering, jumping at phone calls. She hadn't seen him in his world, but today she would. Casey was right. He was a SEAL and Whitney and her little girl, Juan's little girl—they were part of his family. He halted at her front door. Today, he would go pay his respects, merge two of his worlds, and say goodbye, not out of guilt but out of gratitude that Juan had been his brother, his friend.

The door swung open. "Are you just going to stand out there all day?"

Micah's mouth dropped open. Kaylan stood on the other side of Casey's door, her auburn hair pulled to one side. In her plaid shirt and jeans, she definitely looked like she was back to her old southern self.

"I'm sorry. I must have the wrong house. Or state." He stepped into her hug, still confused. "What are you doing here?"

"What do you think, Bulldog?"

He would have failed every awareness test right there. Just past the entryway stood several members from his special team—Jay, Colt, Titus, Logan, and Nick. It was Nick who stepped forward. "You've done far too many of these goodbyes alone and for the wrong reasons. This time, we do it right."

"Together." Micah clasped hands with his best friend and brother-in-law, casting Casey a knowing look from where she stood in between Colt and Jay.

"Jay, keep your hands to yourself, man."

Jay grinned—always a dangerous sign—and held up Casey's left hand. "I don't see a ring, Bulldog. This gorgeous lady is still free game."

"I might be persuaded," Casey said, casting Micah a wink.

Micah growled. Actually growled.

"Down, Bulldog. I've got the kids under control." Titus pounded his back. His blue shirt accented his dark skin and slightly hazel eyes. He and his wife, Lisa, had just adopted their first little girl from Haiti, thanks to Kaylan's influence, and now Lisa was finally pregnant.

"How's your bride?"

"She is happily exhausted. She couldn't be more thrilled with Mia and a little future SEAL on the way." Titus's grin was brilliant.

"A little boy? That's awesome! Congrats, man." Micah hugged his friend. "Tell Lisa I'm so happy for y'all, and I miss her annoying teasing."

"We miss you, too, Bulldog. She sends her love."

"Alright, my turn, my turn. I've missed my surfing buddy." All five foot ten inches of Colt lifted Micah into the air, a wild grin plastered on his face. "We miss you at home, brah."

Right now, Micah was missing it, too. Casey found her way to his side and slipped under his arm. He loved the way she openly showed affection now.

"You found yourself a girl." Kaylan sniffed. "I might actually cry."

Micah laughed as his sister hugged her husband. "Don't even start."

"Technically, I found him," Casey chimed in.

"By found you mean almost ran over." He squeezed her closer, enjoying the teasing glint in her eye.

"You almost ran him over? That's my kind of girl. Are you sure you are content with Bulldog? He really is a grouch in the mornings," Jay whispered so the whole room could hear.

Casey had eyes only for Micah. "He's a little rough around the edges, but I think I'll keep him." She wrapped both arms around his waist.

Kaylan squealed. "You are perfect for him. I told you he had met his match." She elbowed her husband, drawing a groan.

"Now we just need to get you two with good girls." Kaylan pointed to Jay and Colt. "Got any cute friends, Case?"

Already Kaylan was shortening her name. Micah grinned. Kaylan and Casey were going to get along just fine. Another Richards lady would be joining his clan very soon.

"One. But I don't think she's what you're looking for."

"Fair enough. I'll just have to find them girls in California." She crossed her arms.

Jay groaned, and Colt held up his hands. "Whoa, I am a free agent. I do not want to be tied down. I'll pass on that."

"You'll be whistling a different tune when I'm finished," Kaylan assured.

Micah didn't think he had ever seen Colt look so terrified or lost at the same time. "Guys, tell her. I'm a free spirit, not a family man."

The room broke into laughter for a moment. Micah felt at home—with his old team, with his new team at his side, with his family.

"I still don't get how you knew or why you are all here."

Everyone turned to look at Casey.

"Casey..."

"You needed your team with you Micah. You needed to remember that you don't have to do this alone."

"But how?"

"I might have stolen your phone, copied Nick and Kaylan's numbers, called and suggested they come for the weekend, and they took it from there."

"Did you think we would let them come without us?" Titus asked, insulted. "Man, how long did we serve together?"

"We operate best as a team. Even I know that, and I'm the Lone Ranger here," Colt shrugged. "We should have done this with you all along."

"Maybe you wouldn't have felt the need to leave," Jay said.

Micah shook his head. "I never believed I would say this, but it was my time to go. I never knew if I wanted to stay in long-term, but everything that happened earlier this year was just the catalyst to get me where I need to be." He squeezed Casey closer. "Right here. I think I just needed to know that you guys were still there, too. That you didn't hate me." He swallowed the lump in his throat.

"You know how this goes, Bulldog. Any day. Any time. We will always be here for you. Just in different zip codes. Besides, when I became your brother-in-law, you officially got stuck with me for life." Nick clapped him on the back.

"Did you finally earn the title of 'wise one' once I left?" Micah flashed his brother-in-law a grin.

"I'm sorry, I believe Titus holds that title hands down," Jay scoffed.

"True." Micah conceded.

"We all have our roles to play," Titus spoke up. "Jay is the hothead. Colt is the mischievous daredevil. Nick is our eyes and ears. Logan is our leader. I'm the one keeping us all on track. But you, Bulldog," he turned to Micah, "you are the heart of what we do. And we've missed that."

This time Micah swallowed back tears. "You are definitely the wise one. And thank you." He smiled at Casey and then at those gathered in the room. "All of you. I've been dreading today, saying goodbye one more time, looking Whitney in the eye, seeing their little girl, and knowing Juan won't ever watch her grow up. But with all of you, today feels . . . easier."

Nick clapped him on the back and steered them all to the door. "Let's go honor Juan's bride in the way he would want."

They piled into cars and pulled out in a caravan with a direct line to Fort Worth.

CHAPTER 25

A fire burned bright in Mama Rosie's backyard Saturday night. Micah, Casey, and the team had spent the day in Fort Worth with Whitney and her little girl. They'd gone to the park to play with her, swapped stories about Juan, and a few tears fell in the midst of laughter. Now standing next to Casey under the stars once more with the SEALs, his sister, Mama Rosie, Shawn, Teagan, and even TJ and Emery, something sank into place. His team. This was his team. It didn't look perfect. It didn't have a label. They were a combination of the places the Lord had taken him and the circumstances placed in his path. And somehow it all worked, together.

"You're quiet, handsome. What's on your mind?"

"It's been a crazy last few days."

"Guns, SEALs, meeting the fam. I'd say this is a new level of crazy for me."

Firelight danced over her face, now unguarded. She'd let him in. She was letting him see all of her. And he loved it.

"I kinda love you, you know." He leaned in close so that only she could hear, his team around him laughing and talking and roasting s'mores. But in a sky full of stars, he had eyes only for Casey Stewart.

She wrinkled her nose. "Only kinda?"

He held his arms wide. "More than this. Is that okay?"

She tapped her chin, studying him. "This isn't going to be one of those relationships where you fall madly in love with me in the aftermath of every fight, is it?" Casey smirked. "I'm just not sure I can manage your fragile ego every time."

"Not a chance, love." He wound his arm around her waist. From where they stood off to the side in shadow, Micah had all the privacy he needed. Laughter surrounded him and the fire crackled. The scent of pine and smoke coated his clothes, and the faint elixir of roses tickled his nose. He tipped Casey's chin in his direction and tightened his grip around her waist. "I fell for you before this mess."

A flicker of doubt flashed across her face, and he pulled her even closer.

"I'm not going to run away from you when it's hard. If anything, I'm going to run toward you and try to dive in between you and whatever mess you've stirred up, love."

She chuckled softly, her grip on his shirt tightening. "Love, huh? I kinda like that one. Is it too cheesy, though?"

His breath was warm on her cheek. "Never too cheesy, and it can never be said enough. I think it is your defining quality, even when you built your walls. I think it's what drew me to you initially. I could see your fight and how strongly you cared. And I think that kind of love is something we can build a life and a home on. I think love led me here. To finish out goodbyes. Love intrigued me as I watched you in your world. And love is keeping me here. For you. For these kids. For the family you have built with Mama Rosie, Teagan, Shawn, and Al. For the family you have with Emery."

"Mmm, now I really like it." She slipped her arms around him, her fingers tracing circles on his back.

He smiled the smile that now belonged to Casey alone. "I love ya, Casey. And I want to spend the rest of my life learning how to love you more, fighting for you," he placed a kiss on the tip of her nose and leaned in close, "and with you."

Her laugh stirred something in him. Something he had been missing since his buddies died, since his accident, since he'd given up the SEALs. She stirred his warrior's heart to action. In Casey, Micah had found a strong partner, a valiant woman, and a gift worth fighting the rest of his life for. He'd found his team. He'd found his home.

He'd fallen in love with the heart of a tiny warrior.

NOTE FROM THE AUTHOR

This book has been a long time coming. I'm sorry . . . and I'm not, all at once. I needed the time, and I have to say THANK YOU for sticking in there with me.

I finished the first draft of this book during a season where I lost several family members and two more were diagnosed with cancer. We have since lost them, too. I think some of the first draft was therapeutic for me. Micah lost many of his team, after all. Loss is part of life and will be until Jesus comes back.

While the first draft of this book was written and rewritten as a way to deal with grief, the last draft, the one you are now reading is filled with hope, that even in our floundering and pain, there is life on the other side, purpose, joy, and love along the way.

If you've followed along with my stories, maybe you've spotted a theme, that even in the darkest times, we can get through them together. And we can have hope.

NOTE FROM THE AUTHOR

I believe words matter. I believe stories matter. And while you will never read my first draft, I believe it mattered and got me here. I hope this story inspires you. I hope it urges you to find healing, hope, and purpose in a God who gives good gifts and loves us deeply. And I hope it gives you courage to face your fears, your challenges, and your past with grace and find your people along the way. This book is for the family I've lost. For the ones you have lost. And for the believers in Christ, this book is a celebration of the party we will all one day have again.

I believe our heart's cry is ultimately to come. But here in the present, we can find it in hope, love, and purpose and making the most of every day and every opportunity.

ACKNOWLEDGMENTS

It truly takes a team to write a book, and I want to take a short moment to thank the people who have stuck with me through this journey. So in no particular order...

To my husband – You came into this journey later than I wanted, but you've been a gift in your timing! Thank you for never being too cool to read my stories, for providing honest feedback, and for loving me and encouraging me through this whole process.

To my family – You have been my cheerleaders from the beginning, encouraging me never to give up. Designing, editing, marketing, praying . . . just being on my team. And to my new family, my husband and in-laws. You have adopted this journey with me in incredible ways, and I couldn't be more thankful to have you as part of this road now.

To my friends who read this when it was still a hot mess – Adrienne, KyLea, Janell, Ashley, Erin, Mandy, and Alena, as well as my mom and mother-in-love. THANK YOU! For catching what

I was no longer seeing and for believing in me and in these stories. Your support and your ability to talk about story with me truly means the world! And a special thank you to KyLea, who lived with me while I worked on all of my books. You were and continue to be a fun story partner, friend, and confidant. I can't wait to see what stories we'll chat about in the years to come.

To my editors – Charlene and Christian. Y'all worked a miracle getting me to publication. Thank you for your time, energy, and gentle critique that made this story so much better! You dig through the mess so I can make it a masterpiece. I couldn't do this without you.

To my community – Christy, Juliana, Sheetal, Emily, and D'Ann, y'all put up with weird schedules and occasional meltdowns and continued to encourage me to do what God has called me to do. Thank you for being part of my story so I can write these stories. And to my new married community group – Jacob, Adrienne, Sam, Allison, Nick, and Brena. You have already been such a fun encouragement as I finished this new book. I'm excited to have y'all along for the ride.

To my *My Book Therapy* friends and mentors – Susie, Rachel, Lisa, Tari, Alena, Michelle, Mandy, Jeanne, Tracy, and Andrea. Your texts, emails, and time spent at retreats and conferences is invaluable. You were willing to dig in with me when I got stuck, cheer me on when I wanted to quit, and pray with me and for me as I completed this book. And you were just there to relate along the way in this journey of writing. Thank you, thank you for being my favorite writing team ever!

To my readers – THANK YOU for never giving up on me the last few years, for loving the *Heart of a Warrior* series, and for always asking for me. You drove me to finish this book, and I hope you enjoy!

To the Lord – Thank you for choosing to give me the gift of story, and thank you for being a God of second chances, of healing, hope, community, and making all things new. That's truly what this story is about, and I wouldn't have been able to write it without You.

ABOUT THE AUTHOR

Kariss Lynch began her writing career in third grade when she created a story about a magical world for a class assignment. Chasing her dream into college, she received a degree in English from Texas Tech University and fell in love with writing characters with big dreams, adventurous spirits, and bold hearts. Kariss is a die-hard Texan, proud aunt, and a gypsy at heart, traveling whenever she can but always finding her way back home. She and her husband live in Dallas with their dog, Maverick. Connect with her at **karisslynch.com**.

- facebook.com/author.karisslynch
- twitter.com/Kariss_Lynch
- instagram.com/karisslynch.author

ALSO BY KARISS LYNCH

Shaken
Shadowed
Surrendered

Made in United States
North Haven, CT
21 October 2021